THE MERCURY ANNUAL

The Razalians take the sun's contempt in good part. The nature of their planet has long inured them to disappointment – hope, too, but this isn't as bleak as it may sound. They know examples aplenty of what hope can lead to – most notably, in their system, the Twenty Aeons war between Barask and Sehunda, adjacent planets at the opposite end of the arc. There, the hope ignited and persisted on both sides that the other would surrender its world. So powerful did the hope grow that the actual reason for hostilities was clean forgotten by Aeon Three. It finally took the intervention of the sun – tired of seeing its spiral path littered with phosphorescent cannon-shafts and the goggling eyes of garotted helots – to lay all hope to rest. For three and thirty parts of an aeon, it looped around these two planets alone, sending out secondary rays to warm the rest of the arc (apart from Razalia, which got a dab or two, equal to an electric fire left on for half-an-hour every other day). Closer and closer it looped, till the famed serpent's-tail rivers of Barask were boiling and the thousand-foot snow-trees of Sehunda were stripped of their magenta bark. Only then did the planets' leaders cease hostilities.

Michael Wyndham Thomas is a poet, fiction-writer, dramatist and musician who has been widely published in the UK, Europe and North America. His first poetry collection, *God's Machynlleth and Other Poems*, is available from Flarestack, while *Port Winston Mulberry* is forthcoming from Peterloo Poets. His CD, *Seventeen Poems (and a Bit of a Song)*, is now on release from MayB Studios. Publication of his novel, *The Song of the Sun*, is also forthcoming, as are productions of his play, *Mr Culverson's Apostle*. Since April 2004 Michael has been poet-in-residence at the annual Robert Frost Poetry Festival, Key West, Florida. In consequence, he is now Poet-at-Large in the Navy of the Conch Republic of Key West. He undertakes these "bardic" duties with due solemnity and happy bafflement. See www.michaelwthomas.co.uk for more information.

Also by Michael Wyndham Thomas

GOD'S MACHYNLLETH AND OTHER POEMS (FLARESTACK)

See also

MAGAZINE SIX: THE KEY WEST ISSUE, ED. KIRBY CONGDON
(KEY WEST, FLORIDA: THE BICYCLE PRESS, 2006)

SEVENTEEN POEMS AND A BIT OF A SONG CD (MAYB STUDIOS 2007)
(WWW.MAYBSTUDIO.CO.UK)

THE MERCURY ANNUAL

PART 1 OF VALIANT RAZALIA

Michael Wyndham Thomas

Theaker's Paperback Library
BIRMINGHAM, ENGLAND

Published by
Theaker's Paperback Library
(an imprint of Silver Age Books)
56 Leyton Road
Birmingham
B21 9EE

www.silveragebooks.com
silveragebooks@blueyonder.co.uk
www.myspace.com/silveragebooks
www.lulu.com/silveragebooks

Parts of this novel were originally published in
Theaker's Quarterly Fiction,
issues eight (2005) and fourteen (2007).

First paperback publication in 2009.

ISBN 978-0-9561533-0-2

Dedicated to Lynda – and the footloose moons of Razalia

PROLOGUE

Nothing swells or drains the tides. They bubble alone. On the shoreward side, they finger their way through something that crunches like shingle but pulses and burns like the heart of a sapphire. It is shaped like so many miniature scarps and gulleys, headlands and coves. Whenever the three umber moons above are aligned, it redistributes itself. Gulleys rise and level off, headlands collapse like the last sands of an hourglass. It is as though the mineral is as prone to boredom as any kid in its first church pew. It must needs grizzle and shift about.

On the seaward side, the tides ebb only a matter of feet. Then they stop, as if hard against a thread of invisible hands. From a distance, their whitecaps look like sheep going mad to feed, scrambling and rolling on each other's backs. Beyond the tideline is what looks like cracked mud. Bone dry, it has never been so much as flecked by a whitecap. It goes a mile out, flat as a board. But its cracks are no aimless zigzags or spider-trails. Restlessness is as deep in them as in the pulsing shingle. On every night that falls exactly between the alignment of the umber moons, they flex and thrash like sporting crocodiles. This one curves about, meets itself coming the other way, closes in a blind eye's knowing wink. That one convulses through rhomboids, spheres and trapeziums. Over here, half-a-dozen shimmy across the mud like synchronised snakes. Far beyond, a pair interlock and spin, attaining the graceful weave of a Celtic knot, then a dried-up pen's raw scribble.

The flat, cracked board ends at the outwaters. These are nine oceans, shelving down and down, each with its own shape. Their edges are cliffs of water. They are separated from each other by broad highways which meld and split in a maze endlessly curving. Unlike the cracks, the shingle, they never change, whatever the three umber moons might be about. Nor do the cliffs of water slide. Movement out here is undramatic, provided by a host of roots that ring the inner edge of each cliff. Modestly they wave, like windblown hairs on a magnified arm. Sometimes they kink and flex a little, suggesting tiny men at their physical jerks, buried upside down in sand. What they are connected to, what being or plant draws its life from the cliffs of water, is undiscoverable.

The cracks between tide and outwater owe nothing to convulsion or heat. Sliceblossom made them: makes them still, occasionally, but mainly it curves to their patterns. Two-dimensional, huge of leaf, sliceblossom rises everywhere from miles below and feeds on what passes for air. All over the board, the leaves rear and shiver. Once sated, they puff and flatten, again and again, putting forth petals red as coxcombs, blue as the last of day, like a colour-bomb showering all that terracotta. Then they drop as one, and echoes pour like smoke from the cracks.

For the eye that seeks easy beauty, the shore and the outwaters are beautiful. In their own way, so are the cracks and the sliceblossom, although the sudden appearance of those leaves, dark and elephantine, can freeze the senses when first witnessed. Elsewhere, however, beauty is precarious. For Razalia, the home of these wonders, is a half-finished world and thus unique among the sixteen planets of its system. True, its landscape is not unpleasing: verdant without being chaotically lush, rolling without too many steeps and hollows. But it is plagued with gaps: not translucent, allowing sight of what lies beyond, but pure white like a hotch-potch of abandoned canvasses. Sometimes these ambush the traveller, and many have assumed that they offer short-cuts. But to walk into a gap is to surrender all: to "make the horizon's farewell", the nearest Razalian gets to the word "death". The alternative – a detour, often of leagues together – is wearisome but, after all, wise.

Theories abound about Razalia's provisional state. The most dramatic of these is that Razalia's maker, whatever it was, had to scale a mountain to put the last touches to a tricky pinnacle. The ascent was calm and clear, and the maker had just nipped the pinnacle's spike into place when a welter of turbulence – gifted by one of the three umber moons when asleep – clawed it from its labours and pitched it into "forsaken midnight", the Razalian approximation of "space". Another is that the maker was a badly-tutored apprentice, left to its own uncertain devices, unable to contact its master. After several tours of the planet – bodging this, half-cocking that – it had made one last effort to get something wholly right. With the resolve that despair can beget, it managed the mountain with the perfect pinnacle. But then, realising how far short all else fell, it fell itself – deliberately, before rolling on over the shingle and the board of cracks and losing itself in an ocean.

A third theory has the maker on the shoreline, dragging its however many feet or hoofs on the ground, wondering if, after all, shingle amounts to the best use of pulsing gems. The gems quake; a ravine yawns between the maker's legs; destiny posts it to the core of its own work. A fourth, affined to the second and third, insists that the inept apprentice was swallowed by a beast that still frets and lashes at the centre of Razalia. Despite its dwelling-place, this mysterious being once had something of the gregarious in its disposition. It was even intent on clambering to the surface, there to roam and befriend. But then the maker, played false by the shifting gems, had landed in an indescribable heap on the beast's back. The beast's alarm had turned to wrath and thence to hunger. Ingesting the maker, however, the beast also absorbed its peevishness at its pig's-ear creation. Thus did night fall on the beast's humour. Now, it devoted itself to roars and snarls of malcontentment – hence the ponderous echoes when the sliceblossom retreats through the cracks. In a refinement of this last detail, it is also mooted that the sliceblossom grows on the beast's tail. Whenever the beast's pique shifts from fit to ecstasy, it lashes its tail in a long wave that somehow rises through Razalia and buffets its crust, pouring forth the blossom.

There have been many theories prior to these. And, over time (which, in keeping with the whole planet, is a fits-and-starts proposition), these will yield to others. What unites them all, perhaps, is a sense of finish. As little tales, they have a completeness which – through ill-luck or gormlessness – Razalia's maker hardly knew.

And, as with the planet, so with its satellites. No theories circulate about Rezalia's three umber moons. No maker is assumed to have had a hand in their creation. They invented themselves: in defiance, it seems, of all notions of a moon as chaperone of love, horseman of tides, beacon for wartime bombers. In their very colour, they dismiss any lunar duties: duties properly, happily discharged by their fellow moons above the other fifteen planets of the system. Though strangely visible, they do not shine upon Razalia. Instead, they spend the planet's lurching, uncertain time in spasms of tag, dance and leapfrog. Now they pile vertically like acrobats discharged from some circus ship, content to hone their skills in the amethyst blue that envelops the system, indifferent to the absence of watching eyes. Now they juggle themselves, whipping up winds about them, wordless equivalents of "eyyy-upp!" Once, one moon was reported to have landed on Razalia, spending a daylight hour in a slalom between the puffing sliceblossom, bouncing across the nine oceans like skimmed shale, before flying back to its mates and (so the story goes) jostling them like a thief of tender years, bursting from his first spree in a shopping precinct.

Not that they leave Razalia untroubled. Twice in the Razalian month, they align south-west to north-east in the amethyst blue. Bafflingly, it is a business they take seriously. Somehow, in the bulging, deflating balloon of time around the planet, the alignments have a stern regularity. Then, the shingle morphs as it pleases by the tideline. And, exactly between the alignments, the cracks beyond the tide make answer to the shingle, drawing themselves anew for the next lurching stretch of time. Intermittently, the moons line east to west for slumber. Then there arises the turbulence which might have plucked Razalia's maker from his mountain-top. The landscape bends and fusses. The nine oceans furrow and gawp. Only the unfinished parts, the gaps of pure white, are unmoving, although it is said that, from close to, they emit a choral murmur, as if all the strayed, hapless souls within were trying to fight back through dissolution, retrieve their skin and bone and resume their long-interrupted journeys.

Though the planet knows no moonlight, it does see the sun. Once each Razalian fortnight – anything between eleven and seventeen of their days – the skies turn from amethyst to azure. Downs and valleys soften; the shingle beats with a fiercer pulse. There is, however, no majestic rising and setting. Rather, there is a radiant nosing about, a prodding and poking. If this sun had a face, akin to the man in the moon seen from Earth, it would doubtless look with scorn upon Razalia.

The system's sun is a martinet. Its planets are spread before it in a long arc, revolving on east-west axes like beads on a curved abacus, with Razalia at the far, far end. In slow, under-and-over spirals, it warms its charges from west to east, most of the time as far as Carolles, Razalia's neighbour, then back again. It serves these fifteen planets as a source of life should, for it considers them worthy of its fire. Its dawns and dusks are scrupulous, and woe betide any part of any planet not positioned to receive them at the precise point of spin.

But woe never figures. The other planets are complete and well-behaved. Their enveloping balloons of time are perfect spheres. Their minutes and hours flow like buttermilk, where Razalian time can stutter like an engine on a January morning or spring like a cat over half a day or more. But the sun realises, if somewhat reluctantly, its duty of care to the whole system. And so it is that, every twelve or fourteen or sixteen Razalian days, it heaves itself past Carolles, loops to the far end of the planetary arc, and assures itself that Razalia is not dead. Its incredulous rummage may last a whole day or an afternoon only. Then it commences its gyrations westward, and for a good hour after (or a good minute if Razalian time has leapt on: their phrase for that translates roughly as "if nightmares harry the clock"), the planet's air seems filled with the disbelieving tuts and chuckles of a celestial plumber.

The Razalians take the sun's contempt in good part. The nature of their planet has long inured them to disappointment – hope, too, but this isn't as bleak as it may sound. They know examples aplenty of what hope can lead to – most notably, in their system, the Twenty Aeons war between Barask and Sehunda, adjacent planets at the opposite end of the arc. There, the hope ignited and persisted on both sides that the other would surrender its world. So powerful did the hope grow that the actual reason for hostilities was clean forgotten by Aeon Three. It finally took the intervention of the sun – tired of seeing its spiral path littered with phosphorescent cannon-shafts and the goggling eyes of garotted helots – to lay all hope to rest. For three and thirty parts of an aeon, it looped around these two planets alone, sending out secondary rays to warm the rest of the arc (apart from Razalia, which got a dab or two, equal to an electric fire left on for half-an-hour every other day). Closer and closer it looped, till the famed serpent's-tail rivers of Barask were boiling and the thousand-foot snow-trees of Sehunda were stripped of their magenta bark. Only then did the planets' leaders cease hostilities. The Council of Barask signalled its readiness to talk by garotting a cohort of its own helots and firing a million-eyeball salute at Sehunda's moon. Appropriately, Sehunda responded with a cascade of severed flippers. Since then, they have lived in amity – though the rivers of Barask have yet to cool and a report of a patch of magenta on a Sehunda snow-tree has proved false. Such, for the Razalians, is the price of hope. Indeed, mindful of the sun's effect at that time, they coined a new phrase for that dangerous abstraction, which roughly translates as "brass-monkey cauldron".

The Razalian attitude, midway between perkiness and despair, naturally extends to their view of themselves. Interplanetary marriage is not unknown further along the arc, but no Razalian would ever presume to secure the affection of a golden-haired nymph or hero from neighbouring Carolles. Like their planet, the Razalians are half-finished, their Maker having apparently regarded earlobes, lips and nostrils as a novice modeller might regard the fiddly turrets on *HMS Victorious*. Not that their heads lack features. The eyes are there nearly all the time. As for the rest, however, they only materialise when absolutely needed. A Razalian must speak – well, then, lips and teeth will bud out from their skin; another must hear – an ear will bloom like a toy cabbage, often in the right position; the first flowers of spring appear – one nostril will whorl itself into being to enjoy the smell – possibly two if the scent is heady. Occasionally, a strong smell or sheer excitement can call forth three nostrils. Involuntary though they may be, such exhibitions are regarded as vulgar, the phrase for the exhibitionist translating as "greedy trumpet".

It is assumed that the sheer doggedness of evolution was responsible for connecting the Razalians with their world by more than sight. For a race that holds few assumptions, that simple speculation is the nearest thing to a Razalian creed. But, long ago, faith of a sort did play a brief part in the planet's life. Perhaps understandably, it centred upon the notion that Razalia's maker might return and complete its work. Prophecies were legion that it would fly back through space's forsaken midnight and set to, closing the gaps of white, meshing the vegetation, causing the oceans to let fall their cliffs of water and flow as one. For a while, however, this was challenged by the idea that Razalia's deity was the mordant sun. Once upon a time, the challenge ran, there was no Razalia at the fag-end of the planetary arc, and the sun made its lambent way over and under its "noble fifteen", as the Razalian phrase translates. But then it was detained at the other end – possibly due to another interplanetary barney between Barask and Sehunda. In its absence, Razalia's maker snuck in out of the great nowhere, tried its hand or paw at a spot of life and then met one of the fates assigned by theory. Returning, blazing disbelief at this cuckoo in the systemic nest, the sun pondered burning it to ashes. But then, in an instant, it changed its mind and declared itself god of

Razalia. It was a furious god, but with all cards stacked in its favour; and it embraced the very human notion that punishment was most delicious when long spun out. If the planet had somehow half-created itself, then it must pay the price for its own presumption. If some weekend bodger was responsible, the planet must pay for what, in that hitherto perfect system, amounted to vandalism. (Indeed, there is an old Razalian saying, still used, about its fifteen neighbours and the boon they enjoy: "the sun thinks in five and five and five".) And thus began the sun's regime of scant visits and widow's mites of heat for the system's cuckoo.

But over time, these claims to faith dwindled. By all accounts, they never had a strong purchase on the Razalian mind. The "creed of the returning maker" was bound to be a casualty, since it depended on that baleful will o' the wisp, hope. Perhaps more interestingly, the "creed of the furious sun" vanished because, the Razalians concluded, it abused humility. It obliged them to abase themselves before the sun for something they didn't do – even unwittingly. (True, there were some sages of the furious sun creed who sought to offer proofs that their race had unconsciously created itself. But the Razalians have a profound sense of self, to the extent that, if they concentrate enough, they become consciously unconscious, knowing when they don't know that they are planning this or doing that. The sages had their brief season and faded with their beliefs.) If the Razalians worship anything at all, it is humility, which they tend and protect like a scrupulous gardener. Humility without just cause – the basis of the furious sun creed – is, in the Razalian phrase, "a sweating brow in a noon of icicles". In the end, that creed, too, had to snuff itself out.

As well as being the keynote of the Razalians' temper, humility could be called the architect of their physical lives. If the system's acerbic sun could speak, it might well term this a necessity, pointing out the absence of sufficient materials to build, say, a multi-layered metropolis, all floating astroports and spiral arms, such as is found all over Carolles. There is truth in this, although Razalian ingenuity, never to be underestimated, could run to a decently-buttressed sprawl if such were desired. But the Razalians prefer to live as they act, without flourish. Even so, their small settlements, with no building higher than two storeys, would probably call forth a blush of purple in the average tourist-guide prose. Spread gently out, curved of roof and modest of frontage, they counterbalance the dips and cambers of the land as though, mushrooming by nature not labour, they have the trick of symmetry by instinct. They hug the ridges, trickle down valleys like a stream with no urge to be a river. Even Mopatakeh, the Razalian capital, shuns the pomp and multitudes implied by its position, statistically nestling instead between San Gimignano and Gretna Green. Let Carolles have its metropolises. Let Sehunda create its granite awnings, its monkey-puzzle dormitories that nearly overtop its snow-trees. In the Razalian phrase, life is lived most equably "a stoop's length from a fist of soil".

A similar simplicity, or nice distrust of management, defines the civic life of the planet. Each settlement, Mopatakeh included, has a sole leader, invariably named Tharle: a proper name, not a designation, and never prefixed by *a* or *the*. Tharles are not elected in any common way. Rather, each settlement simply knows who new Tharle should be. A telepathic *yes* shivers from mind to mind, and all is fixed. (Telepathic from birth, Razalians normally reserve the power for extreme deliberation or moments of personal risk. They see its gratuitous use as akin to the caperings of a three-nostril scent-hound, dismissing it, in their phrase, as "think-bleeding". Only Tharles employ it regularly, for it is a natural part of their office.)

Once *in situ*, Tharles benefit from their especial, communally-divined wisdom. For them, evolution gets another move on: throughout most of the year, whether dealing with official matters or delighting in quietude, they sport one or two of everything on their faces, all correctly positioned. They have the power to double their height to facilitate ease of address at communal gatherings. But perhaps most tellingly, in the Razalian view, Tharles enjoy a modification to their palate and gastric system. Thus overhauled, they can feast on sliceblossom leaves, invigorating to their bodies while poisonous to all others. It has not been established whether sliceblossom aids Tharlian deliberation, deepens the *gravitas* of their verdicts. But, allowing themselves another assumption, Razalians conclude that it must be so. Either way, the image of Tharles "feasting on the flaps of acumen", in the popular phrase, offers a pleasing antidote to the troublesome flora of remoter cultures: the lotos-flower, the apple of Eden. And, drawing on a folk-belief to whose truth they are cheerily indifferent, Razalians insist that this mastery of sliceblossom not only helps to define their leaders but also, somehow, allows everyone on the planet to distinguish Tharle from Tharle. That this might be a matter of telepathy is doubtless acknowledged in some way. But the "mastery" notion, aside from being more dramatic to proclaim, enriches the esteem in which Tharles are held.

Compared to the other planets in the arc – martial, sophisticated or a mixture of both – Razalia appears childlike, its customs and patterns of life barely breaking out of prehistory. Yet, in a way that possibly irks the sun, the noble fifteen regard it with a kindly curiosity, seeing it as a paradigm of how they once were themselves. No-one has ever invaded Razalia, but this is nothing to do with its lack of super-planetary light to aid descent and landing. Indeed, it receives its share of visitors from across the arc. Once every Razalian year – which, given their capricious time, is a matter of anything from nine to fourteen months – a contingent of Baraskians, enforced by a few slack-jawed funsters from Galladeelee ("the planet of the rouge catacombs") arrives on the planet for a special festival of their own devising. White is a colour unknown on Barask, so the gaps in the Razalian landscape hold a special, almost supernatural fascination for the Baraskians. For two Razalian weeks, under Tharlian eyes, they variously sing, carouse or simply stand before the gaps in mute worship. The Baraskians know the gaps' awful power – only too well, now. Half an aeon ago, a dozen of them took it upon themselves to conclude one evening's festivities, at the gap just beyond Mopatakeh, with a toneless but lusty rendition of the Baraskian anthem, whose theme, perhaps inevitably, is a celebration of the planet's serpent-tailed rivers. Daredevilry or intoxication, or both, impelled them to stand, arms linked barber-shop style, with their backs almost grazing the gap's surface. All was well until verse eight, when a *sotto voce* argument broke out between two singers in the middle of the line, about whether the verse's final word was "flood" or "mud". As the argument waxed, the disputants began tugging mightily at each other's arms, causing a serpentine sway down the whole line. At last, seeking to free his arm, one of them lost his footing, pitched backwards and pulled the whole chorus into the gap, in an movement like the clamping wings of a giant moth. The crowd started forward and, but for the restraining telepathy of Mopatakeh's Tharle, many more would have been lost. As it was, Tharle's mental cordon was a little too slow for one Galladeelean, who thrust his characteristically loose-hinged jaw into the gap, as a curious toddler might lean too far into a zoo's snake enclosure. The jaw disappeared on the instant; the lips of his three mouths all but fused. Ever after, he was obliged to press words out like sheets through a mangle. Worse, he was vilified as a freak on his return to Galladeelee, condemned to count the number of rouge catacombs running below its surface: a punitive task, especially given that the planet is the size of that vaguely-known system in which Earth spins. Nowadays, the Baraskians keep a respectful distance from the gaps – and any stray Galladeeleans remain at the back of the crowd, manning Barask-oak tables that groan, literally, beneath flagons of Barask's favourite tipple, a mixture of stardust, flame and serpent-river sediment.

Perhaps understandably, Razalia's most frequent, enthusiastic visitors are its immediate neighbours. Twice and often three times a month, the water-cliffs of the nine oceans suck themselves in, their edging of roots left stiff and undoused like chin-bristle. Below the cliffs, the dry highways broaden and their surfaces blur in eddies and devils of dust. Then, one by one, the septupedal craft touch down, their huge, parasol-shaped roofs suggesting a Polynesian hut re-cast in sterling silver. After a regulated series of whoops and beeps, their curved, slightly bellied sides slide back and a three-lane down-escalator, pure titanium, unrolls to the highway like an iguana's tongue. Once again, the people of Carolles have dropped round for a concerted gawk at the settlements, the ridges, the umber moons.

Collectively, Carolles' natives are known as the Carollessa. Those who incline to maleness are Carollo; those in whom the feminine has the upper hand are Carolla. Technically, the Carollessa comprise four sexes, but the other two were never properly named, have no connection, intimate or otherwise, with the Carollo or Carolla and are in any case all but extinct. One is shaped like a huge ear. Perpetually airborne, it glows peach and crimson by turns. The other is a head-splitting whistle. Thus do they procreate – or did. Over time, however, the whistle's targetry became inexplicably slipshod, so that it was as likely to impregnate the Carollessan atmosphere – or, on a still night, one of Razalia's umber moons – as any hovering ear. Not that the ears made the whistles' job any easier. Whether through self-assertion or late-blooming coyness, they became less disposed to carry embryonic whistles, tooting like so many toy referees, through the crisp Carollessan air. When they sensed the approach of a lairy whistle, they were apt to fly away, far above the planet's overwrought skylines, leaving the whistle to swing between ecstasy and dismay, the result of which was that its piercing note dropped landward like the swan-song of a heartbroken kazoo. The dominant sexes have tried to preserve their ill-starred peers – even to increase their numbers. But the signs thus far do not encourage. In a special section of Panbestiopolis, the huge wildlife park at the centre of Yathkyeda Falls, the Carollessan capital, the ear-and-whistle enclosure routinely proves the least popular attraction. This is partly due to bafflement on the part of the park's designers, understandable enough, about suitable living conditions for flying ears and misaiming whistles. The decision to house them in a huge dome, continuously filled with the sound of the wind at all its pitches (presumably to get the ears going) is doubtless as sensible as any other. But the ears flap listlessly about or gather halfway up the walls like a flock of question-marks, occasionally opening in the whistles' direction, then huddling again in attitudes of contempt. For their part, the whistles hug the floor of the dome, exchanging boastful trills about conquests of yore and, now and then, tooting at the floor like Victorian topers who pride themselves on missing the spittoon. In one sense, perhaps, the ears' disdain is justified: whistles are notoriously reluctant to settle down.

It is known, throughout the planetary arc, that the terms by which the Carollessa know themselves are relatively modern; and that they have some affinity with an Earth-tongue called Spanish. Were this the case with the Razalians, the air would fill, modestly, with theories ingenious and unprovable. But the Carollessa know the strength of the connection, having sound-recorded, imaged or otherwise bagged every tick of their planet's history-clock. The fruits of these everlasting labours are available to be seen, heard, sniffed and swallowed at Yathkyeda Falls' Aeonodrome, whose official title, in Carollessan, startlingly translates as "a full hindward romp". Here can be seen the planet's five makers, one claw apiece extended as they drop the final rock into place. Here can be seen the graphite brain, the size of a passionfruit, whose ridges, working like pectoral fins, supplied Yathkyeda Falls with heat, light and kyeda-foam, a Carollessan delicacy, for the best part of ten aeons. And here, in grainy, sometimes blurred images, can be seen the Carollessan craft – a primitive, tripedal affair – that hovered in the high clouds above the Cadiz Penninsula in the Earth summer of 1746, badly off-course for Galladeelee but determined to salvage something from the mistake. The craft's sides slide away. Something like the pad of a huge lint-brush emerges. The pad glows bright red, and in seconds the entirety of eighteenth-century Iberian culture is absorbed: a godsend for the Carollessa, as it turned out. Hitherto chafing under the name Carollodidods – more suited to a sub-sect of Galladeeleans, or yet the ears and whistles that pursued their haphazard congress about the skies – the Carollo and Carolla of the time were looking to buff up their self-regard as a new century approached on their planet. Beguiled by the Hispanic sounds from the disgorging culture-pad, they realised that only a little aural rummaging would yield shiny new names.

Breathtakingly beautiful, muscular or voluptuous as their majority sex dictates, the Carollo and Carolla form orderly lines to come ashore on Razalia, leaping gracefully over the protean shingle and hailing Tharle and commoner alike. It might be expected that they would behave like gentlefolk on a visit to Bedlam, apparently kindly but in fact as scornful as the sun towards the unfinished beings who walk with them inland. But a profound respect obtains between Razalian and Carollessa. They know that, beyond fleshly particulars – a proud Carollessan cleavage or a Razalian nose uncertainly anchored – they complement each other in mind and soul. The Carollessa – technological gods of the planetary arc, striding through their world of speed and light, citizens of whooshing airlocks, of nano-second transformations. The Razalians – settlement dwellers, progeny of a botch-meister, innocents in the ways of facial expression. Yet each race salutes the other, their fervour heartfelt; each cares for the other with sibling tenderness. Indeed, there is also something of the parental in Razalia's attitude to the stunning Carollessa. When each Carollo or Carolla is born, they are seven-feet tall, about average for an adult Razalian. But, over their life-span (two hundred years, to use the terms of a crude planet), they shrink to a matter of millimetres. It is thus a mark of reverence to be all but invisible to the Carollessan eye. Unfailingly, this gradual exit from sight arouses a kind of protectiveness in the Razalian breast. Their phrase for the process translates as "slipping into atomhood", and they take especial care if forewarned that a visiting craft contains a cohort of elders. "Let your heels be warmed with no blood": such is the command that Tharles issue to their people on such occasions. Razalians in each settlement are commanded to stand stock still until assured that the elders have passed by. An innocuous toe-tap could do for an epoch of Carollessan wisdom.

Not that the traffic is all one way. Often, Razalians will accompany the Carollessa on their journeys home, spending time on the spiral arms which house pioneering industries, responsible for at least one life-tweaking invention per Carollessan week; marvelling at the myriad beasts of hoof, wing and tentacle from all across the arc which inhabit the Panbestiopolis (and often growing a mouth to sob silently at the approaching doom of the ear and the whistle); or simply roaming the planet to drink in the fact – miraculous to them – of a landscape filled in to the last twig and puddle. But none of this excites Razalian envy. Again, their profound sense of self prevails. Wishing the Carollessa joy of their spangling world, they know that, were they to tarry long in it, a deep ache would start in their sporadically-featured heads. The Razalians are not unduly sentimental: in their book, sentiment ranks alongside humility as something whose justification must lie beyond dispute. Still, their journeys home are a matter of sweet anticipation, complete with sighs and full mouths to emit them.

It should be stressed that Razalians can make their way to Carolles under their own steam. But – in the context of its place in Earth's technological history – "steam" both defines the nature of Razalian craft and describes the uncertainties involved. The craft would have been familiar to the Carollodidods of the Earth year 1100; but today's Carollessa view them with a mixture of bafflement and alarm. They resemble signal-boxes from the Earth era between those two attenuated explosions, disregarded by the rest of the universe, called world wars. Wooden levers, stuck more or less securely in a series of wells, are controlled from the kind of spindly office-stools described so often by the one called Dickens. They can only be powered by a deep draught of telepathy. Tharles find this difficult but not impossible. Sometimes, they will band together in a Razalian dozen (which stabilises at nine for most of the year) and steer their craft through the seven-Earth-month journey to Carolles, needing only a Carollessan day or so to hear again the almost inaudible mind-murmur that tells them their powers are restored. But it would need a hundred commoners to generate the same fuel for the same length of time. Even then, the strain would be notable. Indeed, they would get to know their hosts exceedingly well, since they would have to remain as guest patients in the Recuperation Gyre of the *Subdivaletudion*, Yathkyeda Falls' outdoor hospital, for at least three Carollessan years.

So Razalia calls forth the admiration of neighbouring Carolles and the fascination of the entire arc. But there is nothing about the planet or its people that they actively desire – except one particular: something that, after all, allows the three umber moons to disport themselves in glorious redundancy and possibly excites confusion in the heart of the absentee sun. Most Razalians might be telepathically spavined by a DIY trip to Carolles. But all of them, for the whole of their lives, have what is best translated as "watching-light". From waking to sleep, their faces have a glow somewhere between starshine and alabaster, throwing off a light which allows them to toil, to celebrate, to see their way.

It might be thought that this attribute provides explanation enough for the sun's intermittent jaunts to the end of the arc. Why should it spend itself, the argument might run, on a world of a thousand suns? For the Razalians, however, the gift of watching-light has no bearing on the matter. Even at its height, admittedly temperate, the creed of the furious sun made no reference to it. The sun does as it does, they have always reasoned. If it is confused, even annoyed, by watching-light – if, after all these aeons, it still cannot bring itself to regard Razalia as anything more than a systemic mock-up – then it must weather those feelings as best it can. Occasionally, some tender-hearted souls might feel pity for the sun, locked thus in peevishness. They might wish that the sun would regard watching-light as a sort of evolutionary homage to its own furnace-strength. But, good Razalians that they are, they do not allow the wish to shrink to a skulking guilt or the pity to bulk into self-satisfaction. In any case, such thoughts are brief, fading like the sun itself after one of its disdainful gawps at the planet.

For Razalia's fellow-planets, however, watching-light is endlessly enthralling. Though its passengers might have visited Razalia a score of times, each Carollessan craft hovers for an age above the nine oceans, so that all might look inland through the panoptical lenses on the observation deck and marvel at the small, clear lights moving purposefully beneath the amethyst sky. Now and then, a troupe of happy-go-lucky Galladeeleans buzz over the planet and back, courtesy of an endlessly stretching catapult, the Galladeelee mode of travel. Arms and bodies arranged in a kind of sheep-shank around the frame, they whoop when they burst into Razalia's atmosphere, plunging their heads down on necks almost as elastic as their craft, yelling something that translates (very roughly) as "stars! stars! stars in the water!" – for thus do the lighted Razalians strike them. For the Baraskians, watching-light is part of the miracle of white, another reminder of the colour denied to their planet. Many a Baraskian has offered a king's ransom to a Razalian, pleading with them to return to Barask and perform the service of a night-light or a signpost for one of the planet's notorious pleasure-clubs. Politely, such offers are declined, the suggestion often made that, if white is not meant to be on Barask, then perhaps some natural ill might befall a Razalian beacon and the investment would go for nothing. With gruff good humour – the Baraskian way – the would-be investor ponders, then biffs its impressively creviced brow and usually says something which translates as "Now why didn't I see that? You must think I'm a Gallideelee plunge-head."

But there is one element of watching-light which the whole system calls priceless. Some few have seen it – particularly Carollessan children who, disregarding parental strictures, have crept hopefully at twilight into the room of a visiting Razalian, arching their seven-foot frames over the guest as they drift sleepwards. When a Razalian falls asleep, the fading light figures the entire kaleidoscopic ballet of the system. Lines switch back and forth on their brows like the ebullient flock of asteroids that often follow in the sun's wake. Whorls mimic the graceful eddies of Barask's serpentine rivers, or the pulsing launch-pad of a Carollessan astroport. Patches of white hollow out, leaving the jagged roofs and floorways of Galladeelee's rouge catacombs; or stretch into a tower, the image of the single dwelling on Lachbourigg, in which its dozen inhabitants live. Finally, the magic resolves itself into two tiny catherine-wheels upon the eyelids, whose fade has been known to call forth a sob from the curious Carollessan child – and, indirectly, bounce the Razalian visitor from their bed, an infant Carollessan sob corresponding in pitch and volume to the ire of an elephant weltering in a trap. More than anything else, and whether seen or merely heard of, these delicate fireworks fix Razalia as something special in the systemic mind. While the noble fifteen see the planet as an image of their own long-finished epochs, the ritual disappearance of watching-light strikes them as doubly special: evidence, in fact, that Razalians have psychic custody of a time before time, when all the shapes of the arc – at its beginning and to come – were still brewing in its several makers' minds. Characteristically, the Razalians do not claim this as the truth, but are happy to let their fellow system-dwellers believe it. After all, such a legend plays no small part in keeping a planet uninvaded.

At the far side of Razalia's nine oceans, a Carolla who is not keeps guard on a free-floating pier. While Razalia toils or feasts, while light creeps into its faces or whirls on their drooping lids, she glides back and forth between splendid white columns, under a canopy of teal green, scanning land, ocean and beyond, a graceful hand shading her vision. "A Carolla who is not" is the Razalian phrase for this sentinel, whose arrival has long been a mystery to Tharle and commoner alike. The Carollessa describe her in equivalent terms, for no jot or squiggle in their Aeonodrome records any migration by a lone Carolla to their sibling world. And nothing on either planet explains the construction of the pier, which is unexceptional by, say, the standards of Sehundan engineering but, as the sun would be pleased to observe, is utterly beyond the resources of its pitiful cuckoo. Its form (which might be called neoclassical by Earth's knowing prattlers) emphatically rules out any involvement by Razalia's maker, although the potential theory – half-baked creator nerving up for one astonishing throw of its jinxed dice – is acknowledged as having some romantic appeal. The Carolla's beauty, however, is a different matter. Is she actually Razalian? the race in her charge sometimes wonder. Were we once as lithe and striking as the Carollessa? As expected, the Razalians do not see this as a chance to plume their self-regard, nor yet to sink into a doleful reverie on beauty departed. Like the benefits of sliceblossom for Tharlian contemplation, it is a notion that is entertained with warmth. But then, as the practical demands of life press in, it is laid aside – but carefully, like a modest jewel returned to its serviceable cushion. For their part, the Carollessa are convinced that, were there any evidence for the notion, it would surely exist in their exhaustive Aeonodrome. But their tender regard for their neighbours seals their lips on the matter.

It is known that the Carolla who is not spends more than half of her watch at the far end of the pier, where it floats off the edge of Razalia and points like a squared, unsteady finger at the planet's amethyst sky, tracing its gradual surrender to pitch black. Her preoccupation with that end comforts the Razalians. Though not a fearful people, they are naturally aware that the arc peters out with them and that, unlike their Sehundan counterparts at the other end, they have neither the belligerence nor the firepower to see off any being or beings unknown who may come loping out of the "forsaken midnight". Arguably, this awareness has led them to give uncharacteristic rein to their fancy and speculate upon the non-Carolla's powers. They wonder if, a threat to Razalia appearing, she could summon the noble fifteen to its aid in a trice. At other times, they wonder if she could in fact repel single-handedly any marauders from out of the blackness. No-one, not even Tharle of Mopatakeh, has asked her. Indeed, no-one in living memory has spoken to her. First and last, the Razalians are phlegmatic. Like the sardonic sun, they observe, she has her reasons for being where she is, doing what she does. As for the powers she might possess, these would obviously reveal themselves if the occasion merited. And anyway, they conclude with some slight stirring of optimism, if unknown beings come marauding and she proves powerless after all, the Carollessa would not leave them in the defenceless lurch. True, it would take seven Earth months of travel for the Carollessa to prove them right, but that is not something on which the Razalians dwell. Their phrase for gratuitous worry – "grinding the beads of thought" – is properly disdainful.

The Carolla who is not scans the edge of Razalia with a special intensity. That is not to say, however, that she sees all. She does not always notice when, heaving and furrowing, the ninth ocean receives the singular gift of turbulence from the sleeping umber moons. She does not always look round when Carollessa or Baraskians come whooshing or droning in to land. Certainly, she remained stock still, back presented to Razalia, when a man, stood on the highway that girds the ninth ocean, made to kick the rear bumper of his van, then stopped and gazed about like the first scrap of creation in the first dawn.

"THE MERCURY ANNUAL"

White. White only, billowing, contorting, massing and stretching fine. Far away it is a million ridges. Closer in, a lapping of all the waves that have ruckled any sea. It deepens here, growing a belly of grey, pretending substance. There it pulls to a skein, promising to dissolve and show whatever is beyond. Minutes tick, the skein holds. Beyond stays unknowable. White only.

Then the drop. Shapes of billow and ridge are left somewhere above, for the white presses close now, as though the entire universe wishes to rid itself of fog, once and for all, and has heated and chilled, rained and shone itself into one last soup. The white is hungry for the mouth, would be at throat and lungs if it could – filling, clinging like a new kind of air, thick but mercurial. It needs to invade. Even now, a globule of white detaches, bulking into a mouth-shape as if it would push the lips apart.

At the last second, a rift, tearing open huge distance, daubs of grey and blue at the very bottom. Dropping, dropping. The daubs are coy, resisting surrender of their shape. Some are in a curving line? Some in hollow squares? It's impossible to tell at this moment. Or to say what those other lines are: thin and elastic, stretching around and among the daubs – a peppery colour, perhaps, or simply black buffed by distance. And there are other daubs, that seem to move along the lines, up and down, full of tiny purpose, coloured – no, their colours won't declare themselves. They might not be coloured at all.

Dropping, dropping. Now all below is edged with the smokiness of an aerial view. The static daubs reveal their dispositions: squares and long stretches and, yes, curves. They stretch far under the smoke. Some skirt round glistening water, narrows and lakes of it. Others fetch up against scarps, throw themselves down valleys. And the moving daubs, those tiny beads, are taking on blushes of red, bright blue – and there a yellow, no, two yellow ones. The lines they move on go wide, go thin and have – yes, in places they have three winking lights above them, balanced on the vertical. As each winks on, it flicks off the others. It is as though Razalia's umber moons have got at a paintbox and now spend their days foot-to-shoulder, positioned as they wish forever to be.

Diving now, straightening. Here is overgrowth, thicker than the forests of Lachbourigg, said to rove around in the twilight of the departing sun, obliging the planet's dozen inhabitants – shamans of unknowable powers – to leave their single dwelling, form an equilateral triangle, five per side, fold their arms and squeeze, somehow crushing the forests' motion with that intimate pressure. But this overgrowth is not natural. It recalls Carolles' first jolting steps towards sophistication, recorded and preserved in one of three antechambers in the Aeonodrome. The static daubs must be dwellings – yes, roofs now, blotches of tiling, with black-eyed slants and shards beneath them, like clippings from the arc's forsaken midnight pressed any-old-how onto... brickwork, is that?

Staying straight, dropping deeper. The undergrowth now: slab-work, tilting, broken; small gates, here peeling, there slumped at eccentric angles. And here are the moving daubs: green, black, purple, anything they fancy, their colours sloshed on with a carelessness that would bring a breathy little blub to the mouth of a Carollessan elder. Wheeled and sprung, they jockey on their lines (which are sometimes peppery, yes, and sometimes black) or fan out, or make to graze each other, little red lights pumping away on their rears, making them look like sorry prototypes of the Floribunda birds of Galladeelee. Are they wooing? If so, the parps and blares they emit when closing on each other are singularly ugly. Some daubs are taller than others and make to cut diagonally through the rest when the notion takes them. But now, look, they're slowing. Up ahead is a vertical array of moons, the top one flaring, the others asleep. Now the middle one wakes, the top one dies; now the bottom moon, taking the strain of the others, flashes on, gaudy as the jostling daubs. And now the fanning again, the parps and beeps.

Swerving now, over a huge green circle tricked out with... well, sorts of flowers, presumably, though they look as though one of Barask's gardeners – legendary in their ham-fistedness – has been at their tending. The coloured daubs flow round the circle's edge. Is this a promenade, a chance for random partnering? Or punishment, perhaps? Clearly they're stuck there forever.

Flying on, time passing. The blares and beeps diminish. Here's a smaller circle, just a few coloured daubs spinning round it: the unchosen, probably, wallflowers. Quieter now. A peppery line approaches: wide enough, almost properly surfaced, flanked with – yes, with a tree or two. Spindly things, though, their leaves a sickish green, furled almost into tubes. Are they dying? Is there air to breathe here? Or is it the fog from high above, in transparent doses?

Speeding along the line, which rolls and lifts and curves this way and that. The dwellings seem variously charmed or unmoved by it. Here, a crowd of them, fused brick to brick, bear down on its very edges; there, they stand off in couples, fronted by scraps of green and brown, by parti-coloured tangles that spill and wave; there again, they stand singly, frozen in the midst of more green, more colours in frothings and tides. Suddenly, to the right, a huge lemon daub works its wheels from between two slabs of brickwork, parping robotically: a sorry love-call for such virile dimensions. Will it now roam in search of those wallflowers left to spin round their little circles? Show them that, in one regard at least, they are not forgotten? Skirting sharp around the lemon daub. Speeding on.

Daubs and bad colour and choked-up trees. Set aside Razalia's theories for a moment: its maker dropping off a mountain or down to the core, or somersaulting through space. Did it actually survive? Go flapping through immensity – now slicing on, making a bow-wave in the black; now dead out with fatigue, treading emptiness; considering numberless directions, choosing one at last with no more reason than that its eye or eyes or pads or snout lingered a second upon it? And did it come bent and winded into this system at last? Buffet its way through the ridges, the billows, the miles-high fog and battle against whatever sun might be about? The parps and pepper lines, the tangle-fronted dwellings – are these the maker's second go at creation? Its second betrayal of the cack-hand?

The crest of the pepper-line. Dipping now. Single dwellings on the right – decent enough, though, for different reasons, Carollessa, Lachbouriggian and Baraskian would shake their heads at them. On the left, an unnatural cliff (which might excite Sehundan interest) with prodigious windows, emitting splashes and echoes, hosting lines of wheeled daubs on its own laneway. Dipping, dipping. More dwellings on the left, then a long wall of Razalian quaintness, a patched and bulging thing, emitting a tiny thwacking sound and cries and a sort of applause. On the right another kind of daubing, on a sign

– black script as ungainly as the Galladeelean alphabet: *Kennershalt, District of South Staffordshire.*

And now a certain dwelling on the right, this one here, at the pepper-line's end. Outside it, another sign, *Rowan Tree Lane.* More ungainliness. Swerving in, over surprisingly neat slabs, through its door, up stairs, on a level, up more stairs, on another, then along to the kind of swing-ladder last seen on Carolles five aeons ago, and up into a room of dust and triangular walls where something squats among piles of more colour. This is it. This is him.

He was sitting cross-legged on a forgotten travel-rug. Above him, the loft's single bulb gave its bit of light for the job. All around were tentacles, death-rays, buildings a-tumble, schoolboys grinning through freckles, schoolgirls chatting in groups. He stared vacantly at them, picked up a ghoul, gurning and iron-clad, then cast it down. It hit a pile with a sort of splash, glossiness on glossiness. Others, already taken up and dropped, had sounded no more than they were, paper hitting paper. For more than an hour the sounds had alternated, half-mesmerising him. He loved them all, glossy or rough.

Intermittent light rain had been forecast for that Thursday afternoon: par for the course in early summer. So it had turned out. Good news, at least, for the cricketers up the road: no downpour, no outright stoppage. Some special match, he'd heard, a team sounding like the Oddfellows versus another like the Rotarians. Through the small dormer window came sporadic thwacking, some applause, an occasional lone voice of praise or protest. These alternated with the splash or muteness of his gems as they dropped.

"Can you not see to those comics, Keith?" Thus she had started on the subject – Easter, must have been. Her tone had seemed disinterested, almost kindly, implying that any time between now and Christmas would do. Over the following weeks, however, the tone had changed. Sighs and tuts had woven themselves in. Intimations of peril had appeared: "It was making a right racket, the tank, I thought, so that's why I went up. Damn nigh broke my neck on a pile. Don't know which is worse, their shiny covers or that plastic you keep over 'em. Lethal either way." The tank's racket, it transpired, was only the effect of her Indonesian serenity-oil phase, the proper appreciation of which required at least two baths a day.

By the end of May, she had enlarged her approach. Unspecified destiny entered the frame: "Well, it's just *there*, isn't it? Has been since we moved in. Space and a load of dust. I do what I can up there, Keith, you know I do, but the vacuum's out and I can't risk this back on hours with a dust-pan. It's got... we could really turn it into... oh, you can see that, surely."

Now he rubbed his nose, thinking of that last phrase. He could tell what she saw. She hadn't needed to broaden the hints. A bedroom for Janice's boy – well, he didn't want to be forever kipping down with grandad, did he, when he stayed? Big adventure, up the swing-ladder – well, till stairs replaced it. Or a bolt-hole for Niall after current girl-friend chucked him out, before the next one took him in. Niall's old bedroom was now her meditation-zone, its location apparently chock-a-block with vibes. In one way, the Niall option would be easier, cheaper. In matters of lifestyle and taste, their only son had always been a dust-and-floorboards man. Each successive girlfriend realised that. A day or so later, he was obliged to hit the road.

"Look, Donna," he'd tried, one Friday at the start of June. "Mog's room's too small for her. If you really want that loft –"

"She's fine where she is." Her answer had rushed out like one word. She'd looked at him, her eyes steely a moment. He knew what she was thinking. It was what she always thought when talk turned to their youngest. With years of practice, though, the thoughts now zipped round a well-worn groove. Who in either of their families had been called Imogen? What possessed him to insist on the name? And why bother, since he'd spoilt it ever after by calling her Mog? It was-n't only that, of course. Mog had been a late surprise: for him, a source of unequalled joy, then and now; for her, something else. "Imogen sprawls," she'd said; always she used her full name. "A week of her up there and it'd be your comics all over again. No point in changing a thing."

That same evening, he'd stuck his head round the lounge door: "Just off up to The House," he'd said, meaning his regular pints with Hoj and Philpotts at the White House (*"Kennershalt's Finest"* said its sign; *"Jas Harkley's Moonbeam Ale Brewed At Rear"* – claims which, like the sign itself, had weathered away with the years).

She'd barely tilted the back of her head. Her gaze was on the TV screen, across which a woman dressed for a night-club wove and ducked, avoiding attic beams. Finding the crown of the roof, the woman straightened and flung out both hands: "Pa-ten-shul!" she exclaimed. He saw a notebook hastily taken up from the arm of the chair. Nodding to himself, he sloped off.

After that, the topic had faded – or gone underground, as he should have realised – until that Thursday morning. A ten-minute exchange had sent him up to the loft. It had commenced as soon as Mog left the house for the third time, her average in the matter of schoolthings mislaid.

"Forgot to tell you," said Donna. "Message from Mrs Askills."

"Ebbatson House? When?"

"Yesterday – six, six-thirty."

"Six-thirty? I'd just left there."

"Yes, you must have done." Her fingernail invented a rune on the surface of the kitchen table. "I did write it down," she added a little dreamily, as though the scrap of paper were plain to see but in another time and world.

He sighed: "Bet she wants those aqua-blue sinks after all."

"No, no sinks nor you neither. Some bigwig visiting all the old dears this morning." She looked vaguely about. "That paper's here somewhere. Some Residential Care bod, anyway."

He stared at her: "Well, I'd best phone her. See if a one o'clock start –"

"No, no," she interrupted like the teacher she once was, "no call for you at all today. Tomorrow, eight-thirty as norm, she said."

Pushing up from his chair, he froze. "Why didn't you give me the message last night?"

"I'm giving it to you now," pursued the teacher. He sat down.

"Oh, well, if Ebbatson's off, I'll go down Darkhouse, see the gaffer on that executive homes site."

"No, no. Forget him. Let's worry about your executive home today, Keith."

He made to rise again: "My what? Look, Donna, I've got to talk to him. Water Board are cutting up rough. He's got imminent bother."

"You're facing the same. Two months, is it, since I first said? Three? Those comics, Keith. Today. Now."

At last he stood up: "I'm phoning him, anyway. And Mrs A, to con-firm."

"Oh, so you think I'm pulling your leg about the bigwig?"

He retreated.

"A minute apiece for those phone calls," she called, speculative, annoyed. "And then" – she fluttered a hand upwards – "then them."

Turning, he propped his elbows against the door-frame and sagged a little. Momentarily, she looked to heaven. She'd never broken him of that pose. Forever using it, he was, if there was a doorway to hand. It went through her like a knife at social dos: made him look pie-eyed.

"So what's it to be, Donna?" Now he looked heavenwards, suddenly feeling wearier than if he'd spent a whole day among the straying, importuning inmates of Ebbatson House.

"The loft?"

"Are we kitting it out for Janice's or for Niall?"

"Andrew. He's called Andrew." She shook her head. "*Janice's*. Bad as *Mog*. Can't you hang on to anyone's name?"

"Because I'll need to get the gear and make the time, and that's –"

"I need to see the place cleared, Keith. Then we can decide. Might be one or the other, might be neither."

He frowned. She wasn't thinking of shipping all her relaxation doings up there, was she? Insisting on some jacuzzi of paradisal design? Joists wouldn't take that – plus it would need a double-sized tank, or a second one. He imagined lying in bed, watching Europes and Asias of damp creating themselves across the Artex, twitching his nose as the first fragrantly-essenced drips came down. And why did she bother with *we can decide*? Oh, yes, there'd be joint decisions, here and there, on frills and finishings. But the big decision would be hers, as it always was with the house. His frown deepened, causing her to repeat that it might be something else altogether. When had that happened, he wondered – her having the say-so on everything? Probably when he'd shrugged and agreed once too often. Only himself to blame, then. Odd, though, feeling like he was being booked in and called out to his own home. He didn't know whether to laugh or –

"You'll have that frame all crushed," she was saying now. He looked. One hand was clenched on the frame, knuckles pure white. He stared at her, clenched harder for a moment, then straightened up. She pushed her chair back a little.

"If *we're* still undecided," he said, "what about fitting it up for Mog like I said? It's daft, her still in the smallest room and the other two gone."

"Imogen is fine where she is." Her eyes narrowed. "Unless you're thinking of shifting all your tat from the loft to hers."

"Her feet'll shoot through the wall just now. Though why she couldn't've had Janice's old room –"

"Visitors, Keith, visitors." She sighed like a woman thirty years older, her manner implying that, despite his best efforts, his very presence, visitors still came – once in a way. "Lightest and airiest, Janice's room."

He gripped the door-frame again, launching himself back into the kitchen: "And doesn't Mog deserve light and airy? It's a nonsense, her bookshelf out on the landing in a house as big as –"

"Madam has two more years at school, then she's gone!" Tight, small, her voice suggested that she had something other than university or the big wide world in mind. "Two more, that is, if she's stopped dreaming long enough to write those exams she's got. She won't shoot through her damn wall. It'll hold her that long."

They stared at each other for a long moment. She shifted uneasily: not from awkwardness, he knew that, but because she probably wanted to head for her meditation-zone, beggar about with an energy core or two. A cry came faintly from the road outside: some passer-by, interested in or amused by the cricket. At last, Keith turned as if dismissed and made for his tiny office between kitchen and conservatory. She heard him picking up the phone and caught his change of voice as he dealt first with Mrs Askills, then with the foreman at the Darkhouse site. As he replaced the phone for the second time, she checked her watch. Yes: about a minute for each call. She smiled, satisfied, at the half-closed office door, then slipped from the kitchen before he opened it.

Now, he shifted on his haunches and peered slowly around the loft-floor. Toppled from their piles, their colours clashing, his gems made a strange planet-scape all about him. He stretched a hand, resting it on *Dearest Chums,* December 1957, his fingers obscuring the faces of a skating party on a frozen lake. Through the dormer window came more sounds: shrieks, remonstration. Kids from Christfields Primary being shepherded up the road to the Baths. Moving his hand, he regarded the laughing ruddiness of the skaters. Mog had learnt to swim at Rowan Tree Baths, just after they were opened. The other two had thrashed and choked their way into some kind of technique, fearlessly taking on the waves of sundry resorts. But he'd wanted

Mog to learn properly. In the garage he'd found the learner-suit his parents had bought for him, a one-piece with pockets round the midriff for six plastic floats. He'd offered to unearth it for Janice, then Niall. In turn, they'd looked at him gone out. So had Donna, saying he'd make them a laughing-stock by parading them like that: "Might as well have them in hoops and crinoline," she'd added. But Mog hadn't demurred. Over weeks of steady practice, six floats had become four, two, one, and she was there, graceful and unaided, slicing through width after width.

"She's done it," he'd cried to Donna, phoning home from the Baths.

"She hasn't lost any floats, I hope. We might get a bob or two for that effort. Some folk aren't partic."

Remembering her words, he balled a fist and thumped his knee. At that moment, a drone of torment rose through the floor. She was having a crack at her tension cycles. He recognised the tape, though he couldn't place its title – same for all of them. *Melanesian Timbres,* was it? *Aztec Pulse?* He'd borrowed one once and played it in the car, curious about its effect, which was to make him run a red light at a pelican crossing and cop a mouthful from a mother-of-four. Mog had been with him: "Put your stuff back on, dad," she'd said. A moment later, Buddy Holly was relaxing them both.

He got to his feet, steadied them on a joist and stretched. Mog'd be well set up here, he thought. A princess in her palace. The drone rose. He could feel it buzzing in the wood. Before he knew it, he was bending this way and that, scooping up his gems, flinging them any old how so that they clattered on the beams, skidded along the dust. One hung itself on the dormer window, threatening to slide out. The drone stopped. He braced himself for purposeful steps on a rung or two of the ladder, for "What you doing with them?" But the timbres or the pulse recommenced. Slowly he edged across the floor, retrieving the comic from the window. Then he sank down again, eyeing his scattered gems in remorse. Lunch soon, he supposed. He'd need to get a move on.

But get a move on with what? It suddenly occurred to him that, after all the clashes, he didn't know what she meant by *see to them.* She hadn't made it clear. And he'd been merely concerned with postponing the job – and resorting to his usual hope-against-hope that she'd let it drop. He wondered why that habit persisted: with the bit between her teeth, Donna was unquashable. It was the usual, he supposed. Go along with it all. Anything for a quiet life. Again he laid a hand on a gem, this time covering a cityscape in flames, across which bile-green beams ranged and destroyed. His laugh was almost frightened. For the very first time, he realised that the so-called quiet life was anything but. It was another attic, groaning under acquiescences, capitulations. Airless, damp, it stank of one big gathering grudge.

He knew what *see to them* didn't mean: move them elsewhere in the house. That left the smaller garden shed or the garage. The shed was full of stuff that he really *did* mean to see to. But it was musty and would need insulating if his gems were to survive. A day's work, maybe? Three? When could he make the time? More than plenty on at the minute. He should have headed down Darkhouse since Ebbatson House was no go. Never mind all this. But all this was in front of him now. Anyway, the garage was the better bet for them. Attached to the house, it picked up as much heat as the loft, near enough. But where in the garage would they go? He visualised the space with its broad verges of tools and garden chairs, freezer and clutter. He'd be lucky to get his gems into three piles in some corner, hard against the ceiling. They'd have the life squished out of them, and that kind of pressure was as damaging as damp. Wait on, though: those travel-racks for the bikes could go in the small shed – could go altogether, in fact, since the kids' bikes had gone long since, apart from Mog's, which was in the large shed. And he could shift that old dresser to where the bike-racks were. What was in it but the family history of bits and bobs? Actually, last time he looked, they were all in the bottom drawer. It was almost empty, then – unless Donna had stuffed the other drawers with reserve supplies of healing folderol. Ignoring that possibility, he frowned hard. So: bike racks gone, dresser moved. The strimmers and leaf-vacuum could go in the larger shed, just about, for now, till he sorted out the smaller one. Yes – that would leave the whole back wall, and he could space out his gems so they wouldn't –

Before he knew it, his hand was sliding away from the comic, as though, having wasted the city, the bile-green beams were now angling for his bones. Like a developing film, a terrible image crept over his mind, sharpening in odd places till all was coloured and linked. Donna clicked her key-fob. The garage-door reared up. For the first time, she saw the fruits of the attic arrayed across her headlights. She worked her lips in that way she had, pressed the accelerator, rolled in, watched the ridges of rising shadow from the 'roo bars across her grille. For an age she pressed, mashed, reversed, pressed. The plastic covers crackled like that cityscape; pile after pile of comics collapsed under her bumper, gummed up the arches of her wheels. And now his mind prickled as it had when she'd first said *see to them.* "Has to be the garage," he tried aloud, the loft-beams swallowing his words. "There it is, Donna." He repeated the words, variously going for no-nonsense, outrage, the calm confirmation of a plan agreed. But the image persisted, the rutted treads of Donna's tyres working school chums and astral buccaneers into so much paper snow.

She wanted the comics good and gone. She could have said from the off. Then again, he could have asked. But she hadn't because this was a nag worth stringing out, allowing her to revolve her several selves at leisure: the embattled *hausfrau*, the martyr, the interrogator of a brick wall. And he hadn't because he knew and didn't want to know. Like a translucent predator rising through clear water, the shock was upon him. Over the weeks and months, it had fed well on his dodging, his facing away. Now, like a skinless body, he had nothing to absorb it. Here, at its most punitive, was the quiet life.

Around him, the world squeezed and shrugged and changed forever. Someone was piling on the runs over the road: a megaphone announced it, to claps and whistles either admiring or mock-derisive. He felt as though he'd never known what a megaphone sounded like, or that clapping was a matter of percussive hands. Something bigger than a car went by. Was its groan mechanical, or a chorus of despairing voices? From below, the Melanesians or Aztecs droned louder. He felt rather than heard a beat which rose and faded like someone plucking a long, slack rubber band. Slamming his hands down on the joist, clenching it as he had the frame of the kitchen door, he told himself that for two pins he'd shin down that ladder and give – But the drone ceased, and now there were the little bumps and movements that said her session was done. He hunched a moment, surveying again his comicscape – as heaped and ruinous as that city under the sweep of those bilious beams. With a haunted glance or two at the top of the swing-ladder, he eased forward and finally got down to it.

She halved the pork pie, laying one half each on two plates, between the wreaths of salad. She planted a small mound of mango chutney on the edge of her plate, then dug deep in the jar with the spoon and shook a dollop over his pie. Low-fat crisps cascaded over the lettuce and tomato. Surveying them, she took a fistful of his and transferred them to her plate. Mixed herbs fell evenly as snow for her. For him, a gout of salt exploded on the pie-crust. She swung away from the counter and set both plates on the table. Then she looked at the ceiling, pursed her lips and dragged her chair out with her foot.

Twenty minutes later, wedging a knee-high pile of *Leapin' Loons* against the furthest wall, he heard a rattle like the hatch of a cell. There was her head at the top of the ladder. The tray slid along the floor, causing a small bottle of exotically-christened tapwater to wobble at its edge and a fork to slide off the salad.

"Didn't want you breaking your stride," she said; then, sighing, "this as far as you've got?"

"I'm sorting them by subject." His words almost vanished, addressed as they were to the *Leapin' Loons*. His tone irritated him. If he'd turned, stepped to one side and spread a hand to the pile, he couldn't have seemed more like a kid starved of merit-points.

She snapped her fingers. "Now that's your best idea in an aeon," she said, her tone suggesting that she was now at least three steps ahead of him in the matter of the comics' fate. He didn't like "aeon" on her lips. It wasn't her word but his, along with "demoleculate", "Crikey, Tich!" and a million others. He braced himself to erase years of slippage with a firm declaration. She was sighing again:

"Wonder the whole shooting-match didn't give way under this lot."

"I'm putting them in the garage."

"Neatly played, sir," came the megaphone over the road.

"In the garage?" Each word was a bubble of disbelief. Then she was sinister-quiet – "Oh, no, boy. No garage for these. No anywhere inside this gate" – and he heard a hundred vetos from her teaching days, saw dozens of young faces, puckering or angry, turning from her desk. "You do know what I meant by *see to them*, Keith? You got that drift?"

"You never said." Worse and worse – he was their own Niall, eight years old, a model of petulance.

Now she waved a hand as though starting on that stuff she sometimes commandeered the lounge for, that Inca soul-weaving.

"How long have we been married, Keith? Long enough for me to put up with your faffing, your *mañana, mañana* business. Well, that's all played out. So – time for your bit. You can hear me, can't you, Keith? You do understand?" Her lips worked as though, about to make herself clearer, she'd decided there was no need and bitten back the words.

He left the wall and dodge-trod round all the other gems until his toe-caps rested at the edge of the tray, forcing her to strain up at his face. She looked strange, cut off below the arms. She looked fragile.

"So where do they go?"

"Imogen's a growing girl. Growing girls have growing needs." She pointed at a stray issue of *Solar Salvation Cops* (June '55), then rubbed fingers against thumb as if conjuring a wad of crisp tenners. "Like you should have done years ago," she added, drooping a wee bit as she used to at Niall's umpteenth *Yes, but why?* Then she descended, timing "Keith, Keith," to each strike of her foot on the ladder. On the landing she called back:

"My plans are firming up, by the way."

Those words. They were hers.

The rain got heavier, rattling on the dormer window. Across the road, voices rose in genial confusion: *Dear, oh, dear. Lunchtime any-way, gentlemen – and she's sure to ease off. I need eight pairs of mitts, silvouee plate – line up the cover just in case.* A little later, shouts and squeals came bowling along. The Christfields kids had evidently stayed at the Baths to have their lunch, to judge by the wan chiding of their minders: *Vez, don't drop your silver foil – no, pick it out of the drain now – here, into this bag. Hood up, Tessa, hood up. What good's that tangerine now, Gareth, with your finger waggling in it?* By the time the rain had eased, he'd eaten the pie, picked at a leaf or so of salad and let the bottle of water roll where it would in the gloaming. He'd also settled into a deft rhythm. The *Leapin' Loons* – the whole catalogue, 1945 to 1952 – had been easy to abstract from the chaos. Theirs was one of the most distinctive mastheads: a cart-wheeling spider spinning threads of radiation red into the slogan *Wacky Critturs, Nutso Worlds.* But now he was ranging more broadly, digging and picking with care. Humour, Horror, Sci-Fi, Yarns Ripping and Sinister, School, Historical, Radio Favourites, Television Greats – piles of each began to rise around him like the posts of a stockade. Aligned to a knife-edge, they looked newer, sleeker than they had when dotted about in those squat, plasticated bundles. Initially, he had thought to arrange each type by title as he had with

Leapin' Loons. But that could come later – and he might even hear it described as his best idea in a second aeon. Anyway, it would buy him a little more time while he decided what to do. He wondered why he'd parcelled them any-old-how in the first place. Was it because, if she'd known, this rainy, loft-bound day would have come much sooner? He started: here was a stray *Leapin' Loon* (November '48). How had he missed that? Then he realised that the spider's thread was plaited red, white and blue. Ah, yes, presidential election year – Truman's second go. Not that the *Loons* were politically partisan. After Truman, they ushered Eisenhower in with Uncle Sam on a flying wombat's body.

"Off to Nanette's." The voice echoed up the ladder and round the loft in a way that his own never could. "Hope you're motoring up there." Nanette was the key link (her own phrase) with Greville Oldstead of *Tight Focus Surveys*, a pollster outfit with special responsibility for TV shopping channels. Every Thursday, Nanette, Donna and six other women met to evaluate the week's output in terms of phasing, content, breadth of goods and quality of star buys. Oldstead supplied them with forms, tick-box efforts with two lines of space at the bottom for *Summative Report In Accordance With Ordained Terms of Reference*. Completed from Thursday to Wednesday, the forms would be discussed. Then Nanette would "make that call" – a staple of *Tight Focus* phrasing – and giggle and purr the collective findings into Oldstead's ear. Each month, Donna received a cheque for her efforts, concealed behind a West Wittering postmark. A day or so later, a new cushion or two might appear in the lounge, or the back porch might sing to a replacement wind-chime.

"Lunch all right?" she called now. Too bad if not, implied the question. Minutes later he heard the garage-door rumbling open. For the first time that day, he smiled. Thursdays – just him and Mog at tea. His turn: that ready-meal Moroccan lamb she loved. Donna usually stayed till evening at Nanette's, although sometimes she returned earlier. This evening she'd be back like a bullet. Loft inspection was required. "No slacking, boy," had been her final yell before she left.

Suddenly, Gabe Tomorrow was staring at him, tough but kind. Gabe had just wrested control of Vulcana from the Aquadons, a race bred in and made of water. Vulcana lurked round the back of Mars, self-effacing but rich in minerals, particularly *auris oceanis*, which the Aquadons had wildly plundered, thinking only of its benefits for their liquid muscles, indifferent to the effect of their pillage on the planet, which was collapsing inwards. *Horizon King!* screamed the cover. *His Now Is Your Then!* Gabe himself was discovered on a rocky incline. One foot planted above the other, he jutted a proud knee like Scott or Amundsen. Around him, Aquadons paid dear for their selfish fixation. Variously they splashed to the ground, or curled helplessly airward like kettle-steam, or simply plopped as raindrops on stone. The next cover was Gabe again, this time streaming through the heavens, his face filling the cockpit of his *Horizoglider*. A zoom line declared his velocity: fat, white, fishtailing back to some point in deep space. Above him were legions of five-tipped stars, which seemed to be waving – as indeed was Gabe himself. Again his stare was steely and human together: the stare of William Tell, the Lone Ranger, Lt. Joe Friday. They had modest swathes of creation in their keep. Gabe seemed to have the rest. But he understood his duty just as they did – his readers' duty, too. "I'll guard the heavens," his stare proposed, "if you guard Main Street."

Absently, he dropped Gabe Tomorrow on his destined pile. He was thinking of the *Horizon King* Intercom Set he'd had for his twelfth Christmas. Two microphones, large teardrops with blue and yellow swirls, trailed – for miles, it seemed then – from their sockets on the Interplanetary Transmitter, a miniature Chrysler Building topped with what looked like a Blackpool Tower of orange matches. Communication held up for a day or so. From Patrol Base, between telly and mock-log fire, his dad had crackled questions to young Gabe, far away on Horizon 12, a station shaped like a car-port. Had the Oxydrator been found? Was it safe or had it, as they feared, been the object of Kadyadovoran sabotage? Would the colony survive? Young Gabe assured him that it was good as new, though its heat field readings were nearing the top of the scale. A brown splash of some kind was visible at the rear of its power-deck, though mercifully it bore no mark of a Kadyadovor pincer. Patrol Base crackled his pleasure, then instructed Gabe to remove the Oxydrator's panel and double-check the thermotransistors. "And be real careful, good buddy."

"Aye, sir," said Gabe, and was just reaching for the panel when the Queen Kadyadovoran materialised, impounding the Oxydrator for the pork roast. By New Year's Day, however, the horizons were silent. Young Gabe's hands roamed the Chrysler Building and Blackpool Tower, tracing each bulge and plane of plastic, trying to feel out the glitch. He checked socket and flex. Deliberately, he pressed the "Comm. Thru" and "Comm. Standby" buttons on the microphones. Nothing brought them to life. He was left to drift along the landing between Horizon 4 and Horizon 9, with nothing above him but anaglypta in a frozen star-fall, nothing to port or starboard but the squared, magnolia sunrise of the airing-cupboard door. Back on Earth, Patrol Base regarded the mock-flames beneath their logs and intoned, "Read me? Read me, good buddy?" before lapsing into despair. Roaming up and down her own universe, the Queen Kadyadovoran effed and blinded at the microphone flex, which seemed to snag her foot at ever corner. At last, the Interplanetary Transmitter found its way to another loft – except for the microphones, which Keith managed to revive, rigging them up as spares for his tape-recorder. One evening his dad came into his room, watched as he solemnly plugged one in and sort of sang the Beatles' "Paperback Writer", then listened to the playback. Unlike the exchange between Base and Horizon 12, it was crystal-clear. His dad took the mike: "Twelfth Night coming up," he said, singing what he assured his son was an old ballad lamenting the end of Christmas: Anthony Newley's "Do You Mind?" as it turned out. Then, employing Patrol Base's generic US accent, he recorded the first four lines of Longfellow's "The Village Blacksmith". On song and poem, his voice was relaxed, even vibrant: qualities denied it in his everyday life on Earth. After playing everything back three times, father and son had sat for a good minute, smiling, nodding to each other.

The rain had eased off again. Over the road, runs were again cheered, decisions contested. Waving goodbye to Gabe and the Kadyadovorans, Keith worked more quickly. As soon as a pile of comics reached waist-height, he dropped to his knees, his arms encircling them. Gingerly, with a skill acquired from years in other folks' lofts and under their sinks, he shuffled each pile backwards, lining them up by the *Leapin' Loons*. As he moved, his shadow feinted this way and that. He could have been a plucky arrival on a bald, sun-hardened planet, hunkering down as his cadet-training had taught him. In his earthly life, down below the swing-ladder, he'd hunkered and ducked for days out of memory.

Of course she wouldn't wait. She wouldn't salute his idea of sorting them by title and give him extra time. Before she first asked him she'd have measured out her tether. Gabe, the *Loons*, the *Dearest*

Chums – they and all were in peril. He could hear her voice that evening, leading the neat tap of her feet up the steps: "Right, then, how've we done?" "We": the breezy motto of the sham libertarian, the airy imposer of self-will. Oh, his gems would be safe for a day or so, standing to attention in the gloom of the far wall. Like well turned-out pupils, their sheer tidiness would soften a bit of her heart for a little while. But after that... well, her plans were firming up: she had said so. And her plans had a way of accelerating. If he dallied by so much as a week, he'd doubtless find the loft empty, with no explanation but the sigh of an exasperated parent – and, if he was lucky, words on the order of *How long have I waited, Keith? All right, so you stacked them nice and spruce – was that supposed to magic them away?* He thumped the pile he'd just worked into place. Just as well tomorrow was Friday and the White House. Just as well he'd be seeing Hoj – and Philpotts, more to the point.

George Philpotts was the proprietor of a wonderland. He knew this himself – knew also that, despite its weakness for gizmos, for whistles and bells, the present age didn't know how to value wonderlands, which was why he'd named his *The Last Emporium.* Double-fronted, their old-gold sign reminiscent of an Edwardian fruiterer's, his premises lay on the outskirts of Sedgley. The outmoded, the bizarre, gradations of tat from sub-artistic to pointless – over his counter they flowed. Nationally, internationally, he had contacts for the sale and supply of military paraphernalia (pre-war Baltic a speciality); Government stock; cards commemorating the stars of world cricket, European football, US baseball, Canadian hockey, Irish hurling and camogie, Australian rugby and (somewhere out the back) the victorious Charentes-Maritime *boules* squad, unassailed victors in the *Departement* championships, 1904 to 1907; girlie posters (beach, boudoir, forest and industrial units, including the mock-up for *Heavenwing 820–LL* tyres, Turin, featuring Amoretta Go-Vixen with monkey-wrench pointing to six o'clock – a rarity of the form); deities of all nations in wood, ivory, bronze, malachite, beaded and clawed, feral, serene or enigmatic; antique radios and televisions, hi-fis and reel-to-reel recorders, most notably a model of the 1957 *Königsapparat* four-track, the first commercially available machine with overdub (lid-clips missing); a global line-up of mags, DIY manuals (including instructions for the Freetown extendable palm-awning, the chattering drum of Nanking and a board for playing *myong-phet*, a Thai variant of ludo); hobby-guides; patterns for knitting, macrame and latticework; annuals; comics. "The chappo": thus, in conversation, did Philpotts bundle together his army of suppliers and purchasers. In fact, he used it for just about everyone, singular or plural, on the face of the earth. Edna, his wife, attended to the accounts and, two days a week, dealt with correspondence. Once a fortnight, she and Mrs Nicklin, wife of the publican at The Belknap Junction, would gingerly dust and clean the displays. Now and then, Edna would open the door to the labyrinthine stockrooms, duster in hand, intent on the same. Often, after wise reflection, she would simply retreat.

Big-boned, ruddy and round of cheek, George Philpotts looked like a farmer. Though kindly, his face was curiously indistinct. It seemed to change subtly when he turned this way or that. When he held the same expression for minutes together, the twinkle in his eye would sharpen or dim at will. It was as though half-a-dozen slightly different faces were lined up behind his skin, each ready to take its turn in wind and weather. Having had this pointed out, he claimed that his birthplace was responsible: Adbuckrilas, between Hereford and Ebbw Vale. "Changed countries umpteen times," he'd say. "At least twice when I was growing up. The boundaries chappo having a joke. Welsh, English, what am I? Celt one minute, Saxon the next. So there you are – where are you?" Edna was from Rotherham and had no time for this theory. For her, his only changeability came in the matter of promises. "Outside of that shop, you can't be trusted with a thing," she'd tell him, not without affection.

The doors of the Last Emporium had been open for twelve years. Before that, George had made a precarious living on the road. Antique shows, air displays, craft fairs, the elaborate gates of lesser known historic properties, themselves fighting for survival – he had fetched up at all of them with his mixed lorry-loads of strangeness and ephemera. Many a long, cold day had seen him sharing a wet field with vintage car zealots and enthusiasts for *Keep The Pound* or the animal kingdom. He just about broke even although, some months, it was a matter of pennies rather than pounds. Back home in Leeds, Edna grew ever more concerned – not least about George's welfare. Luckily, she put her foot down at the same time he decided to call it a day. The day in question was the summer solstice. George had set up his stall for five days at the Medlicott Fayre just outside

Yeovil. Usually, it was one of the more bonhomous fixtures in his calendar. The previous year, he'd even turned an unlooked-for profit. A troupe of six fire-eaters, regulars like himself, had arrived with tragic news: their entire kit had been filched from a platform at Exeter St David's station. Diving into his rig, rummaging mightily, George had unearthed an array of props which (he'd been assured) once belonged to Chinese tumblers from Wuhan at the time of the Boxer Rebellion. True, there were only three fire-sticks among them. But the propless troupe, improvisors to a man and flush from a lucrative engagement almost outside the National Theatre, paid him handsomely. The following year, however, the happiness of Medlicott Fayre was destroyed at the dawn of the third day, the solstice itself. With no reason at all to use the Medlicott site rather than any other, supporters of *Beasts of the Field*, an ecumenical charity for animals' rights, had closed bloodily with members of the nearby St Lavery hunt. The Fayre's exhibitors had stumbled from their caravans and lorries to find the air thick with staves, spurs and (so one witness insisted) a somersaulting pisspot of Aramathean design. The police had arrived hours later, explaining their tardiness by the fact that, as a regular fixture lasting for more than twenty-four hours, Medlicott Fayre was technically an "abode". Thus, any affray on-site was a "domestic", a class of incident they strove to avoid. No arrests were made. George saw the master of the St Lavery slip something to one officer; moments later, his neighbour stallholder saw the same transaction between another officer and a man who, obviously wishing to secure salvation from all angles, was clad in a skull-cap, frock-coat and gold-picked stole. Early punters had loitered to witness the fag-end of the battle (a draw, more or less), then drifted away, pointing and tutting at the churned, weapon-strewn land. Word must have got round: the fourth and fifth day were a financial washout. George had packed up by the last lunchtime. He stopped only once on the trek back to Leeds, phoning an acquaintance from a service station, a property chappo who'd been on at him for some while about attractive leasing opportunities for premises in the West Midlands. By autumn, he had spoken winningly to the banker chappo, Edna had found a house in Chivsull, a hamlet near Sedgley, and the Last Emporium had been painted, stocked and placed on the Local Traders' Register. The morning of the move, a parcel had arrived: an ivory-shafted firestick. The accompanying note read, "Just back from Florida – August gig down on Key West – coined it – here's a practice-stick if ever you want out of the antiques game – thanks and blessings, the Medlicott Six." The stick now had pride of place on the counter. George dusted it personally.

Heaving another pile of comics into line, Keith remembered the tale of Medlicott Fayre, the business of "abode" and "domestic", and laughed for the first time that week. Through the dormer window, the sound of engines roared and faded. The Christfields run had started: a brief-ish run. Smart cars did not crowd the gates of the local primary. Few of the parents could offer much for its bring-and-buy stalls. Soon there would be a good thirty minutes of footsteps walking or pattering, of childish protestation and adult rebuke: the real end of the Christfields day. *Ladies and gentlemen, the last three overs – sorry, two,* came a megaphoned voice from the cricket ground. Keith's labours were nearing their end: just four piles left. As he set to work on the next one, he tried, as so often before, to pin down when he and Philpotts had first met. For some reason, the details always escaped him. Having a sharp memory for all else, he was baffled by this uncertainty. It was as though he'd been infected by Philpotts' blurriness, by the changeability of which the man's wife gently despaired. Whenever he asked Philpotts, he got a different story: he had come to the shop; to a comics-fest in Wolverhampton, Wednesbury, Lichfield, Bridgnorth; they'd got talking on a bus, in a newsagents, waiting for a train, for their cars to be repaired, for their pints to settle. Each version was delivered with absolute conviction, deepening Keith's confusion. He hadn't taken a bus or a train in years – had he? As for Lichfield, he'd only been there once, as a kid, by accident. A family holiday to the Purbeck Downs had been all but doomed on the outward journey. "Now," his mother said, rattling the map just outside Burton, "half a mile on this A-road, then it's left, right, right, left for Warwick." He knew what would happen. His father, head full of songs and rhythms, of stars and far horizons, let the rights and lefts knot up like twine. The row turned to peevish snarls and thence to silence. A mental fandango of lefts and rights sent his father rocketing through the Midlands, till they found themselves at the steps of Lichfield Cathedral with some type in a surplice leaning down at the window and eyeing their summer clothes in some alarm: "Are you in the bride's party or the groom's?" he hazarded. "If you park at the head of the close, you might just get in for the exchange of vows." That was his only time in Lichfield, thought Keith. He was sure it… no, he wasn't sure at all. Shuffling back from the wall of the loft, he vowed to dredge up, once and for all, how Philpotts had come fuzzily into his life. It would be a small triumph to pit against the oppression of present circumstances.

"One more crack from you, Karl, and that skateboard goes back where you stole it." Through the dormer window, the father's voice mixed vexation with that's-my-boy approval. A little later, as the last childish wails and admonitions died away up the road, the megaphone blurted again from the cricket ground – *Gentlemen, draw stumps* – and there was genial applause, punctuated by one rogue whistle. Keith worked round the last three piles, lining up their edges. Puncture, he thought. That's how he met Philpotts. The only one he'd had with the Transit. He sold it soon after, so that was, yes, six years ago. It was Mountford Lane, running out of Sedgley. No jack. Niall had borrowed it: no, just taken it. He was going through one of his phases: making dodgy friends, this one was. Older than him, they ducked, dived, drove cars and vans in various stages of collapse and seemed incapable of using indicators or applying for road tax. "Fazmo's got a delivery on," Niall had explained. "Up Stockton. Be down the tubes if he's blown out with no jack. His Transit's only a reg. or two older than yours. He's back Friday, Sunday, something like… I'll bring it back."

Keith had wondered at the nature of Fazmo's cargo – then shuddered. Donna had taken up the cudgels, enjoying the chance to play hard-pressed mother and breadwinner's consort at the same time: "And what's your father supposed to do if a tyre goes on him? Thought of that at all? His time is money, Niall." She'd paused then, working her lips like mad.

"He gets the breakdown boys." Niall's tone was the one he often used on Janice and Mog – and, latterly, young Andrew: a slow delivery, slightly pained.

"And this Fazmo can't?"

Niall had tilted his head and sighed: "No, he can't," he'd said in hurt tones, as though Fazmo were a fine citizen who, through some perverse misunderstanding, was denied the services of his own country.

So there Keith was: Mountford Lane, no jack, back nearside tyre flat as last week's beer. And he'd actually… yes, he'd been on his way to buy another jack, rightly assuming that his own was gone for good. An old chap, seeing his quandary, had come to his gate: "Just a mo," he'd said, disappearing and returning, staggering and red-faced, with an outsize breeze-block. "My son's got one of those Ford efforts. We've used this before, no bother." Wondering if his son was the buccaneering Fazmo, Keith had watched as the man shoved the breezeblock under the Transit's bumper, then tried pulling one side upright. "You'll have to give a hand," he said reproachfully, his corduroy rump swaying before Keith's eyes. "Try flagging someone down first. We always get three or four on the job, if poss, only next door are away." Despite these instructions, the man clearly had a fair bit of strength in him. A moment later, the block was wedged at an improbable angle under the bumper, which was already pulling up and away from its brackets.

"Look, I do appreciate this," said Keith, "but Barwell's is just at the top of the road. They still got their Accident shop round the back? I can just nip –"

"Loving suffering!" The man sprang up with a sprightliness that would have shamed Niall. "He only wants those cowboys up the road," he added, addressing the breeze-block as if expecting a tut of disgust from its core. "And here I was, helping like a good 'un." Groaning, the bumper bent further up and released the block, which thumped down on Keith's right foot. The man regarded foot and block like a prophet who sees a parable of ingratitude come true. "Go on, then," he said, gesturing banishment. "I'll have to get this round the back again – somehow or other." He indicated the block with his foot, lost his balance and trod on it. Yelping, Keith somehow wangled his foot free.

"I'll bring the block round," he said. "Honestly, thanks for your –"

"You haven't got time, have you, my friend? Panting for Barwell's, you."

As he hid the last-but-one pile of comics in the gloom, Keith felt again the weight of the block and the man above it. Before he knew it, he was raising his foot behind him, working it left and right. Never mind breeze-block: pig-iron, that thing was, especially with the old bloke balanced on it. He pictured himself limping up Mountford Lane, convinced as he went that the man's thundery eyes were burning the back of his neck.

At Barwell's, an ageing punk had said that the tyre-change would take two hours easy: "The trucks are out, chief, and I've got to stay on the pumps." Over the punk's shoulder, Keith saw the station shop. A shock of white hair and pair of starting eyes were visible between a stack of coolant and a special-offer kiddyseat. Keith recognised him as old man Barwell.

"Can't your gaffer see to the petrol?" he asked, nodding towards the shop. "Or if you've a jack about, I'll take it and pay the hire."

The punk shook his head: "Let you have it? No chief. I'd be unauthorising, see?" He leaned close. "And the gaffer's gone doo-lal. If I take off –" He made a grabbing gesture, then took an imaginary swig.

"He drinks the takings?"

At this, the punk snorted: "Before they get to be takings, chief." He jerked a thumb at the pumps and swigged again: "Them."

"He what?"

"Diesel's his tipple, though he don't refuse Lead Replacement. Even tries it on when we're here, sometimes. We had the Mayor's car pull up Bank Holiday last. Packed with the big nobs. I come out from the back, there's gaffer lounging on the bonnet with the nozzle over his face, trying to do the old nose-to-mouth drip – the Tenerife trick, you know, like with them wine-jugs?"

Kneeling under the loft-light, regarding the last pile of all, Keith couldn't remember what he'd said then. Words of commiseration? Certainly words of advice, because the punk had said, "Tried that, chief. Had him put in Ebbatson House, down Kennershalt way, yeah? Lasted two days. He got into their emergency paraffin."

A car had pulled onto the forecourt then – no, bigger, a Range Rover or such. Keith remembered seeing old man Barwell splay a desperate hand on the window, obviously willing it to brake at the Diesel stand. The punk swivelled and caught the look in those wild eyes. "Oh, we're here, we're here…"

"Listen, I'm with All-Britain Accident. I'll phone them – just thought I'd take a punt with you."

The punk turned back: "We'll do it in an hour max," he smartly corrected himself. "I'll get one of the lads back." He pointed down Mountford Lane to Keith's van. "Is that him? Right – give's your keys, yeah? Go and have a pint." The punk ran for it then: the Range Rover was at the Diesel pump and old Barwell was slavering through the door.

Now, Keith recalled every limping step of his way into Sedgley.

He'd never heard a time estimate slashed in half before. It wasn't the kind of madcap claim he made to his customers. But his foot was throbbing and he needed a sit-down: he'd take the punk at his word. And perhaps one of his breakdown lads would manage it. Looked like they had to catch any passing trade, to make up for all that sorry leakage at the pumps.

Before long, but still longer than was good for his foot, he'd been hobbling down Aikenshaw's Walk, to the left of the Rowlandson Arms. Narrow, with no pavement on the pub side, the road had somehow escaped the notice of the one-way system planners years before. By unspoken agreement, the locals only used it to drive out of the town centre. Strangers, however, were at the mercy of their own ignorance. Sometimes they found themselves in a Mexican stand-off with a council lorry or a shopper in a laden car, eager for home. Then the pub's hardcore regulars would turn out, ranging themselves round the Bar door, even betting in pints on the outcome, while Dawes the landlord (teetotal himself, curiously) shook his head behind them – whether at their shenanigans or at the inherent lawlessness of Aikenshaw's Walk, he never said.

Finding himself on the pub side and thus in some peril, Keith had shuffled across as quickly as he could – but not quickly enough to avoid a blaring horn and a royal mouthful as a truck rattled past, *Barwell's Breakdown* lettered on its side. He'd staggered in its wake, shocked as well as footsore now, and looked around vainly for a bench. Finally, he'd lowered himself onto the edge of a brickwork box from which a sapling, apparently nourished by cigarette-wrappers, mashed cans and a single mauve sock, reluctantly probed the air.

It was the first time he'd noticed the parade of shops. Now, reaching forward in the loft, flicking a trail of dust from the top of the final pile, he nodded, fixing the truth of that thought in his head. A near-local, he only used Aikenshaw's Walk to get out of Sedgley, always keeping his eyes left in case an ecstatic tippler came flailing out of the Rowlandson Arms (which he never drank in: scruffy, reputedly unpainted since the summer of the moon landing, it struck him as less of a pub, more an expression of Dawes' contempt for his patrons). He remembered leaning from his throne of cans and papers, gazing along the parade. *Hair Trigger*, a salon was worryingly named. A graphics and printer's outfit seemed no more than a door with a multi-postered window over it. The strip-blinds of a closed insurance office were discoloured, a tipsily horizontal line of brown seeming to hold them together just above the sill. Then – Keith had rubbed his eyes. What was he looking at? The one surviving branch of the Home and Colonial? A general store from one of those costume dramas that Donna was forever taping? Its gold letters, generous above the open door and either window, seemed to waltz his gaze incomprehendingly about, till it came to rest on something iridescent in the shop, angled as if to shoot through the door. He'd stood up, weathered a fresh surge of pain and walked towards it. It was a distress flare. No, a marathon torch. A rocket from a civic display? A fire-eater's doo-dah? Though unlit, it seemed to illuminate all around it – including a poster crying *His Now Is Your Then*, the words arching over Gabe Tomorrow's squared jaw and searching eyes. Recalling the sight now, Keith was filled again with joyous astonishment. At the time, it had taken a more dramatic form: his mouth had sagged open and he'd reeled like a sailor in the depths of shore leave. Recovering himself, he had peered deliberately at the shop sign, this time making out *Emporium* before a man's voice called, "A chappo walking and wounded." Looking down, he'd seen someone utterly unlike Gabe the Horizon King in the doorway. "Saw you struggling over," the man had said, pointing at Keith's foot. "That doesn't look clever at all. You'd best come in."

"Honest to God, you'll be the death of me, Denise Nicholas." The woman could have been in the loft. Squeaky, roll-up-rough, her voice broke through the dormer window. Keith expected to see her words splattered on a joist. "Ha-pa two I was there, soaked to the skin. All the others come out and went. 'Seen Denise? No. Seen Denise? No.' Mel says you've gone with Jody, then Jody comes out, says you've gone over the shops. Bloody hell, Denise."

In reply, her pimpernel daughter repeated, "I was helping Miss Watkins. She's buggered the lid of our stencil-box."

Keith let the voices go, and, after, the revs of cars from outside the cricket ground. Had the Oddfellows won, or the Rotarians? A draw, probably – even though a little calculation, a little attention in the matter of the score-plates, might have produced a clear winner. That seemed to be the way with most matches played over there. He shuffled right up to the last pile, still glowing from all he'd recollected. Yes – that was the first time he and George had met, whatever George might say. It all fitted: the puncture (which was sorted out in an hour, apparently, though it was nearer two when he got back: "Thought you'd immigrated" the punk had said, looming past the pumps with old Barwell in tow cackling, then almost swooning as a DERV truck eased onto the forecourt with fresh supplies); the breeze-block (still reproachfully propped against the old chap's gate when Keith had driven away, the chap himself opening his door for a last baleful squint); old Barwell like an inventor after a life of fumes and residues; the sapling with its compost of rubbish; *Hair Trigger*, with squiggly lines around the letters – meant to represent smoke, presumably, or perhaps it was just the wrong paint on the wrong wood; the luminous stick; Gabe's jawline. And George's greeting: the words of a kindly stranger, not someone met already. He imagined himself raising the subject again at the White House. "No, we definitely met in Birmingham," he imagined George saying. "Convention Centre. DC Comics Day – slides, talks on the outfit's history, veteran chappos autographing special issues of their artwork. Clear as this morning to me. You and me, we were standing in line for the tea-and-cakes chappo. No, we had a moan about the Gents – hand-dryers kaput. No…" Bright but unconvincing, his voice faded from Keith's mind. Niall's mate had brought them together, the tricky Fazmo – who, it turned out, hadn't needed the jack for any Stockton trip. HM Derriton gave him bed and board for five years; his accomplice enjoyed three elsewhere. Luckily, the security guard at the computer warehouse recovered completely from his head wounds. Equally luckily, Niall was cleared of all involvement, though Donna spat her share of fire: "What kind of buggering friend's that, Niall? Honest to God, we could've all been summonsed." From then on, and without parental prompt, he became more discerning about the shoulders he accidentally rubbed.

Keith couldn't remember what he and George spoke of, that first time in the Last Emporium. It didn't matter – and anyway, he'd probably forgotten by the time he returned to the punk at Barwell's. All he could recall was a sense of magic unfolding, among the Assigai spears and horn gramophones, the sets of *Davy Bridge's Floating Castle* (bi-monthly, 1950 to 1973, an Anglo-Indian collaboration) and the "Speak Your Weight" machines retrieved from the Zip-Thru Caff, Runcorn, whose owner, George later told him, had lobbied to have the M6 make a sharp left at Knutsford and run straight past his door, his head full of bold, rather sinister plans for the erasure of whole communities. The magic had deepened as George unlocked this glass case, spun that revolving comic-rack. Of course Keith had spoken of his own treasures – probably with a candour which, Mog aside, he'd never risked with his own family. He remembered thinking from the off that George was no mere caretaker, no johnny who'd breezed into the emporia market for the money alone. He was businessman, connoisseur and acolyte together. He clearly understood the beauty and worth of all that passed through his hands – and was generous-spirited enough to give a home to some things that had neither.

The magic had deepened further over numberless visits to the shop and the house at Chivsull. George had visited Rowan Tree Lane, smiling benignly at Donna as he sipped his tea in the lounge and waited for Keith to descend from the loft with a pack of gems. After the first few visits, Keith remembered, the benign smile was not returned. In fact, unbeknownst to him, Donna was even then pondering life without an infestation of comics in the loft. She hadn't given it much clear thought before. At the time, she was still working – busy in the classroom, busy in a home from which only one child had been shed. But the niggle must have been at the edge of her mind, for, when George appeared, she surprised a yearning for magic in herself – along the lines of "I'll give you two thousand quid for the lot" from the mouth of this burly man who obviously drank more than was good for him. Such words not forthcoming, she had begun to employ discreet tactics of freezing-out: a sighed exit to another part of the house, and the proferring of tea without biscuits, without saucer – and, finally, no tea at all. Another barmpot, she concluded, as bad as Keith – worse, since he could have made an offer of advantage to himself as well as her – well, them, then. She knew how much these merchants marked prices up. Greville Oldstead, her man at *Tight Focus Surveys*, had told Nanette as much once. How they'd got onto the topic, she never said. Out of the blue he'd phoned her, middle of the day. Questionnaire business, she'd told Donna, but never said what.

Niall had still been living at home during George's visits. Drifting through the lounge, spotting George, he used to catch his mother's eye and pretend to bore a finger into the side of his head. Mog, however, grew fascinated by George. Partly it was to do with his sharing of dad's interest ("call it interest, for want of a better," as Donna would cryptically remark to herself and friends); and his visits made dad happy, which delighted her. And partly, it was his liking for dad's particular comics. She adored them. They took the word "possibility" and painted it in fairground letters; they shattered the word into more meteors than the universe could hold and then put it back together, bigger and bolder than before; they proclaimed other worlds, yelling as loudly as that town-cryer she'd seen on a school trip to Worcester Christmas Fair. And dad looked after that word, which made him even more special. Whenever she thought of "possibility" in terms of mom, she could only see as far as the front wall, the lounge windows, the garden sheds; beyond that, everything faded like the close of day. But also, George fascinated her because she'd picked up on his blurriness: "Cloudy George," she called him to herself. His strangely changeable face was like a comic itself. Watching his head turn was like getting ready to flip a page of *Davy Bridge* or *The Nebulae Posse* or any of them. What was waiting on the other side? What expression would take hold for a moment, before giving way to the next like the flow of pictures in a cartoon?

Donna had quickly noted that Imogen liked hanging about when that Philpotts came calling. After his first few visits, when it was clear that he wasn't going to do anything sensible about the comics, she'd used every pretext to bundle the child out of the way. For his part – feeling more uncomfortable each time, less able to concentrate on the selections that Keith laid out for him – George finally let the visits tail off. Thereafter, he and Keith met up at the shop, Chivsull or the White House. Sometimes, Mog would come with her dad to the Last Emporium. Once or twice, she'd visited the house at Chivsull, where Edna had fussed mightily over her. As time went by after George's last visit, Donna's annoyance settled back into a dull resignation. She braced herself for another stretch of life with those bundles of tat hanging about over their heads. Even then, she nursed a half-hope that something would happen: that Philpotts would talk Keith into a deal after all, or that Keith himself would up and advertise his daftness in the "For Sale" columns. She also made a secret pact with herself. If nothing of the kind happened, she'd suffer their presence so far and no further. She didn't know how long she'd wait – only that she'd know when the waiting was over.

There was a chirring sound above Keith's head. A moth or some other insect had zoomed fatally in on the loft bulb. He looked up but saw nothing. Then, bowing his head, he seemed to pay homage to the final pile. It was nowhere near as high as the others; it would barely reach halfway up his calves. Nor was it destined for a place along the wall. Keith hadn't sorted it out: hadn't needed to. The pile was neatly sealed in a plastic bag, red and capacious. He'd got it from Donna – or rather, the school she was in at the time. *O'Sullivan Educational*, ran the legend along one side. A pair of chunky display boards had arrived in it, for a project she was doing: *Life On Other Planets*, it was. He – no, Mog – had suggested that she make use of his comics, which at the time had been lying about uncovered in the loft: "Bit of fun, mom," Mog had said. "It'd be great. I wish Mr Carson would do something like that. No chancy, Clancey," she'd concluded, quoting Gabe Tomorrow whenever some scheming alien tried to enlist his aid in a spot of intergalactic tyranny.

Donna had merely worked her lips at her last-born. A day or so later, however, she had arrived home with the bag: "How about keeping your planets clean and tidy in this?" she'd asked Keith, her voice curiously neutral.

"They won't all fit."

"Well, ask your wholesale bods to keep some bags and sheeting on one side," she replied, all reasonableness. "And there's that new stationer's on the Tovington Road." She'd looked at the ceiling then. "Attracts all the dust in the house, your stuff does."

Mog had stuck her head round the door: "Less housework for you then, eh, mom?" Donna had glared as though she were a pupil who'd just fired off a mouthful. "No, Imogen," she'd said. "Same amount." And, rubbing the small of her back, she'd made for the kitchen. "*Wignall's*," she'd called, clattering a pan onto the cooker. "That stationer's."

Father and daughter had stood silent for a moment. Then Keith, hearing again the call of the quiet life, had written the name down on a pad by the lounge phone. Mog, picturing the way her mother had rubbed her back, had blinked and bitten her fingernail. She'd gone to the kitchen door then, hovering, willing her mother to turn round and smile. But Donna had clattered on, and Keith had appeared at Mog's shoulder: "Call you when the meal's ready," he'd whispered, gently dispatching her to her room.

Now, half-hearing footsteps on the front paving, he slid a hand along the side of the bag and eased the masking tape away. Inside was a tightly-wrapped tablecloth. Inside that was cardboard, folded like a self-assembly filebox. It looked complicated, as though its contents were to remain secret forever. But Keith's fingers made light work of the flaps and edges, and in a moment he seemed to be looking at the spines of an nine-volume encyclopedia. Each volume was further cossetted by padded envelopes, wedged between one spine and the next. *Clapham* was embossed in gold at the base of each spine. Down the middle, a winged figure, golden also, looked poised to flee the wine-coloured cloth. Not the most elegant of publishing addresses, Clapham. But in all else, from the contents of their titles to their trademark's determined stance, the Mercury Guild had had elegance to spare. They produced encyclopedias – among other titles, and it was one of those that Keith now slid from between its envelopes. In 1945, the Guild had come within an ace of routing Raphael Tuck & Co. as appointed purveyor of adventure, history and hard fact to the offspring of the Royal Family. Tuck had survived the attack, but no matter: the Guild's response was to produce nine of the most diverting and beautifully crafted annuals ever destined for Christmas stockings up and down the land, their marvels a reminder, perhaps, that the House of Windsor should have trusted the promise of their gilded messenger. In fact, the first *Mercury Annual,* 1946, was angled to celebrate the forthcoming marriage of Princess Elizabeth and Prince Philip. On page after page, silver bells swung for noble and commoner alike. Feisty shopgirls cut a swathe through bilious papas, lorlummying mamas and a tide of cloth caps till they were clasped tight by the princes of their dreams (who, in an especial flight of fancy, really were charming). There was even a page of advice to young ladies and gentlemen on how to behave at a wedding, including tips on maintaining posture through lengthy sermons and how to remain attentive if bedevilled by a restricted view. The 1947 *Annual* simultaneously marked Indian independence and the consequent Partition, offering six tales of Shashthi, the Snake-Boy of Berrar, a mythical village exactly on the border of India and East Pakistan and claimed by both without a hint of rancour. Consumed by pride in the Festival of Britain, the *Annual* for 1951 dizzied itself with futuristic architecture. Whether the stories concerned the pluck and ingenuity of William Caxton or Communist spies posing as haymakers on Lord Edgar Dellow's estate at Kingham, there seemed always to be a spherical tower or serrated platform lurking just within the frame. The very last one brought 1954 to a close with whoops and voluntaries, celebrating the fact that, at last, rationing was no more. Had Lord Dellow's sinister farmhands been on their mission in that year, they would have found it difficult indeed to make hay, let alone whisper codes into the soles of their boots, tempted as they would have been by the hills and ziggurats of chocolate on offer throughout the pages. But elsewhere, ruddy-faced, mud-smeared schoolboys seemed to swear off the stuff with the resolution of medieval ascetics, preferring to enjoy their japes while wolfing bananas, dates, figs and (in "Heigh-Ho Bransleigh Shines Again") a pomegranate diced with a stolen hand-saw. ("Suppose I'd better give this thingummy back to our carpenter-fellow," mused Heigh-Ho. "Or pay him for it. No." His jaw tightened. "By the cut of him, he'd drink the doings away.")

Keith was looking at the *Annual* for 1950: a parti-coloured prom-ise of a glittering decade ahead and, by implication, a relieved good-bye to the one just ending. Its cover showed a boy, a girl and an English sheepdog standing on the edge of a cliff and looking out to a sea on which sunrise glowed. Above their heads, bluebirds fluttered and swooped. As with the others, more than half of the annual was taken up by cartoon stories, four generous frames to a page, each one supported by twin plinths of text elaborating the scene above. Now and then, speech bubbles also appeared, usually for the purpose of emphasis: inexplicable noises off might require "Whoooooo-whooooo," or some such, with the point of the bubble piercing the frame's edge; or some functionary, a servant or postman, might suf-fer assault by the villain of the piece and be discovered in a crumpled heap by the hero and heroine, "Groan, Groan" captured in a bubble above his sore, belaboured head. There were poems, too, and puzzles and quizzes. There was also sustained prose, but even that was illus-trated, and it rarely ran for more than a couple of pages. Certainly there was no determined march of paragraphs such as Tuck's annuals offered. Perhaps it was this – the more earnest face of storytelling – that recommended the Guild's rivals in the regal eye.

1950 was Keith's particular favourite. The absence of any defining event on the national scene, a fairytale wedding or festival, seemed to allow the *Mercury* regulars a more generous billing, with at least three stories apiece. Now, heart aglow, Keith began to turn its pages, discovering Eddie Beplate, "Clarinettist Against Crime", a metropol-itan cross between Hercule Poirot, Al Bowlly and Artie Shaw. Eddie moved with ease between banners of neon and alleys of dank gloom, no stranger to either the sulks of the apprehended footpad – "Ere, 'ave a 'eart, mister" – or the smart click of the cocktail shaker. A fixture at the Riverside Riga, WI, he played with Jack Swingway's Jazz Bombardiers (featuring Clara Grosvenor, "The Lynx With The Larynx", with whom he sometimes sang). But he also found time – during sets and between them – to pursue the case of the moment. Nightly, the Riga's audience included a string of fellow law-enforcers, official and casual, waiting for a decisive sign from the clarinettist that a body had been discovered, a note deciphered, a cache of diamonds unearthed. Chief Inspectors in mufti, small-time narks with hair punitively oiled, undercover agents posing as waiters and cloakroom girls – all rubbed shoulders with each other and, in several stories, closed in on the chief felon, usually the picture of arrogant unconcern at a prominent table. Eddie's decisive signs were apparently improvised phrases on the clarinet, derived from popular standards. Maestro that he was, he dropped them effortlessly into whichever number the Bombardiers were about. A bar or so of "Goodnight Sweetheart" meant that the trail was hotting up. "Stardust" played straight meant that a crook's next victim would be male; played with a blizzard of trills, female. The middle eight of "White Cliffs of Dover" meant that some outrage or other was the work of a whole gang, unscrupulous and foreign. Hearing such sweet music, those for whom it was intended would variously stride or scamper off to hasten the tale into its next handful of frames. Policemen would sweep past tables, their billowing coats brushing penguin suits and naked shoulders alike. Narks would make for the fire escape, there to whistle piercingly into the West End night and set their own web of subordinates to work. A hat-check girl might appear to faint; a waiter might drop a trayful of ten-year-old malts by way of diversion. And soon enough, good would triumph. Incredibly, given the number of arrests actually made at the Riga or involving a known patron, neither its owner nor Jack Swingway nor Clara nor the Bombardiers ever fathomed that someone at the club might have played a part in them. The stories would invariably end with Jack Swingway, dapper and somewhat dim, ticking Eddie off for gilding the lily too much: "Go easy on that tweeting," he might say, tapping the clarinet-case. "We are not in Chicago, young 'un."

Then there was Rowena Baines-Redland, "The Chum At Chapelvale". Feted Senior Girl of this renowned school (whose founding date sometimes shifted between 1820 and 1843), she would target bullies, skulkers and other miscreants like a divine arrow, her shoulders broad and comfy enough to soothe even the weepiest, most violently homesick "titchy" from the Lower Third. Smoothing a left-hand page, indifferent to the ache in his knees, Keith lingered now over the ending of "Torn By Temptations", a tale which saw Rowena in full retributive spate. There she was, giving a jolly good what-for to another girl, sunken-cheeked, unprepossessing on all counts, a supplier of illicit cigarettes (and thus headaches and swoons) to trusting, ingenuous Fourth Formers, assuring each and all that they were special, medicinal, a known cure for winter sniffles. The artist had frozen Rowena's index finger in its furious wagging. Her other hand, though dormant on her hip, was probably poised for similar theatrics. Below the picture, the words almost sang Rowena's dudgeon: *Caught red-handed on Big Dorm corridor, Balkan Sobranies bouncing from her cuffs, Margie Dibbenham can only submit to Row's wise and fearsome judgement. Row and her friends know that cigarettes are for Mummy and Daddy at the theatre or with a well-earned liqueur. If one starts that lark when one is young, it will not end with a harmless puff now and then. It will not end at all! It could lead to far worse!! Just consider the weasely, hooded eyes of Alf, the under-gardener's ne'er-do-well gambler of a son. What tale do you think they tell? A tale of dark dens, that's what, thickly curtained against the glories of the sun and full of wailing souls; a tale of the madness that has him by his grimy, malnourished throat.*

Keith smiled as he leafed on. He shook his head, remembering how Donna had caught Niall on the brink of Alfhood. Eleven, he was, just started at secondary school – and, on that particular afternoon, a furtive shadow in the bushes by the cricket-ground. Some older boy, it turned out, had sold him cigarette papers and a compound which he said was tobacco. Keith wasn't around: he had that big plumbing contract on, the new estate over Tellers Hill. (New for about a month, he thought now – then suddenly decrepit, and grown even worse over the last eleven years: wood facings rotted off, carport struts rusting, a right shanty town.) But Donna was, dusting the sheen off some knick-knacks in the bay window. She might not have spotted Niall, for all that the bushes were a daft place to seek concealment. Mrs Bannerman, however, was out on the pavement, flapping a hand across the road, and Donna followed its line of agitation. The Bannermans lived next door in the corner bungalow, officially on Pembroke Rise. Keith liked them a lot, but Donna, in a well-worn phrase, "didn't put in or out with them" – largely because, their own children having long left home, they'd always indulged hers to beyond a fault. And of course it later transpired that Mrs B had realised what Niall was up to and was trying to shoo him to greater safety. Instantly suspicious, Donna had gone striding across the road, even holding up her hand at an ice-cream van which had just come rocking and chiming into Rowan Tree Lane and which, according to Mrs B, braked so hard that its interior was a mess of cornets. His mother had beaten Niall from the bushes. Moments later, he stood before her, a three-paper roll-up in his hand, flaccid, shedding its motley contents. When Keith got home a while later, Mrs B was in her front garden. Seeing him, she'd twisted her jaw leftwards, stretching her lower lip: a familiar signal – storms beneath his roof. In the lounge, Janice and young Mog were flattened with fright against one wall while Donna bawled the odds into Niall's ear, squeezing the lobe like putty. She'd given Keith a breathless account of his misdeed, almost working her lips off between phrases. Then, clutching her back, she'd let go the ear and collapsed on the sofa: "Talk to him, Keith!" she'd screamed.

"Row and her friends know that cigarettes are for Mummy and Daddy at the theatre or with a well-earned liqueur." The words had come out before he knew it.

"What?" mother and son had said together.

"Who's Row, Dad?" Janice had demanded, trying to reproduce her teenage notion of an unillusioned gossip.

Only Mog, to whom Keith had read "Torn By Temptations", had recognised the words. At the time, she was hardly old enough to make complete sense of them. But she loved their music – and the music of everything he read to her. She alone had smiled, almost giggled, feeling a release from the tears that had begun pricking when she saw her mother's hand at her back.

Later inspection showed Niall's compound to be a smattering of tobacco mixed with stove-ash and fried-onion tips. Despite much pressing, he never revealed the identity of his supplier – who, in any case, never had his custom again. In fact, Niall never tried another smoke of any kind, at school or after. Keith had often wondered if, far from showing common sense, this was actually a ruse to keep his mother in agony, braced for the moment when she turned out a lighter or nub-end from his blazer. He wouldn't have put it past him. Then again, it wasn't all that long after the roll-up incident that he'd begun to take a more obvious revenge, palling up with the Fazmos of this world.

"Dad." Had Keith heard the voice or imagined it? He assumed the latter, having just returned through time to meet his children, scared or arraigned in that differently-painted lounge. A moment earlier, he might have paused in case it wasn't a cry out of family history. But a few left-hand pages slipped past his thumb, Row disappeared and he found *The Voyagers Twain*. A voice right at his ear wouldn't have pulled him back now, nor yet a squeezing finger.

The Voyagers Twain had eight showings in the *Mercury* for 1950: more than Eddie and Row combined. The stories were an attempt – admirable yet faintly absurd – to blend a definable time in British history with the murk of the yet-to-be. The title referred to William Broome and Joseph Anstey, gentlemen map-makers in 1720s Somerset. Their Christian names were routinely shortened to "Wm" and "Jos", forms which, now and then, they would jokily use when addressing each other. Possibly they were pre-echoes of Charles Mason and Jeremiah Dixon, surveyors of the Pennsylvania-Maryland boundary and founding fathers, so to speak, of the division between enslaved and free before the Civil War. If they were, the echo never deepened. In fact, they seemed to make few if any maps, though they were forever sallying forth with boxes and tripods and weights on string. Not that they lacked commissions. Among their clients were landowners who desired them to scout out tracts of estate – huge, remote and hitherto neglected – to go under the plough; or burghers of small towns, at each other's throats over some boundary matter; or Excisemen convinced that their coastal maps were a child's scrawl, hopelessly out of date and no match for the evidently superior documents in the swarthy hands of some master-smuggler. But these claims on their time were merely pretexts to get the pair on the move. When they arrived at the undulating ridge, or shingled beach or tidy, tucked-away hamlet, a few carefully trodden-out paces would be enough to launch them off the planet. A frame or so later, after a depiction of Wm and Jos flailing through space or sprawled in the natural saddle of a whizzing comet, Georgian Britain gave way to a silver megalopolis from the thirty-fifth century, or a desert planet, all storms of burning sand and dwellers like swollen molluscs – or any destination that took the illustrator's fancy, provided it be fantastical and allow the colours of the rainbow to light up its frames.

That they weren't, after all, somewhere round the Quantock Hills or Watchet Bay never fazed Wm and Jos in the least. However unlikely the beings who reared, scuttled or flew up at them, the pair invariably greeted them with a "What ho!" or a "Dash me, here's a thing!" The beings seemed prepared for such salutations. They never responded in bafflement but instead with a pretty fair stab at the King's English, naturally gingered up with the *patois* of that particular neck of infinity. The whole premise, of course, was as it should be. Scientific wizards all, these beings had raked creation fore and aft with lenses, microphones and the kind of cine-projectors of which the manager of the average Roxy could but dream. The most sophisticated had even roved through time and space, some in gilded torpedoes, others in metal-clad balloons kept aloft by rows of bike-frames and serfs to pedal them. They all knew, therefore, of Messrs Broome and Anstey: the niceties of their calculations, the bold confidence of their lines. Thus it was that, en route to the latest manor house or blasted headland, the pair were routinely scooped off the face of the earth, finding the nature of their commission extravagantly mirrored on whichever planet they What-ho'd. Whether the pair were expecting these forays, or whether each was an accepted surprise which slipped from the memory when their boots thudded back on West Country soil, was never made explicit. For one thing, the writer's jiggery-pokery with time always meant that, however long the foray, they always got back in the same moment that they'd taken off. Sometimes, Keith had detected some hint in their final exchanges, some awareness that new knowledge had conferred itself upon them, fitting them more than admirably to stop, say, the incursions of Mad-Beard Blackshott, the Rum-Runner Grandee. But he didn't mind either way. Similarly, it never troubled him that, with the flower of gadgetry at their disposal, the alien beings felt obliged to call upon a pair of Augustan lens-gawpers to solve their woes. Such questions belonged to the world beyond the *Mercurys*: the world of the rooms downstairs, of the drive and the garage into which Donna's tidy little 4x4 would soon enough roll.

"The Magenta Line" was the *Voyagers* story that Keith was looking at. Squire Evershed had summoned Wm and Jos to Shepton Mallet. A deal of trouble he was having with Goody Trower, who insisted that he was moving the loose old wall that divided the western edge of his lush pastures from her lone, sorry field. Her cot was some distance from the field, so she couldn't be hobbling back and forth all the time to see what he was about. It was all she could do to tend her few goats every day; sometimes, she had to send an oik in her stead. As she put it when her frames came round, "Fair gobblin' 'er up, Evershed is, look – won't be scrap o' chawing grass lef' fer my nannies nor they babbies." And not only that: she had long maintained, on the authority of a map that had been in her family "sin' afore Queen Bess could whimper", that a good hundred acres of his pastures were hers. It was tricky – and for other reasons besides. Goody Trower might be physically frail, but she was suspected, in the Squire's words, of having "special tricks clapped in her bonnet, d'ye see, sirs?" Though she was an amiable soul, in the main, it had been said that her displeasure could poison wells, chop wheels from speeding coaches, visit ordinary, righteous Shepton folk with a dense rash which, if viewed with a squint, looked like a toothless grin.

In truth this was all a ruse. Through intelligence of his own – the last testament of a hoary old salt who had died of scurvy off the Greater Antilles – Evershed had learnt of a casket of gold buried in Goody Trower's field. He was indeed gobbling it up – or rather, slyly grazing. The salt had claimed that the casket was somewhere near its eastern perimeter; so, in the dead of several nights, Evershed had set a gang of hooded reprobates to dismantle the wall, move it forward, dig up each yard gained and then, if the effort proved fruitless, fill in the trench and turf it over. He himself was braced for each fresh morrow, when he would meet the increasingly restive Goody with an expression of innocence, spreading his hands wide at her accusations: "Gypsies camped nearby, Mrs Trower," he might say. "Must be them at their strange larking." But thus far, these efforts had yielded nothing. Besides, his tactic belonged to the ebb-and-flow school of cunning, requiring a patience that he did not possess. And there were Goody's "special tricks" to consider. How long would it be before, abroad in the town or entering his Sunday pew, he felt an unholy fire in his withers? And what of his wife, young and beautiful, skin like roses, expecting their firstborn? What if a special trick took root in her mind, turning her into a crazed thing who shunned himself and the babe?

So he had summoned Broome and Anstey – as sacrificial lambs, really. He was waiting for them with a particular document he had caused to be made. Trumping Goody Trower's claim to a portion of his land, it alluded to the Doomsday Book, identifying her field but stating that it was only a tenth of its present size: specifically, twelve strides east to west and north to south at the centre. The rest was the property of Piers d'Evarre, clearly his ancestor. He would tell them that this document had only just come to light; then he would set them to work on re-mapping Goody Trower's field from its antique specifications. That way, he could play the regretful landowner, sorry indeed that so much of her field had to be swallowed up, before swiftly adding that he must perforce honour his ancestor's memory. "Work at night, you were best," he would tell them. "That woman won't trouble you then. She sleeps like" – here he'd chuckle, sepulchral and low – "the dead." Then, when the fine gentlemen were stumbling about with wires and lanterns, he'd get word to Goody that the gypsies were at it again, she'd forget her old bones and descend on the field in the full splendour of her witchery, Wm and Jos would pay the diabolical price, Goody would be hanged and he would have proper daylight leisure to unearth the casket and indulge his passion for horseflesh.

In this story, Wm and Jos had just made their first visit to Goody Trower's field when they were swept away. Keith knew the rest by heart. They found themselves on Farhanva, Planet of the Rising Age, where they were greeted by Evershed's counterpart, a twenty-foot high seahorse drawn as if made of crazy paving. The Farhanvan leader, it had gained its position through a mixture of duplicity and main force. It told them that the Penumbrae, inhabitants of the neighbouring planet, had accused it of fiddling a boundary: in this case, a magenta line slung like a rope-bridge through space, equidistant from both worlds. The Goody Trower character was an ancient Penumbress, revered by her people and granted rights since time out of mind to breed *voidlings* – amoeba-shaped fragments of space, a delicacy on Penumbros – along the fertile strip of nothing that bordered their side of the line. Apart from protesting that the seahorse was already nudging the line towards her planet, the Penumbress told her people that it was culling her *voidlings* on the quiet. She had her document, a talking kaleidoscope whose dialect occasionally recalled Guernsey, which declared her to be sole and uncontested *voidherdess*. And the seahorse squire had its document, a disembodied snout resembling its own, whose assertion of its ancestral right to shift the line in its favour suggested an Edwardian masher singling out an ingenue for the evening's sport. The seahorse set Wm and Jos to work on its calculations. Soon enough, when darkness fell on both worlds, they found themselves on the Farhanvan side of the line, plonked in baskets attached to pulleys attached to wisps of green fog tied in reef-knots, flanked by hooded seahorses ready to help them push the line the ninety-six Farhanvan leagues which, according to the Edwardian masher, were the seahorse squire's due.

But the gents had rumbled the seahorse. An earlier trio of frames showed them examining its document after it had retired to its chamber early (a necessity, since it would shortly give birth to the next generation of Farhanvan rulers). Through some stage-business with a prism, Wm and Jos found that it was a fake and the Penumbress's claims were all true. ("Odds bobs!" said Broome, as grimly as the phrase would allow. "This Farhanvan's a rum stager, Jos, tan me nethers if he ain't.") They hatched a plan, bided their time. And when, frames later, they were in their baskets, about to signal the big push of the magenta line, Wm held the prism aloft and somehow, in all that blackness, flashed a message to the Penumbress (on the page, a speech-snake coiled itself round the edge of the frame with the words *"Ye have been most grievously used, Madam – do as ye see fit!"*). Waiting on Penumbros, the *voidherdess* spread her arms wide, causing the *enceinte* seahorse to be sucked from its chamber, barrel through the air and hit the magenta line, the back-twang sending it far beyond the Planet of the Rising Age or any age at all: *Past planets dying or yet to be,* said the supporting text, *it plunged on the path that right and proper justice had decreed. Past beringed Saturn and mighty Mars, past our own Earth with Evershed plotting, Goody Trower fretting, you and I sound asleep. Why, what galaxies –* Keith started back, lost the page, thumbed his way back to it. Unusually, the frame he'd been looking at was stretched across the width of the page, the better to show the seahorse's plunge into nothing. From left to right it flew. There was Saturn, as the text said, and tiny Mars, and Earth with its moon, flanked by Evershed's scheming profile and Goody Trower's narrowed, suspicious eyes. And then – Keith bent close, looking at the right of the frame. Astonishment was on him, intensifying, turning to joy. He looked again at the text: *Why, what galaxies and suns did the foul Farhanvan not pass on its journey to doom? It even sped past the Arc of the Sixteen Planets, past the humblest of them all: Razalia, unfinished, overlooked, the very runt of that system.* Above the words was a world foregrounded, with a vague stretch of planets beyond it. It was ridged and valley'd; nine teeny swirls of ocean blue marked its face, separated by sandy lines. At the top of the world was a mountain – even on this scale, clearly the most complete feature of the lot. And, here and there were inexplicable daubs of white, as though the illustrator had been called away as he was about to colour in, say, a canyon or the delta of a river. *Once past Razalia and its fifteen fellows,* said the text, *what hope had the seahorse of return?*

Keith sat back on his heels. He clapped his hands and whooped. For a second, he thought he heard a noise, another call like the one he'd imagined when he found "The Magenta Line". This time he was sure it was in his head, a triumphant echo of his happiness. He did remember something from his first talk with George. George had just explained the history of that glowing firestick, how it had been a gift of gratitude from those juggler types at that Fayre. Now, they were looking up at the *Gabe Tomorrow* poster.

"'Tomorrow's Rezoon'," said George. "That's my favourite Gabe effort." Then he'd gone on about Tomorrow's quest to find the last surviving planet in the Spiral of the Green Twilight, a system that had become choked in a deadly gas created by his sworn enemies, the Kadyadovorans. "Funny old pitch, Rezoon," George said. "Unfinished, according to Gabe's materio-data readings."

Now, Keith recalled rocking back on the chair that George had provided for him, shaking his head furiously, till his leg gave an almighty throb and he rocked upright again: "No, no," he insisted, "Rezoon was the first planet to die in the Spiral. The minerals planet, it was – except the Kadyadovorans had sucked them all out. The only unfinished planet I know is Razalia – not one of Gabe's."

But his host had shaken his head in turn, and – yes, Keith had noticed straightaway that curious haziness about his face. It was a wonder that Mog's nickname for him hadn't popped into his own head: truly cloudy, his face was, with a shift in expression at every shake.

George had pressed on: "The Kadyadovorans," he said, "were planning to" – then he came out with something about their "Prima-Portal Rays", how they were set to stockpile those infernal weapons on Rezoon and thus prepare a doomsday attack on the other five Spiral systems in that part of the Orbiterra galaxy.

"Kreegitz," challenged Keith. "The Lone Planet of the Daluthan Ridges. That's where they stockpiled the Rays. About to blow apart the Ridges and cut through to the Slumbering Universe on the other side. Gabe coated the Ridges in ur-Xenon, bent the rays back on the Kadyadovorans – got 'em all, too –" Keith paused in his recollection, seeing and not seeing the elongated frame, the dispatch of the sea-horse. No, he'd got that wrong. The Queen escaped, with two of her drone escorts. How else could the Kadyadovorans have survived and multiplied – for at least five or six more clashes with Gabe? But he'd got the story's title right: "Prima Pandemonium". And he'd revealed it to George, he remembered, most emphatically.

"So where's Razalia from, then?" George had asked.

Now, tracing the planet's circumference on the page before him, Keith spoke softly, in unison with his memory:

"One of the *Mercurys.*"

George couldn't credit it. "No *Mercury* chappo would come up with that. Which year, then?"

Again, Keith heard his younger voice and spoke alongside it: "That I can't place, offhand."

But now, by accident, he had. He knelt low, studying the gaps and swirls on the planet. Suddenly, he blinked hard. For a moment, it looked as though another picture had crept in: a figure, a man, stand-ing against some kind of vehicle by – a waterfall, was it? Beyond and above him was a woman – a bit of all right, to judge by that costume – walking along some kind of bridge, or ledge. He rubbed his eyes, opened them. As before, there was Razalia, all on its own at the right of the frame. Just as well the sorting was done, he thought. The loft might well be a refuge, but it was time he returned to light and spa-ciousness. Besides, he ought to make the most of the house before Donna returned. He smiled as he thought of tea with Mog, who should be back any time now.

Keith closed the annual and slid it back in its wrapping. He didn't bother with the end of "The Magenta Line": he knew it well enough. Although they might have forgotten entirely about seahorses and *voidlings*, Wm and Jos were equipped with extra savvy when they landed back near Goody Trower's field. His trickery laid bare, Evershed flew through the air to his come-uppance, a standing pool of rare pungency. Goody Trower's document proved as genuine as her grievance. In addition to her field, she regained the hundred acres which, at some stage in the dim-and-distant, Evershed's ancestors had filched from hers. Indeed, she became lady of the manor. The end of the story showed Evershed, a reformed man, boarding the London coach with his blooming wife, bent on a missionary's life – *somewhere in the innards of Africa,* the text vaguely observed. As for Wm and Jos, they strode back home, their knapsacks filled with a fresh batch of Goody's loganberry scones, to await their next commission with its hidden promise of otherworldly junketing.

At last Keith stood up and stretched his legs. The *Mercurys* could go with him to his bedroom. Bit of luck, that, finding Razalia. He could tell George at the White House tomorrow night. Yes – the unfinished planet. Funny he'd forgotten that it was tucked away in "The Magenta Line" – and that it had cropped up in that first conversation. Heaven knows, the dispute hadn't rested there. George had persisted in his belief that the planet was bound up with Gabe Tomorrow's crusades. Now and again – at Rowan Tree Lane or Chivsull, at the Last Emporium or in sundry pubs – its name had resurfaced. And despite making promises, often of liquorish solemnity, that each would locate Razalia, neither actually tried. One time, they had left their cars at the Widow's Peak in Roseville and got a taxi home. For once, the evening had turned, well, purposeful, with Donna and Edna's likely reactions wholly forgotten. On the way home, George had suddenly claimed that Razalia must have featured in "The Collapse of the Gods", the only Gabe Tomorrow story to appear exclusively in *Erstaunlichreise,* a 1965 compendium of worldwide science-fiction, published in Munich with parallel German and English texts and distinguished by a breathtaking tonal range.

"No, George, no, no, no," Keith had said. "'Collapse of the Gods' takes place entirely on the mountains of Acaranta – apart from that valley scene where Gabe crash-lands. First line of frames on page two," he'd added.

"All right, perhaps some illustrator chappo pinched Razalia for – for the backdrop, before he crashes."

"It's just not possible. There was enough hoo-hah about releasing the story to the Munich outfit – all kinds of barney over copyright. The Christmas '65 issue of *Fantasy Scribe* was full of it. Munich wouldn't have risked putting in something that wasn't in the original."

"Do you have a copy?"

"*Erstaunlichreise*? Rare as hen's teeth, George. You'd be hard pressed to find a copy, let alone afford one. But I've read it. Special display copy at the Poitiers Sci-Fi Festival, oh, must be five years gone. Family holiday – I just stumbled on it. I had to read it under supervision, bloke with plastic gloves turning the pages. So I took it all in – and there's no Razalia."

"Ah, but you're a much-read chappo, Keith. You say you took it all in, but you can't be sure that" – George had tried tugging inspiration out of the seat-belt – "that one of the gods didn't sneak off to Razalia – to have his collapse where the others couldn't see."

"It's all on Acaranta!"

"Might just be one frame, Keith, two at the most. That white-glove chappo breathing down your neck... you know... your eyes might have slipped –"

"George," said Keith, "no god ever came a cropper on Razalia" – a remark which the taxi-driver subsequently smuggled into his working chat.

Now, looking at the *Mercurys'* bedding, *O'Sullivan Educational* in stretched black letters along its side, Keith slowly nodded. Of course, if either of them had discovered Razalia's origin, it would have spoilt the fun. But it had been more than that, and more than any showing-off. Keith knew that George had returned to the fray so he could revel in his friend's knowledge, his mastery of all the wonders that two dimensions could hold. And Keith himself had found a proper audience for his passion. Thoughtfully, carefully, he had gratified George's curiosity, humbled – then and now – by the man's capacity for admiration.

"Dad!"

Keith turned. The face at the head of the ladder was framed in blonde. Pretty, it was fuller than oval without being round, the eyes nicely set, the nose just a little snub. Now it was wrinkled in despair.

"I called five times, dad! Honestly!"

Bending a little, Keith made for the ladder: "Mog, Mog, sorry. I've been seeing to these. Put the oven on and I'll –"

"It's on, dad. I'll see to it." She frowned, noting the bag of *Mercurys*, craning to look round the loft. Her voice softened: "You've done it, then." Now it was his turn to frown, but she smoothed it away with a smile: "I knew something was up this morning, dad. Mom was mad to get me out of the house. It had to be this."

He sighed: "Yes, love, had to be." At these words, realisation of his labours hit him. He'd put the time in up here, easily equal to a full day at Ebbatson House or the Darkhouse site. The bending, sorting, shifting about... leaning against a beam, he fell silent.

"The Moroccan lamb?" coaxed Mog. "Peas and chips? The whole gourmet bit?"

"Great, great – be right down. Just let me – actually, Mog, could you – ?"

Next minute, heedless of her clothes, Mog sprawled over the trapdoor, her hands either side of the *O'Sullivan Educational* bag. Below her, Keith had it porter-style on his head. As he lowered himself, step by step, so she wriggled forward to steady it for as long as she could. She still had her fingertips to it when his feet reached the landing. Bowing his head, he let the ladder take the weight of the bag, guiding it as it slid down the struts. While Mog followed it and made for the kitchen, he worked the bag along the floor and into his room, noting how it turned back the carpet-pile, telling himself he'd better get the sweeper out to brush it back. The ladder he'd leave out. After an evening of important focus talk, Donna would want to make a determined, unbroken ascent to the loft.

A while later, Mog reached into the very back of a cupboard and returned to the table on exaggerated tip-toe, something behind her back.

"Ketchup," she mouthed. "Bad, seriously bad." Then she resumed her seat and watched as her chuckling dad made free with it on his chips.

"I found chutney on my plate at lunch," he said. "Full mango."

Mog slumped like a rag-doll in her chair: "This gaff," came her best Cockney, "is goin dahn'a pan."

"Well, at least the chips are low-fat."

"No-fat, dad, the pack says."

He cocked his head at the ketchup label: "How do you get no-fat chips?" he asked it in cheery disbelief.

They tucked in: "Exam today?" asked Keith.

Mog shook her head: "Tomorrow morning. Last one."

"Ah, thought you were at the end. Why'd'you go in today, then?"

"Lib–" she began, then fingered away a drizzle of juice from the corner of her mouth. "Library. The Flemish weavers. Stuff to check. Methods and dates. And Miss Ryakis just got a DVD on tapestries – wanted the group to see it."

"For the exam? She's cutting it a bit fine, isn't she?"

"No, we've covered what we need to. It was out of interest, really – well, and to show what can come up at A-level. There was only me and Lucy Sadler there." She gave her fork a slow, reflective tap. "Hope there's more than us doing A-level – the Big End might say we can't. *Group viability*," she warbled, quoting her Head. "Honestly, he keeps coming out with this stuff to everyone in school – first years, too – like we were all as geeky as him."

Quivering slightly, Keith put paid to a moutful of lamb: "Oh, your Mr Endsleigh's a good sort," he chuckled at last. "He won't do you out of that. You're their best artist – he said so at the parents' do. How could he – ?" He trailed off, feeling as though he were talking aloud on his own. He knew, without looking up, that Mog had moved onto something else. When at last he did, she was poking the air above her head with her fork. Catching his eye, she looked meaningfully at the ceiling.

"So, dad… is Cloudy George getting them?"

Keith swallowed a mouthful, then planted knife and fork either side of his plate.

"Yes and no, love."

Mog giggled: "That sounds like him," and she turned her head from left to right, making as many faces as she could without choking. "Gotta chappo, Keith," she mimicked expertly. "Mustard-keen. Have them off your hands in half-a-twinkling. Earnest, he is, earnest." Dropping her knife, she rubbed thumb and finger together.

Forgetting that Donna had made the same gesture in an utterly different spirit, Keith chortled. "Well, Mog," he began, "what it is –"

He paused. What was it, exactly? In truth, George had never made a bid for the collection. Admiring it from the start, he'd taken pride in… well, watching it grow wasn't really the phrase. It had been many a day since George had set foot in Rowan Tree Lane, knowing the frosty gaze and working lips that would await him. But Keith had brought each new prize to Chivsull or the shop (though not the White House – as George himself had counselled, "You take *The Nebulae Posse*, first issue – October '49 as I'm standing here – and someone parks a pint of Harkley's on it... well, it's like chopping up a Stradiverity, yes?"). So George had, in a sense, kept abreast of its expansion – had aided it, in fact, tricking the collection out with a copy of *Yuks-a-bundle* here, a *Splendiferous Hols* annual there. He wouldn't hear of payment for such: "Came drifting my way, Keith," he'd say. "A tale of a chappo and a favour."

Beyond all this, George didn't want the collection to leave Keith's hands. The treasures, after all, had found their perfect curator. Oh, he knew enough about Donna's attitude by now. But he'd always hoped that his own enthusiasm would turn itself to courage in Keith's heart. Something – sheer perversity? an excess of friendship? – had made him will Keith to hang on to them. Once, not so long ago either, he'd even stood Keith an evening's drinks at the White House and treated him to a vision: "In that loft of yours," he'd said. "An exhibition. Don't worry about stands and cases. I've got a pack of chappos who could fit us out. Occasional, I'm thinking, by appointment – I could put up a card at the Emporium, you could have one in your porch. Few select hours a week, you know, like those shops that never sell anything. Could even charge – if that was to anyone's way of thinking." Keith had turned that last remark over in his mind, knowing that it would be, briefly wondering if he should suggest it. But then he pictured feet tramping the oatmeal stair-carpet, trays of necessary refreshment, a visitor's car blocking the driveway – and, above all, one frosty face thawing out before coming to the boil. George must have seen all in his eyes: "A wild thought, sir," he'd said. "A wild, wild thought. I'd suggest the Emporium but... well, you know what the shop's like. And my stockrooms –" Stretching arms and puffing out cheeks, he'd tottered like the world's fattest man.

It was with this episode in mind that he now looked at his quizzical daughter:

"He wouldn't sell them on, love. Matter of fact," he added in a rush, "he's keen to show them somewhere."

"Where? The Emporium? I wouldn't think he had the space."

"No, we'll have to look into –" Keith stopped, startled by the skyward jab of Mog's knife.

"Up there," she half-whispered, as though they weren't alone in the house. "Would have been perfect. As long as folk watched where they were treading. OK, so you couldn't have a whole bunch of them at once. Still, half-an-hour each, dad. That's what they did at Worcester

Guildhall. Miss Ryakis told us. Special exhibition on fashions during the Civil War. Didn't think they had any, but there you go."

Keith gazed at his daughter. He'd half-expected her response, but that only made him wish that he'd told her of George's vision at the time. His mouthful of lamb lost its taste. Now he felt he'd let her down as well as himself, although, as he shortly realised, his next rush of words hardly made amends:

"Ah, now, the loft, love. We have plans for you."

Mog sighed in tender exasperation: "Dad," she said quietly, "I know *we* don't. I stay where I'm put till I go." It wasn't often she mimicked her mother.

By way of awkward apology, Keith picked up the ketchup bottle, reached over and crafted a straight, reddish-brown line on one of Mog's chips, which, broad and long, seemed to have a third of her plate to itself.

"Dad, it's not sealant," she giggled. "Hey!" Holding her knife like a sword, she parried his fork's descent on her chip.

After a moment's contented silence, Keith said, "Anyway, I'm seeing George as usual tomorrow. We'll sort it out from there."

Mog looked across at him, somehow managing to top up her fizzy drink without swamping the table.

"But you're keeping the *Mercurys* here, dad, yeah?"

Lifting a forkful of peas to his mouth, Keith nodded. "They stay. Oh yes, they stay."

Suddenly the air was all plumminess: "*Row and her friends know that cigarettes are for Mummy and Daddy at the theatre or with a well-earned lickyurrr.*" Unwisely, Mog hadn't emptied her mouth before trying this party-piece. Keith reached over and raised her drink to her mouth. The coughing subsided and she was beaming again. "Remember, dad? Niall and his fried-onion ciggy? When mom commanded you to rollock him? Jan and me thought you were well boozed. *Mummy and Daddy at the theatre,*" she repeated. But her smile wavered, as though she were pondering the image of affection created by those words. "Glad you came back when you did," she finished. "Mom was out of control. Wetting ourselves, Jan and me."

Keith had planted a chip amongst the lamb. Now he was leaning another against it, then a third. For a second, they made a perfect little mountain, then fell over. His smile was thin. How could he rescue her from that remembered madness? His eyes widened:

"I found Razalia," he said.

"You never!" Mog perked up instantly. "Where?"

"1950 *Mercury. Voyagers Twain.* 'The Magenta Line'. "

Mog frowned: "That the one with the witch and the goldfish?"

"Seahorse."

"That too."

"Right at the end. I'll show you."

Mog sucked in her breath: "Cloudy George won't like that, dad. Don't tell me, you won't show it him and your big debate can kick off again." Shivering her knife and fork like divining rods, she made her voice tremor: "Where is Razalia? Wooooh…"

About to capitalise on his success in getting her back to the now, Keith found he couldn't speak. The mention of Razalia had revived that picture, the one that had crept onto the broad frame of "The Magenta Line". Now he was the one standing by the vehicle and the wall of water. Up on the ledge or whatever it was, the woman was turning to him. Donna.

"Keith!" she screamed. "It's a wonder your customers aren't up in arms!" She flung out an arm. "Call this a planet? Bodge job here, make-do-and-mend there. And what are all those bits of white in aid of? I bloody near vanished in one. I've been patience itself, Keith. Waited and waited. No more. Time's up. Deep space, boy. Deep space for you." In her agitation, she began striding up and down the ledge. But her clicking heels seemed to echo from overhead, as though she was simultaneously strutting her wrath and inspecting the loft. And now she was on about a Sunday. What about it? Which one? Was Sunday the deadline for the planet to be finished – the comics to be out?

With a jerk he found his daughter's face filling his vision: "Is that OK, dad? Dessert? A sundae?" She sank back in her chair. "I smuggled 'em in. Full fat. Push out the big old boat. Dad? You all right?"

He shook himself: "I was on Razalia, love." Then, as if talking to someone else, "That's fine, fine." As she rose to get them out of the fridge, he murmured, "Fine. Sunday it is, then." The words baffled him. Underpinning them was the continued clack of heels – as he'd hear soon, too soon, for real. No worries about her back, he reckoned. No complaints about having to bend here, dodge there. She'd move like a dancer round that loft, her triumph making her more lithe with every step.

"Come on, dad." Mog plonked herself down. "Best eat up if we want time for the sundaes."

He smiled at her: "Sure thing, lady," he tried, Gabe Tomorrow-style. "I'll just get these rations down the gullet."

She understood: "Well, less chat, then, Horizon King."

She started on the rest of her meal. Looking at her in happy wonder, he was about to do the same. But then the clacking heels returned, increasing like that blasted *Aztec Pulse* or *Melanesian Timbres* tape through the floorboards hours before. Abruptly, they stopped. Whether out of thankfulness for the silence, or one last hope against hope, he sensed a faint scrap of faith in the quiet life, his old and discredited god. Perhaps, after all, the words meant what they said. Perhaps, with the day's work behind him, it could at last be his. But, like a strip of celluloid, the scrap caught fire and melted.

THE WATCHFUL TAWNY

Soon Donna was on Bright's Way. She felt great relief, and not only from the beaded seat-cover flush against her back. A good hour till the pubs turned out. If she'd left Nanette's much later, she'd have found herself in a stream of anxious crawlers, snaking through the villages and junctions that Bright's Way connected. It amazed her constantly – everywhere full on week-nights, pubs and what-have-you. Some folk didn't need to keep the belt in. Or maybe they did and just didn't give a hoot. She pursed her lips as though seeking a nascent sore. Niall's philosophy, that was – especially if it was someone else's belt. He always picked girlfriends who would give him a roof and a happy wallet – till they got wise, by which time he was usually lining up the next one. And Imogen was showing signs of mistaking money for water. Some disillusioning was needed on that score. If Miss Brainbox was off to university, she'd have to manage by herself. No rolling requests for cash and upgraded phones. Yes, she'd have to get in good and early with that warning – offset his nibs's readiness to give the girl a month's earnings at the drop of a hat. Still, he was growing up at last, thanks to her belated prodding and shoving. Nice little pile, those comics would make. She'd had it confirmed that very evening. Donna worked her back against the seat and smiled. Lovely voice, Greville had. Cultured but not snooty. Quietly persuasive. You could tell he was cut out for PR and that.

Summer Oak, a sign flashed up. *Please Drive Carefully.* When did she do otherwise? Her relief deepened. Sedgley in six or so miles, then three miles home – and, with luck, she'd still miss the pub crowd on the Birmingham Road. Cottages and houses fell away to right and left. Nice village, she thought – she'd always liked it round here. Some tasty properties. Might be worth keeping an eye out for "For Sale" boards – for sometime down the line, of course. His nibs had to convert the loft first, turn it into a useful space – and, if and when the time came, a selling-point. Again she thought of Greville Oldstead and his reassuring advice. Yes, goodbye comics, hello

Imogen's survival pot. That was absolutely the card to play with the girl's father, over and over if need be. Never mind what she'd said to him before she left, about growing girls and growing needs. Madam wouldn't get a sniff of it now. Her greatest need would be when she was faffing around at uni for however long. She could have it in monthly slices – if she blew a slice, she'd just have to wait on the next. There'd be a fair bit of interest by then, if they found the right deal. And that wouldn't be a problem, given the kind of circles Janice's Mark moved in – accountants, loss-adjusters. For a moment she considered her son-in-law: a regular rock, he was, not a surprise in him – Greville Oldstead, really, albeit without the polish. A bit of all right to look at, too, which helped. And a doting dad: loved young Andrew to bits. Shame he was away so much, but there it was... nature of the job. If you were in Customer Liaison for a chain of hotels, you had to get out and about, check their standards, smooth feathers, bear the latest message from Head Office. Good old Mark: His Steadiness, as she thought of him. He'd make the right enquiries. He'd find the best fund to, well, pour the comics into. Her smile broadened. Two birds with one stone. All those bits of tat gone, and Madam taught once and for all about the value of money in the real world. In fact, if the fund His Steadiness found for her had good prospects, where was the harm in creaming off a little comic-money now, for the loft? Nowhere, she told herself, as another sign thanked her for driving safely through Summer Oak. Nowhere at all.

By the time she was approaching Uphawksford, she had it all planned out, even surprising herself with regret at how she'd spoken to his nibs that afternoon. But that could be turned around and smoothed over. Of course his tat could go in the garage until properly disposed of. She would even help him, her back allowing. No: Imogen could help him – it was for her good, after all. Sunday – that's when the two of them could do it. Janice was coming round Saturday. They all were, last she'd heard. His Steadiness had been going away this weekend, Janice said: *The Ravensbank Motel* near Alnwick. "Weakest link in the chain" was Mark's assessment of the place – and, indeed, they required his untangling fingers on a regular basis. This time, said Janice, it was some dispute with the outfit who delivered the morning papers for the guests. But he'd had a call just yesterday. The crisis was – well, not over, but subject to – what was the phrase Janice quoted? – "interim strategy". Could he go up next

Tuesday instead and meet with all parties involved? "He was most unchuffed," Janice had told her. "Well, he'd scheduled everything else around the trip, hadn't he? And he does very nicely out of week-end expenses." Still, thought Donna as the Uphawksford sign now took its turn to counsel her on her driving, Alwick's loss and so on… she could have a natter to Mark about funds and nest-eggs. How specific she could be would depend on how far she'd got with the Imogen card before they came. As for that, she could set to work tomorrow teatime: dust off her thoughtful voice – and, who knows, even a splash of affection? His nibs would be seeing Philpotts at the White House anyway, so she'd need to drop it in his ear before he went, get it circulating. Would it be pushing it too much to tell him that, since it was for Imogen's future benefit, he'd still have the comics in a way? That the piles of old paper would live on in her achievement? Course it wouldn't. The more she thought about it, the more irresistible it sounded. Maybe, by the time he'd reached that grotty old pub, he'd be ready to talk figures with Philpotts – who was still obliged, she felt, to correct his attitude from all those years ago and write out a cheque. "The garage," she said aloud, something else striking her. Keith'd fret about conditions in there, imagine creeping moisture and whatnot. He wouldn't want them there for too long, would he? Not with his daughter's education at stake, her passport to the world of work. Curling edges might knock a tidy bundle off their value. Could he put his daughter's fate at the mercy of depreciation? Now she laughed outright. Where had all this inspiration come from? An evening in the virtual company of Greville Oldstead, that's where. In its turn, Uphawksford thanked her for her considerate driving. Moments later, she saw a leftward sign to Chivsull. That's where the man with the hidden cheque-book lived. An omen, she declared to herself. Success, success. "Madam's survival pot," she breathed, "and starter-dosh for the loft." Thinking of which, she'd have to make a definite choice on what she wanted up there. She'd told his nibs that her plans were firming up. It might have to be a case of eeny-meeny-miny-mo in the end. That was all right: the alternatives were all sensible. No, more than that: each promised a whole new phase of life at Rowan Tree Lane. And, in a while, there'd be yet another phase once Madam was gone. The main thing was that, with the comics dislodged, his nibs would soon have tape measure and spirit-level in hand. "A false ceiling," she said to herself, as though it were a cryptic clue. Yes, definitely one of those, whatever she decided on. Nice anaglypta job. Magnolia. Or Sweet Solar, like in her meditation zone? Naturally, she'd speak to Keith about her decision in the same way as with Isobel's uni money. She'd shelve the chippiness and whisper him round. She'd prophesy a perfect blend of elegant achievement and practical use of space. Again she worked her back against the seat, slowly, luxuriously. She could just imagine Greville succumbing to her best routine.

At the roundabout just before Two Mitres, an ancient Morris Traveller joined the road in front of her, slowing her right down. For a moment, her lips worked with their wonted fury, parting now and then for a breathy eff-and-blind. But then she went over a pot-hole and heard the tiniest clink from the seat behind her. Quickly turning round, she saw the box, a bit of tissue hanging down its side. She was all smiles again. The git in front could go as slow as he liked. In her plans for all sorts of future, she'd forgotten her Watchful Tawny.

It all happened at their meeting a month ago. The shopping channels had been full of retro stuff, grandfather clocks in sturdy imitation-wood plastics, 1940s-style radios in *nostalgene* ("more bakelite than bakelite," the ad revealed), TVs on stilt legs. That Thursday, the meeting had been the liveliest ever. Nanette was in the chair, of course, all pert and mighty. Around her, the rest of them clamoured like schoolgirls, trying to outdo each other about why they'd ticked particular boxes on the survey forms, why their *Summative Report* for Greville should be read out ahead of the rest, why malacca curtain-poles would or wouldn't catch on, why the possible comeback of winceyette was a dream come true or a complete non-starter. Then, when drinks and snacks had calmed the hubbub, Nanette reached for her special phone and pressed the storage button for their guru's number. Her face settled into its familiar cat-with-cream expression as that gorgeous, chocolatey voice came through the phone's loudspeaker. Via Nanette, reverent where they'd been shrill, they took it in turns to satisfy the voice's owner with their opinions.

"Well, ladies," he'd drawled, once each had declared her tick-box choices and delivered her *Summative Report*, "it sounds as though our friend the retro style has, shall we say, unbuttoned one big debate." Widening her eyes, Nanette had held the receiver out like a torch so Oldstead could hear for himself the knowing giggles, the dreamy murmurs of agreement. He sighed like one replete, then said: "Of course, as in the retro world, so in the real one. I mean the real old one. Antiques. Collectibles. You'd be amazed how matters of beauty divide opinion. Of course, you have some collectors... oh, I'm so sorry, ladies. Here I am straddling my hobby-horse, all set to ride hard, and here you are, job done, itching to get home. Please forgive –"

"No, no, no!" Nanette almost screamed into the phone, a response echoed by the whole circle. "We had no idea you were" – she winked at the others – "into all that, Grev." The giggling grew uproarious, Oldstead joining in. Only Donna had held back. It needled her when Nanette called him "Grev." An abuse of her position, it was. Besides, her Ted was six-foot-four-inches of jealousy: not surprising, the kind of up-to-the-backside outfits Nanette favoured. He would be less than chuffed to know she was playing flirty Gertie with, well, her employer. And besides all that... Donna had slumped back in her chair, her lips pressed together. Besides all that, she just didn't like it.

The giggles subsided. For a moment, there was only Oldstead's voice, quietly noodling away at further, precisely-phrased apologies. Then Rose Dunbar had leaned forward.

"Yes, Scottie?" asked Nanette, a little aggrieved, about to press her own advantage with Grev.

Donna's lips tightened further. The woman had a name. Just because she came from Scotland, it didn't mean she'd lost it. "Scottie," for God's sake. Common, really, Nanette was. Probably thought Irish people said "begorra" from morning to night. She turned: "What, Rose?" she corrected.

Rose gave her a sideways look, which Donna identified as grateful solidarity, then said, "What was that about beauty?"

Nanette had covered the phone: "Just what I was going to ask him," she said in her all-in-good-time voice.

As she did so, Donna breathed, "I'll bet."

"Beauty, beauty, beauty," serenaded Oldstead through the speaker. "Divides the worlds of the auction room and the one-man outfit alike. Of course, the vulgar are always with us: *Don't care what it is, long as I make a killing with it.* But the discerning – ah, something might fetch its weight in rubies, but if they think it's pug-ugly" – his voice turned mock-posh – "*then aih regret that it's thenks baht no thenks.* I very much think," he continued normally, "that there's a lesson there for our retro friends. Reproduce the beautiful alone, not everything old. I mean, I wholly agree with whoever gave the thumbs-down to the malacca curtain-poles."

"I did!" screamed Cheryl Richardson. Nanette, who hadn't, wearily extended the phone: "He won't have heard you," she mouthed. With some satisfaction, she watched Cheryl swallow and self-consciously repeat herself. Donna, who'd likewise dismissed the curtain-poles, stared hard at Nanette as if willing her to combust.

"I know two or three of you did," said Oldstead. "I have my notes here in my sweat– Forgive me, ladies, my perspiring hand." Nanette thrust out the phone, and he received his due of fresh giggles. "And you're hardly alone," he continued. "In fact, advance research on that line should have told them –"

"Are you discerning, Grev?" Nanette cut in, her fingers splaying and closing on the receiver. "I mean, do you collect?"

"Indeed I do, Mrs Fowell, indeed I do. Rather why I thought I'd broach the subject. I feel bad, you see."

"Ah, Grev, why?" Nanette spoke in a dying fall. Donna and Cheryl exchanged glances. A couple of the others cleared their throats.

"Well, here I've been, picking your brain-cells like there's no tomorrow. I pay you, I know – enough, I trust?" Again the phone shot out at the circle of faces, accompanied by Nanette's prompting nod. The response was positive, except from Rose, who gave a little shrug and said, "I guess." Clutching the phone to her *décolleté* sweater, Nanette frowned at her and pursed her lips, as at a child who'd messed up a prize-day recitation. But Oldstead obviously hadn't heard: "Good, good. But, I feel, insufficient. Now, we've been gathering of a Thursday for quite a while. I think of you as, well, special friends" – here Nanette gave an eye-popping look of girlish happiness – "so I think it only right and proper that I should share my –" He stopped. Nanette stared in anticipation at the phone speaker. Even from where she was sitting, Donna could see her tongue flicking between slightly parted lips. Oh, God, he wasn't going to feed her more naughty niceness, was he? She didn't know how much more of the woman's gurning and squirming she could take. "Passion": was that the next word through the speaker? Or did he have taste enough to discourage the slapper's carry-on? When they came, his words seemed to answer her prayers: "Share other concerns with you," he said, his tone most professional – even a little sharp? "I don't know if any of you ladies go for collectibles? I readily confess that I'm next door to an ignoramus on matters antique. But I have good contacts – knowledgeable, fair-dealing – to put me on the right track. And I would be happy to act as go-between if any of you wished to add to her –"

"I do!"

"Strewth, Donna!" Rose jerked her glass, feeling melon-juice all over her wrist.

"Sorry, did I hear someone?" asked Oldstead.

Nanette caught the phone as it was about to tumble into her lap: "'Scuse us a mo, Grev." Then, incredulous, "You don't collect anything. And you're well sick of Keith's rubbish."

But Donna was on her feet and advancing to the phone. She hadn't a clue why she'd yelled out. Well, she had. She wanted her moment with Greville and she didn't care how she got it. Besides, how did Nanette Fowell know she didn't collect things, or didn't want to? Could have been on her mind for a while. In fact, she thought as she bore down on Nanette, she rather fancied it had been. Besides, there was a world of difference between ten-armed, bug-eyed doodahs and the kind of quality that Greville could line up.

"Donna Huxtable," Nanette told Oldstead dully. "She thought the curtain-poles were useless, too." With a sniff, she vacated her seat.

A minute later, before largely admiring eyes, Donna was the complete thinking-woman, laughing softly where Nanette had shrieked, speaking low where she had trilled. She resolved to listen as long as possible to that chocolatey voice. But almost at once the voice asked her what she collected

"Oh... now," she said, "what don't I?" Cheryl clapped a hand to her mouth. Open-mouthed at the side of her own chair, Nanette smoothed her hands down the brief reach of her skirt. "Get out of that one, Huxtable," said her eyes. Luckily, Oldstead was hungry to share the knowledge gleaned from his contacts. Donna listened while he itemised all manner of collectibles, large and small, whose desirability was on the rise. She followed the ebb-and-flow of his voice, punctuating it with "Hmms" and "Ahhhs" in which interest and indecision were strategically mingled.

"Come on, Donna," hissed Nanette, arms now folded. "If you wanted just to talk to him, we needn't have had this –"

"Yes, teapots!" said Donna, twisting completely away from her.

"Teapots are my" – briefly she glanced back at her hostess's tarty skirt – "passion," she exhaled.

"Aha!" said Oldstead. "That being so, Donna, I have a particular contact with an undeniable love for all things spouty." The snort was out before Donna could help herself. She could only pray that he'd think it superior to Nanette's trills and gurgles.

"And who is that, Greville?" She lingered on his name – just long enough, she hoped, to cancel out the snort and show that she disdained over-familiar abbreviations.

There was a moment's silence, as though he were unveiling the name: "Marius Appleyard," he said.

"Off the telly!" shrieked Nanette, taking a step back. Oldstead heard. He and Donna chuckled together, Donna now hoping that, amidst its calculated lightness, her laugh would communicate the words, "Greville, there's always one."

"The same," said Oldstead. "Good old *A-Haggling We Will Go*. He's doing a new series, he tells me. Start of next year. Not studio-bound, either. On the road again. I gather they're sorting out venues now. Perhaps I could put in a word for your part of the world?"

Hearing this, Nanette began some concerted pulling and smoothing, as though her house itself had been chosen and Marius Appleyard was looming already beneath her carriage lamp. Rose Dunbar watched her, then sighed and scratched the back of her neck.

"But this is something from our purpose, Donna," continued Oldstead. "I shall confer with Marius touching your passion. Get a proper feel for pots and prices. And you and I shall" – a delicious drop in tone – "talk next week."

There were appreciative murmurs and pats on the back as Donna resumed her seat and Nanette icily confirmed next Thursday's arrangements with the promiscuous Grev.

"Way to go, girl," said Cheryl.

"I was going to pack this in," said Rose, "but you've made it fun again."

Now, beyond Two Mitres, the Morris Traveller no more than a dream in her windscreen, she lived the rest of the fun as if for the first time. The following week, she had again usurped her hostess, this time learning of a range of sought-after teapots which were, said Oldstead, competitively priced and attractive to a fault. Reading from what he assured her were Marius's notes, he described each at loving length while Nanette stalked up and down by the chair and muttered about money, trees and her phone bill.

"Of course, Donna, you don't have to decide now," he said, at which Nanette's pace accelerated. "The proper step is to let you see them." Nanette drew herself up to her full height and gave Donna a don't-you-dare glower. Oldstead got them both off the hook: "Bit tricky, that, logistically. I could most certainly send you the pics and blurbs, though."

But by this time the others, having speedily appraised the choices, were barracking Donna like a game-show crowd.

"The Penitent Monk!"

"Go for the Dodo, Don!"

"Cottage of Content! Cottage, Donna, Cottage!"

"I can hear them pressing you hard," said Oldstead, sympathetically. Then, in a whisper just for her, "Look, I'm not rushing you, Donna, but my esteemed source tells me you couldn't do better than the Owl. Or The Watchful Tawny, to accord the beauty its proper title."

"The Owl!" she echoed, at which whoever had lobbied for the Owl cried "Yessss!" and Nanette tossed her hair by way of thanks to God.

"The price, Don," said Cheryl. "What did he say the price was?"

Oldstead confirmed it, to some "pfwarrs" and sharp intakes of breath. Nanette steadied herself against the back of her chair and gawped at Donna.

"Most reasonable, Greville," said Donna, sounding like an veteran of bidding wars. Given the amount she had in her own private savings, it certainly was. At the same time, it didn't hurt for the others – especially Her Majesty by the chair – to assume that Keith was so flush that, even if she'd bought the lot, the Huxtable purse would remain handsome.

A horn blared into her thoughts. Suddenly she found herself coming into Sedgley and nearly in the back of the ancient Morris. A tweedy arm extended from the driver's window and waved her on. But she dropped back, mouthing "Sorry" through the windscreen. Surprise at her own courtesy soon vanished, and she was back in the evening that had just passed.

The Tawny had been waiting, exquisitely crafted and with the promised watchfulness, on Nanette's occasional table. "Sorry, Donna," she'd said sweetly. "I couldn't resist." Donna hadn't minded.

The sweetness and apology were well-nigh genuine. Taking receipt of the hugely-wadded Private Delivery item, Nanette had, in her own eyes, regained her position of authority among the focus group – consolidated it, even. For her part, Donna had been happy to specify Nanette's address. After all, if the Tawny had suffered any damage, responsibility would drop with a thud on her over-displayed shoulders. Besides, if it had turned up at Rowan Tree Lane – ahead of her big push with the comics – that would have been awkward. No: fatiguing, she corrected herself as she slowed down further, letting the Morris turn right. Of course, she had her story for Keith worked out now. The thing was officially valuable, as attested by no less than Marius Appleyard. It would help furnish a room – as might others after it. It would be a talking point: not much talk to be had from piles of old lumber at the top of the house. Quite simply, it made sense in a way that comics didn't.

"Your investment pleases you, Donna?" Oldstead had enquired that evening after the focus business. Replying, she strove for an understated gush.

"I didn't include the papers of provenance with our Tawny, although I'm sure he'd have guarded them to the death. But they'll be on their way. Always best to send these things separately."

"Ooh, posh and proper," came a voice from the room. Hearing it, Donna prayed that she would sound likewise.

"About settling up with you, Greville. I haven't… I mean, I wasn't sure –"

"Oh, heavens, heavens, Donna, don't even think of fretting. This isn't a catalogue shop. Had to ensure your happiness first." Nanette leaned over the chair, and Donna felt an almost sisterly nudge.

"Now," said Oldstead, "we can kill this beast in one of two ways. I could hold back your Thursday payments till we reach the amount…"

"Wouldn't go for that, Don," murmured Cheryl.

"God, no," said Rose. "What we talking about?" she speculated, "Best part of six months?"

Donna wasn't about to go for that. Having led them to believe that she was a persuasive wife, she didn't intend to act like she was a name in a tally-man's ledger.

"I'll send you a cheque," she said blithely. Enjoying the public nature of the exchange, she also knew that, if Keith were to conduct the same business in the same way, she'd kill him. But that, too, she enjoyed.

"The hole-in-one it is, then," said Oldstead. "And just for that, I'll waive the delivery cost on the Tawny."

"You're most kind, Greville." Donna upped the chocolate in her own voice. "To the *Tight Focus* address?"

"West Wittering as ever was. Recorded post, if I may trouble you."

Bending into the circle of chairs, Nanette cupped a hand round her mouth: "He'd be trouble, mammoth-time," she told the assembly, who gave her a round of brief smiles.

"And Donna," Oldstead was saying, "if at any time you'd like guidance on a fresh investment..?"

"Actually, Greville, could you spare a little guidance now?" She had winced imploringly at Nanette, mouthing "just another minute". To everyone's surprise, Nanette had extended her hand, urging Donna to be her guest.

"You desire a companion for our Tawny?" he asked. "I had the jolly old Monk as first reserve. Now I really shall send you the low-down on him before we take one pace further."

"Oh, no – well, not yet." And she told him about Keith's tat.

"Ah, you're the comics gal! Or married to them. Yes, it's come up a time or two in my chats with the good Nanette. So your question is, what price the funnies?"

Donna didn't catch his final words. Like the others, she was staring at Nanette, who swept the room with a smile of top-dog defiance. She remembered her offhand reference to just such a call, weeks before. But how many times were a time or two? Bit thick of the cultured Greville to announce it like that. Or had Nanette wanted him to, as a way of showing, yet again, that she was queen of proceedings? If so, no wonder she was all bounce that evening. Good God, girl, she thought, if your Ted finds out – but then righteousness had become a stab of jealousy:

"... if that would be acceptable," came the chocolatey voice. Donna jumped, realising that its guidance had just passed her by.

"I'm so terribly sorry, Greville, what was that?"

Patiently, he doubled back: "I was saying that comics aren't a field that my contacts traverse in the normal way of things."

"Of course," said Donna, relieved to hear it. What would the likes of Marius or Greville himself be doing with spotted locusts from the planet Zilch? Oldstead's urbanity re-established itself in her mind, banishing his admission of non-focus chats with her ladyship. His voice grew extra-chocolatey. The stab of jealousy began to heal.

"From my gleanings, however, and if we're talking the usual routine – complete runs, first editions, rarities –"

"Oh, yes, indeed we are."

"– then the comics gal should do exceeding well. But if you have any problems finding a new home for the darlings, I can always nose out contacts of contacts, people with an interest" – he gave the faintest chuckle – "of that kidney. If, as I say, that's acceptable to you."

"Oh, most certainly, Greville. I'm pretty sure I can – that a home can be found. I just wanted confirmation that… it… ."

"That it would be properly flush with welcomes?"

Her gaze on the phone's speaker, Nanette trilled at these words, giving Donna a moment to cotton on. Then, "Yes, yes, properly flush."

"Sounds like you'll have nary a worry. But remember my offer, do."

"Thank you, Greville."

"And if you yearn for the Monk… He is still available for prayer, I understand. No rival connoisseuse has made off with him – yet."

"Greville, I'm all appreciation. Look, I'd better hand you back," she added conspiratorially, passing the phone to the bejewelled hand of its owner.

Donna left Bright's Way. Heading for the Sedgley roundabout, she caught sight of Aikenshaw's Walk and wrinkled her nose. She knew where Philpotts' junkyard was – facing the Rowlandson Arms. If ever two dives deserved each other… But again her thoughts drifted. The way Greville had said her name. "Comics gal", too – sweet or what? Of course, he hadn't exactly deepened her wisdom about the comics, but he'd confirmed it – added to her ammunition – and that was just what she'd wanted. Could there be something else for her down the road? Something more… informal with him? Well, not if madam with the phone had anything to do with it. Safely alone, Donna let out a double-snort. That bloody phone. Her thinking she was higher-than-high-tech with it. Cheryl's Will worked in communications – said those phones were old as Noah, that Nanette should get a full-conference effort so Greville could talk to everyone. Of course, she wouldn't wear that. Donna could hear her now: "Oh, think of all the blather in the poor lamb's ear." In truth, she damn well wouldn't give up her routines: purring, schmoozing, thrusting the thing out so all her kiddies could chorus on command.

But as she turned down Perry's Hill for the Birmingham Road, irritation faded into thoughtfulness. Perhaps the timing was right after all. Nanette was so bloody obvious... the endless wiggle, thong a mile above her jeans. Let her do her worst, get Ted suspicious, make herself a proper noose. Then, when everything had exploded – when, perhaps, Nanette was no longer queen bee of the group, or in the group at all... Donna smiled, hearing one of Rose Dunbar's favourite sayings: *What's for you won't go by you.* She imagined her mobile phone going. It was Greville's PA – he must have one – a fella, perhaps, with a nice dollop of chocolate in his own voice. *Greville for you,* he intoned.

Quiet time or no, Perry's Hill was always a race-track. She tried hard to concentrate, showing as much deference as she had to the Morris driver. But her mind persisted, pressing at her caution, holding out all her delicious thoughts like rainbows in an open palm. Before she knew it, she was watching herself in the kitchen with Keith and Imogen. She was reasoning it all out for them – about the comics, the loft, Imogen's survival pot, the Tawny and the wisdom of investing in friends for him. "God, you're good," she told herself and again thanked Oldstead's presiding genius. "My choc boy," she giggled. "Choc and velvet... mmm, sticky, sticky." But then she vanished from her own picture. Struggle as she might, all she could see were her husband and daughter at the kitchen table, chortling, filling their faces. The tears were so abrupt, so fierce, that they frightened her. Why couldn't she love them any more? Why couldn't she love the girl? The Birmingham Road junction swam up with its guard of traffic-lights. She knew why. She kept the answer locked in a loft way beyond Keith's imagining. For ages it had stayed put: she'd done well. But it always broke loose when she thought all was safest, when she was furthest from the door. It was never to be captured till it had told itself through. Now, with the lights approaching, it began. The tomboy forbidden to clamber on the garage roof. Her unthinking defiance. She herself sunbathing on the lawn below. The cracking, the scream, the full weight of the little body as it plunged and squashed. The bowing of her own naked back, all her guts in a hard ball round her navel, firewheels spinning through her neck and shoulders. The screams, mother and daughter together, their last moment of unity. Countless hands, gentle, fearful, on and under her, voices swelling and breaking up. The rag-doll days – miles of corridor, the *scrit-scrit* of trolley-wheels, Jeyes Fluid, that nurse from St Kitts with a thing for Johnny Cash. The couches flat and raised, the pulleys and injections. The months with two sticks, the months with one. The retirement on indisputable grounds – unwanted, baulked and screamed at. The regretful murmurs from the Head, the LEA bod who kept saying, "Now, let's weigh it all up." The earnest advice from the Union. The benefits package, those form letters with the too-wide gaps in which her name almost disappeared. The farewell to all that she'd been. That place near Oldswinford with fake hay-bales and hanging stirrups, "all-you-can-eat-for-£10". Colleagues laughing a bit too loud. And then the nothing.

For the second in which she saw it, Donna's light was green. "Focus, Huxtable," she half-sobbed, hunching forward. "Chuck it – chuck it now." But even as she chided herself, she sank again. What if she was OK most days? What if, now and again, she could even spend hours in something higher than flatties? The woman she'd been was gone, broken from a great height. His nibs had always seen it the other way round: a sacrifice, their youngest saved. He'd loved her the more for what she'd done, or so he said. True or false, she'd never wanted to know. What could it be but wrong love, pity for damaged goods? As for her love, she'd – no, not withdrawn it – lost it among the bitterness and pain. It was that other woman's love, anyway, the one who'd stripped to sunbathe, wife and mother attractive and complete. And something inside her, one hard nugget, could not forgive – even though she wanted to, wanted so much to feel the girl's smile warming her own face, not just kept for him, like now, in the scene she saw, at that table she couldn't reach, the two of them laughing –

"Christing hell, missus, what are you on!?"

The voice, male and raw, dragged her upwards. Donna broke the surface to find that she was on the grass verge to the left of the lights. Petrified, she shut her eyes, huddling tight into herself. Then she looked down, took a deep breath and thumped both sides of her seat. It was there, it was real. Frantically, she rubbed her arms and shoulders, stroked her hair, her legs. Yes – all in one piece. God, what had happened? Something must have steered her there. Some part of her mind not mired in yesterdays must have seen the need to get her clear of – turning, she half-squawked, half-hiccupped. Something must have made her wind her window down, too, though the shaven head leaning in made her wish she'd fought it. Before she could find words, the head withdrew and she saw, parallel to her, a half-ton truck at the side of the road, traffic struggling by. Hands on hips, the man now stood before the truck, theatrically scanning her 4x4 from front to rear. There was exaggerated wonder in his eyes, as though he were asking himself if her car had given up on its driver and simply saved itself. Then he darted forward, filling the window again. She sensed that he was about to repeat something he'd said, perhaps more than once.

"You were on red!" he yelled, his voice bouncing from the interior into her head and out again. "It's not a filter light, that left! Perry's Hill, one red light, everybody waits! I'm tooling down" – his hand shot out at the Birmingham Road – "then you're there and I bloody near stove you in!" Shaken though she was, Donna began to catch the tone – someone who knew his rights, who played fair if played fair with – someone who was actually enjoying all this. "So, right, I think, I'll risk getting one up the rear and let the tosser out, though I'd like to find the court of law as says I had to. Just my bloody luck, with a new rig as don't belong to me. So I flash you on, bugger up the horn. Next thing, you're well nigh stopped and I'm up your arse. Then you're on the cowing verge. You pissed?"

"I'm sorry, sorry." It was hardly a word – the slightest breath of wind, really, just as Imogen had said it when the screams had died down that day, and in the weeks and months after. She trembled violently. The something that had got her off the road had vanished. Her mouth was full of all that had dragged her through the red light. The man made a face of cartoon astonishment:

"What you on about now? Who's this you told and told? Not to climb up where?"

Donna trembled on.

"I'm bloody sure you were sunbathing, missus. Heat's fucked your brain up." The slam of a door shook her back to the present. Oh, God, he didn't have a mate with him, did he? The man seemed not to hear it. Instead, he produced a sheet of paper, looking as if he meant to cram it down her throat.

"I've been stuck a bloody half-hour at Burnt Tree Island. Cowing road-works," he added with a your-fault-too look. "Should have been at Great Bridge by nine-thirty. My time-sheet's down the shithole." He pushed the paper through the window, rattling it in her face. When he spoke again, his voice was quiet, like a grotesque send-up of Greville. "Now, what we going to do about all this, eh, missus?"

Pressing herself against the passenger seat, Donna watched his eyes. "I know what we can do," they said, "to make good all my trouble."

There was a rap on the passenger window, so sharp that Donna felt it right through the crown of her head. His mate, she thought, who'll pin me down while – But the man had left her side and was now arguing across the bonnet. Twisting round, she saw a woman's face, middle-aged and kindly, against the passenger glass. She reached back for the window button, and a small fire ignited at the base of her spine.

"Are you all right, love? We pulled up when we saw. My Wilf's just shooing this one off."

Donna looked out of the windscreen. The woman's Wilf was himself on the nearside of the bonnet, withstanding the trucker's imprecations like an oak in a gale. When the trucker paused for breath, Wilf slowly made elaborate hand-gestures as if gauging distances. The trucker started up again; again Wilf stretched confident arms. Now the trucker made to throw his time-sheet at Wilf's face, but instead wheeled about and stumped off to his truck.

"You're talking bollocks," he threw over his shoulder. "Shag-bag shouldn't be on the road." The couple's car was parked some yards along the kerb. The trucker drove straight for it. Only at the last minute did he pull out, deliberately grazing the rear bumper and nearly sending a biker over the median line. Fresh aggravation filled the evening air, horn mouthing off to horn. Moments later, the biker overtook the truck, whose full beam slammed on behind him.

Donna sat completely still. She was frozen, except for the small fire busy at her spine. Wilf joined his wife at the passenger window.

"Where'd'you live?" Wilf asked quietly. There was kindliness in his tone, a real concern. Clearly his wife hadn't badgered him to stop when he was all for shooting past. His manner restored Greville to her thoughts, unsoiled by that fleeting connection with the trucker.

She told them. "Through Roseville, is that?" He nodded. "Oh, I know, down by the cricket ground. I'll guide you back, then. Josie'll sit in with you."

Josie assented.

Their kindness held off the sunbathing, the screams. Donna began to say what she meant: "What did I do?"

"From what I could tell," said Wilf, "you must have come out a split-second after your amber. Just bad luck. We were behind…" His mouth worked silently through several words, settling on, "him with the time-sheet."

"Ages behind," added Josie. "And there was nothing in the outside lane. Plenty of space right round him."

"Space!" said Wilf. "He could have been on a country road." He smiled at Donna. "All right, so you mistimed it, but it was as safe as that situation could get."

"Came full at you, he did," said Josie. "No need for that. You did right to pull on here. Don't know as I'd've thought to. Shame he stopped, that's all."

Wilf flicked a hand: "Ah, a try-it-on merchant. Anyway, there's three speed cameras between here and Parkfields. He's probably got the full nine-points by now. Working with six already, I shouldn't wonder."

Now Donna pointed at their car: "I heard something iffy when he took off."

Wilf shrugged: "Well, that type would, wouldn't he? Had to get his last little kick in. 'Salright, it was just the plastic."

"We're getting rid of it anyway," said Josie.

Fifteen minutes later, they were winding off the Birmingham Road and round the back of Roseville High Street. With much thanks, Donna had declined Josie's offer to drive. After all, if she let this keep her from the wheel, she mightn't get behind it again. Similarly, she'd shaken her head when Wilf produced his own piece of paper: "I got it all. It's a Birmingham reg. I know, I know, the fault's yours, technically, but he was getting ready for common assault."

"It was harassment anyway," Josie had added. "Think about it, love. There was no accident, you're a female driver on your own. They're getting hot on his kind of malarkey. It'd go your way, I'm sure as sure."

"And we're your witnesses." Wilf had been adamant, as though he and Josie had been called into the world for just that purpose. "I've put our number on. Like Josie says, think about it." Despite another shake of the head, Donna had pocketed the paper.

Now she watched the back of Wilf's car, working her lips as her lights picked out the splintered bumper.

"I am sorry," she said again. "Your bumper. And dragging you into all this."

"Aww." Josie flapped her hands. "We've wasted a mint on that thing. Round and round and round." Finger by finger, she told off its inadequacies. "Bodywork, electrics, suspension, electrics again, bodywork again. Last time we go near a car auction. Of course, wouldn't you know, it all started just as their special warranty ran out – and that wasn't worth the printing anyway, probably. As for the other – well, we saw you were on your own. Woman to woman, love, you were in a right pickle."

Smiling, Donna made to turn to her. But Roseville Island was coming up, with the Kennershalt sign pointing right. Instead, she gave Josie's arm the lightest pat and then indicated.

"Now that's responsible driving," said Josie. "Wilf's good, but he's a bit of last-minute Charley with signals." Putting a hand up to the windscreen, she jiggled it rightwards. "Has he seen that sign?" she asked herself, but then his indicator flashed on.

Having burned awhile, the fire at the base of Donna's spine was doing its usual. Streaks of heat were hitting her neck like tiny, erratically-lit rockets. But she hardly noticed. Such good people. Strangers out of nowhere. And not in the least fussed about their car. They needn't have stopped. Or, having stopped, they might have thought better of it with that bully in full spate. And Josie – back at the verge, she'd sounded like she'd be a real chatty body, bending Donna's ear till she was glad to make her escape at Rowan Tree Lane. But no: she'd said just enough, the right things in the right way. No I-know-best stuff, no going on about the bloke's registration and phoning the police. You'd think she was some kind of counsellor, a therapist-type, like that woman she'd had to put up with in hospital. No, no – there wasn't any of that archness – no grave head-nodding, no pausing to weigh words. Swinging round the island, following Wilf onto Le Manquis Avenue, Donna wondered whether she hadn't spent too much time with the Nanette Fowells of this world. Then, for a moment, Janice's Mark filled her mind's eye. She heard a typical line of his spiel: some palaver about a hotel's cleaning rota that only he could sort out, an apparently offhand reference to a new pal at the gym who was going places in a big law firm. For the first time, his sexiness seemed strangely bland; his finger-in-every-pie routine grated. Oh, she'd still ask him about investment chances for Imogen's *arrivederci* money. But perhaps he, too, was a bit of a pain.

Where Le Manquis Avenue became Rowan Tree Lane, Donna took a speed-bump awkwardly.

"Inventions of the devil, those things," said Josie, then pricked up her ears at a chinking sound from the back seat. She craned her head round: "You been shopping?"

"Sort of." Donna managed a proper laugh and described the Tawny.

"Oh, my sister-in-law's mad for all that," said Josie. "She goes in for – what d'you call them – fairings? Stuff you'd win at coconut-shies. Shepherdesses, jolly old Joes in sou'westers – all over her house. Give me the willies, they do, all those dotty little eyes following you about." She chuckled at her own foolishness. "*Another gift for the dust,* I tell her. But she loves them. And one or two would fetch a bit. Not that she'd part with them, mind. Still, she'd have something to fall back on" – another chuckle – "if she ever threw my dopey brother out."

Donna started. "So are you... from near here?" she finally said, though "Are you human?" was what nearly came out. For a crazy moment, she wondered whether Josie and Wilf weren't scaly green beings in human form, dropped out of some comic's badly-painted sky to... what? ...suggest possibilities? ...predict the shape of her remoter future? God knows, she'd had thoughts. Not like Josie had said, maybe, but... getting away... starting over... They were dreams, of course, born of bleak moments. After all, tidy though they were, how far would her savings take her? Still, like the heat of that sunny day, like the feel of the sun-lounger against her breasts, the dreams returned... Meanwhile, Josie told her where she and Wilf lived. As with Greville's advice on the comics, she realised that she hadn't caught a word. But she'd been able to beg his pardon. No chance of that with her kindly companion. Wilf was slowing. Here they were by the cricket ground.

Walking back to Donna's car, Wilf bent down and rubbed his damaged bumper. He gave a quick shake of the head: no problem, it said – at least, nothing to lose sleep over.

"Now, you sure you'll be alright?" Josie's hand was solicitous on Donna's arm.

"Honestly, I'll be fine… thank you." Now, Donna sounded almost chirpy. If Josie sensed the effort required, she didn't let on. "I've got my owl to cry to," added Donna.

"Ooh, not only him," said Josie. She looked across the road. Following her gaze, Donna saw the lights of her house burning. A shadow moved behind the lounge curtains. She gave a single nod as if unkinking her neck: "Oh, yes," she said. In her mind's eye, her younger, sunbathing self rolled from back to front. Again that day might have replayed itself, but Josie said, "Thanking you, sir," and Donna turned to see Wilf opening her door. He leaned in:

"You'll be ok now," he said, his words confirming rather than questioning; he, too, stared across at her house.

Donna straightened up in her seat. A single rocket flew up her spine, but she ignored it. She looked purposeful. Then, "I'd invite you in," she said deliberately, "but I think I'd better have a quiet five minutes – and I've got to make sure that my peculiar husband has finished dealing with a load of mad old clutter." Relief settled on her face. Ah, she was in control again; she'd passed her own test. She knew she'd only thought that last bit, not said it – and in any case, Josie had held up her hand after "quiet five".

"Donna, Donna, family's best for times like these."

"And remember that bit of paper," said Wilf. "His reg. Our number."

"Call us anyway," added Josie brightly. "For a proper natter. Tell us how your owl settled in."

"Owl?" said Wilf, at which Josie laughed and told him not to fret his head.

"Girl talk, is that?" Wilf sounded surprised at himself, as though he'd failed a test of his own and hadn't meant to speak out loud.

"Now, where'd the likes of you hear that phrase?" bubbled Josie and got out. Leaning round her, Donna smiled broadly at him. Sweet, he was, coming out with that, then looking embarrassed. For a bloke of his vintage, he looked nice, too.

The couple waited till Donna had swung across to her gate. Then they pulled slowly away, Josie's hand fluttering a goodbye at the edge of their roof. Donna eased round Keith's van, parked more awkwardly than usual on the drive. Ordinarily, she would have had a quick eff-and-blind, chiding herself for not telling him about it before she left. But the strangest feeling ambushed her – something like thankfulness. Somehow, the small annoyance eased her back into her world, doubling her resolve to manage it all more briskly. Really, she had let the whole business of the loft drag on for far too long. There'd be no more of that – no more indulging the disinclination of others. Apart from all else, there was her health to consider. External aggravation meant internal misery: that was one useful thing the hospital therapist had said. But, like a chump, she'd all but forgotten it and put the good of the family first. Well, that couldn't happen again. As if seconding her decision, the base of her spine obliged with a raw tingle.

Taking the key out of the ignition, she clicked the fob button for the garage door, which juddered open. Anyway, she thought, her world would improve enormously once those comics were gone and the money put to intelligent use for young madam. And, of course, she now had Tawny: first arrival of many, perhaps. Then there was that generous-hearted couple, whom she would ring. For a giddying instant, part of her wondered if the eruption of the trucker had actually happened. She might be returning straight from Nanette's right now, the misunderstanding with that old car at Sedgley the only faint blot on a – yes, a most wonderful evening. The fantasy seemed to bathe and empty her mind, just like those bathsalt pyramids Rose Dunbar had got her. *After the Storm,* they were called. Didn't she deserve such bliss? Weren't storms forever edging round her life? She still had half a jar left. Yes, she'd have a good, deep bathful right after checking the loft. Practically serene, she pulled into the garage.

Once she was in the house, however, serenity came undone. The shadow on the lounge curtains must have been Keith, now settled in front of the TV, absorbed in some item about the Ghost of Fazeley Canal on the local news. At the edge of the commentary was a faint, relentless thump. Imogen's music. Robot rubbish, too loud and too late. Donna tried the thought once, twice, as she looked up the stairs. But for some reason, the enjoyable irritation it usually brought her would not come. And now, here was Keith, turning the sound down, swivelling in his chair, smiling pleasantly at her:

"Good meeting?" he asked.

"Yes, it was." She found herself trying to match his tone. Suddenly she felt rather uncertain about… well, everything. She tried to think of the box whose pricey contents, carefully unpacked, now stood on the dining-room table. No warm glow there, either, aside from another rocket up the spine. Keith swivelled a little in the chair, this way and that. She hadn't seen him so relaxed in an age. He looked for all the world like he had something particular on his mind. Something good. It seemed as though the warmth she'd been striving for in her own thoughts had been diverted into his face, his eyes. Relief, she tried insisting to herself – that's what it was. He'd realised that he was free of his own foot-dragging game. He'd done what she'd asked and now the load was off him, too. He'd learnt the worth of action. For a second, like a thrown ball at the top of its arc, her theory comforted and persuaded – then plunged. Nervously, she searched his unchanged expression. Was she about to hear some barmy plan? Was he about to trump her about the future of the loft? Had he (she tensed; another rocket flew) decided to keep the bloody comics?

"Everything done and dusted upstairs?" she pressed on.

"Oh, yes – all finished." His mild tone tugged at something. She folded her arms as though the tugging were real. What was going on? Did she find his words gentle or annoying?

"Well, I'll check that all is correct, boy," she tried, but there was no edge to her voice. Even "boy," one of her favourite wallops, failed her and her mouth soured a little. More pleasant than ever, he gave a be-my-guest nod and smile before restoring the television's sound.

"'Lo, mom!" Donna squinted up the stairs to see Imogen heading towards the main bathroom. "How was the focussing?"

"Good!" Donna spoke over the question.

"How was Nanette? The usual pain?"

For a second, Donna didn't reply. Here it was again – the tugging. She'd expected her "Good" to close the exchange and give way to the thump of Imogen's feet, the slam of the bathroom door. Fondly, she'd anticipated her usual irritation at the girl's airy gallumphing about, but she couldn't connect with it. Instead… moving to the foot of the stairs, she unfolded her arms.

"Nanette? Oh… you know."

Imogen chuckled in response.

"She gets worse," pursued Donna, stunned by the eagerness in her voice. But Imogen seemed to invite it. There was openness in her manner, real interest… and more? And she was still there, at the top of the stairs. Donna looked harder. Some voice whispered that father and daughter had been hatching something: "Get out," Donna breathed. Oh, damn the shade on that landing light! Even though

Imogen was just underneath it, her face was ledged in shadow. But there was a smile there, surely – yes, a full smile, such as she gave her dad. Wasn't there? Donna looked back into the lounge. Keith's profile retained the pleasantness with which he'd greeted her. Aware of her eyes upon him, he turned expectantly, then opened his mouth as something occurred to him:

"You get past the van all right? I should have shifted it over."

"No, fine, fine." Donna's eyes whizzed almost comically between Keith and Imogen, who was now on the top step, asking what the group had discussed. Suddenly Donna was back at the lights on Perry's Hill, seized by the thoughts that had propelled her into the trucker's path. She saw love before her, solid as a statue. Questions filled her mind, briefly more alien and frightening than the trucker himself. What was it all worth – her scheming, her planning, her life as a stranger in her own house? She had saved her child that day. She could love them both again. She'd tell them about that godawful man and her terror, about Josie and Wilf. She'd tell them everything. And now she saw Nanette Fowell's cawing face, heard Greville Oldstead on the phone, deep and menacing: "Let's forget the gew-gaws, Donna. I know what you want." Disgust made her pucker her face and step back. Those were their true colours. Her real life was here after all.

Keith half-rose from his chair.

"You all right, Donna?"

But Donna looked up as though her youngest had spoken. Imogen had now descended a step or two. The shadows from the shade were rising from her face like curtains. That smile was broadening, wasn't it? Blooming like a flower? A smile just for her. She'd been a complete fool, she could love them –

But suddenly the fire roared up her spine, flinging itself round her body. Again the shadows fell. Again the old patterns found their place. He'd bloody better have finished up there. Didn't she have an exam next day? What had they been saying at their precious kitchen table? When Imogen echoed her father's question, Donna all but shrieked, "Yes, yes, I'm all right – as I always have to be. Now, let me at those comics." She mounted the stairs, defying the flames that spat with every step. Imogen scuttled aside, patting the loft ladder to ensure that it was firm.

"Do you want me to hold – ?" she tried.

"I want you to shut that music off, lady. You've got something to do tomorrow, yes? I haven't forgotten, though you obviously have." And she swung past the girl like a demon fleeing its own conflagration. At the foot of the stairs, Keith looked dully after her. Then, catching Mog's eye, he made a turning gesture, and she darted to her room. The music subsided: "And now, Craig with the weather," called the TV.

A while later, an observer out of nowhere – Eddie Beplate, maybe, or Gabe Tomorrow – might have decided that this wasn't the Huxtable address or any private house. This was Ebbatson House for the Elderly. Keith hadn't touched any comics that day: he'd gone to work at the residential home, as arranged with Mrs Askills. He'd been approaching a bathroom, set to deal with a troublesome sink, when a black-robed figure had appeared by the doorway, swaying a little, steadying itself against the frame, then shuffling forward as surely as age and disorientation would allow. Keith had looked this way and that for an attendant – even called out. Nobody appearing, he'd tried to help the figure as best he could. Such, at least, was suggested by the scene on the landing.

"Dammit, Keith, I'm all right!"

"Did you really have to go up, Donna? You saw how it was all going at lunchtime."

"I wanted to make sure it'd kept going – didn't want to find you'd chucked them about the place again, like they were before."

"They weren't chucked! I had them in those little piles."

"You had them where a body could twist their ankle. Well, there's an end of it. No square inch of this house is going begging again. No more dreaminess over common sense."

Easing off her robe, Donna moved to the edge of the bath, into which, on her instructions, Keith had scattered Rose Dunbar's bath-salt pyramids. "I can manage," she called over her shoulder, then lifted a leg and winced.

Keith watched her swaying back, his hands tight on the doorframe: "I'll have to rig up some steps instead of that ladder," he said, "even before we do whatever it is up there. You"re clearly not up to –"

"Nothing wrong with that ladder!" Donna's foot was now in the water, dispersing such bathsalts as hadn't dissolved, so that they washed about like the tatters of an iceberg armada. After a moment's thought, Keith started forward to help her climb in. Seeing him between patches of mist on the wall-mirror, she worked her lips, warning him back. Again she swayed, clamping a hand to the small of her back as though that gesture alone would hold her together. Then, tentatively, she stood up straight in the bath.

"Going up there with my lunch. What was that in aid of?" Donna tensed at his tone. No pleasantness now. Even in the midst of pain, she wouldn't have been surprised to hear him going on about missing a delivery at Great Bridge, about a ruined timesheet. "I could have come down to eat –"

"Keith, leave me be!" Her cry was more strident than ever, sustained for one moment of pure wrath. Then it dissolved into a long, wavering "Aaaaaahhh" as, cuffing the air in his direction, she turned and lowered herself among the pyramids. Keith picked up her robe and threw it over the toilet-seat.

"Chair!" she bleated. But he just stared, as though committing her to memory. Stabbing a finger at the wicker chair, she brought on another "Aaaaah". Slowly he draped the robe across the chair-back, fingering it as though his touch, too, wished to remember.

"Don't make a meal of it, Keith. Just go!"

As he closed the bathroom door, his mind filled with that strangeness of hours before – in the kitchen, while Mog was getting the desserts. Again he saw that phantom scene from "The Magenta Line", those brief, unfathomable details of Razalia. Again, he himself was standing by a wall of water and Donna was up on that ridge. Now, she was even more haughty, more savage, her legs apart, her back ramrod straight. She gave him the same mouthful about the planet they were on, holding him responsible for its spatch-cocked condition, then harping on again about some Sunday. A moment passed, during which he looked about. Yes, he was in his own home. There was the landing, the stairs; there was the loft-ladder, which he was too weary to push out of the way for the night. But there was something else. He felt as though his head was being used for deliberations by... by what? Before he knew it, he'd whispered, "Sunday it is then," just as he had in the kitchen. But his lips moved on, silently, as though warming up for some design that had yet to break cover in his thoughts.

Turning to descend the stairs, he looked at Mog's door, thought of knocking, decided against. He'd drive her to school tomorrow. He'd see she was all right for her exam. Looking up, he thanked heaven for that lucky moment. Before the bathroom palaver, some spirit – benign and unhoped-for – had moved Donna to push the door open and wish the girl good luck. Briefly, in the midst of her agony, her voice had rung out, tender and kind, the way it hadn't been for... well, years. Keith tried to make sense of the moment. It was as though something had allowed her a minute with her old self, like you'd allow a prisoner with his family. Then she'd been pushed, or pushed herself, back into her world now – her world of pressed lips and sharp comebacks, her world of untimed explosions where everyone was "madam" or "boy". He thought of the number of times he'd tried to understand that world and given up. And here was another. But tomorrow, he'd echo her "good luck" for Mog; he'd say it over and over. Mog would be all right. She'd remember her mother's voice in that moment. Besides, she could focus her mind like no-one else he knew, for as long as was needed. Only after the exam would every-thing start to... to – he gave up on that thought as well. He'd have a word with Mrs Askills. She'd understand. He'd get away for an hour or two and collect Mog. Pub lunch, he thought with a smile. Plenty of ketchup.

He went through the house switching off and locking up. Emerging from the lounge, key outstretched for the porch door, he saw a silver curve suspended in the dark of the dining-room. It looked as though some unearthly being had drawn energy from the street light and breached the curtains. "Razalia," he said without thinking and turned the dimmer-knob. When he dropped the keys, the Tawny seemed to measure their fall. When he staggered back, it seemed to puff out – ready to swoop and see him off.

THE STEALTHY CRAVING

The sun heaved itself into its westward spiral. Its after-light fanned
out like a bow-wave, then blurred like spillage on a cloth. All round
Razalia, the skies turned amethyst as the raging galleon steered further away. Another fortnight had passed. Another grudging visit was
over – a full day, this time. Razalia had been poked and prodded, its
surface daubed with a bare sufficiency of warmth and light. And now,
as always, its lower air seemed to thrum with solar contempt, nipping
at Razalian ears, turning the planet's term for space on its head. For
Razalia itself would now become a "forsaken midnight", while the
silences beyond crackled with energy and the vast emptiness became
a spring of fire, hugely uncoiling as the sun spiralled in slow majesty
towards Carolles. As if defying their planet's fate, the three umber
moons darted in turn at the tails of the burning bow-wave, like kids
who cheek a bobby's retreating back.

And, as always, the wake of the sun caused temporal havoc. A
Razalian hour passed normally enough, then shrank to ten minutes,
then sneezed out a good half-day, then stabilised at an hour and a bit.
Bobbing on the top of planetary time like corks in a bucket, the three
moons spread out and were still – this time like kids glued to a screen.
For, as the sunlight disappeared and the minutes passed more confi-
dently, Razalia shook off its desolation. Across its face, a million
torches shone under the amethyst skies: Razalian faces, each its own
sun.

On a heathery knoll just beyond Razalia's capital, one face shone
with especial intensity. Tharle of Mopatakeh had long disregarded the
haughtiness which defined the sun's visits and departures. Like most
Razalians, he felt neither belittled by the sun's manner nor saddened
that its visits were so rare. The sun was haughty, he reasoned, in the
same way that a stream was wet or a sapling green. Should it wish to
change, to smile long and benignly on Razalia, it must needs look
deep within itself, not expect change in others. If it saw the glow of
Razalian faces, their "watching light", as a mockery of its own splen-

dour, the sentiment was its responsibility alone. Besides, he had other things to consider. Evening was coming on. He knew it, and it had nothing to do with the forsaking sun. Though the glow on his face was bright, he could feel a nub of darkness at its core, heralding an end to the day's toil and, presently, the descent into sleep. All over the planet, his brothers and sisters, young and old, were sensing the same.

Turning round, planting his feet apart on the knoll, Tharle regarded the fields and thoroughfares, workplaces and dwellings of Mopatakeh. Tiny ovals of light were everywhere about their business. This one nodded along behind a plough. That one bent down in a doorway, above hands that shook a mat or wiped themselves on an apron. Here, a crimson-tinged oval reared back as a hammer set sparks dancing on the amethyst air. There, amid cries and laughter, a jostle of especially tiny ovals broke apart on a street corner: the young of Mopatakeh, their learning done for the day. Tharle smiled upon the place of which he was leader. It was a full, broad smile – indulgent, some might say. After all, as Tharle, he wore his mouth nearly all the year round, only sealing it off when he felt that a period of fasting would sharpen his judgement. But it was a smile of deep affection, too – although, as he turned from Mopatakeh and braced himself to look elsewhere, affection became sadness, a sadness pricked with fear.

On the opposite side of the knoll, two mighty arms of water converged and raced into the distance. For Mopatakeh was spread out on an island, southernmost in a chain of seven. The chain was washed by the generous waters of the Billomingow, a river so broad that, even from the knoll, its banks were barely visible. Mopatakeh was the largest island, the others decreasing in size from south to north. Aside from the Billomingow, they shared a common shape, something like a teardrop. Viewed from high in the air, with one island seeming to drip onto the next, the chain suggested the grief of some inconsolable horizon. Now, watching the course of the Billomingow, Tharle tried not to think of tears and grief. Allowing himself another minute or so before he looked where he didn't want to, he considered Mopatakeh's happy position. Not only was it the Razalian capital – it also stood smack dab in the middle of the planet. To use the crude linearities of Earth, the zeroes of longitude and latitude crossed on its fertile ground. This was as it should be – symbolically, of course, but practically as well. For Razalians loved to visit their capital whenever they could, and the fact that none of them had to come excessively far took the pressure off the planet's transport system, a fleet of twenty-seater chara-jets. Fragile, apt to loop the loop if a passenger stirred suddenly, or even sneezed, they loafed rather than sped through the air. Many moons since, they had been gifted to Razalia by the ever-upgrading Carollessa. A corps of Razalians had been trained in their maintenance, the knowledge passing from one generation to the next. Sadly, the stock of spare parts had long dried up – as had the minerals, peculiar to Carolles, from which they were made. Scouring the technical archives of the Aeonodrome, their famed planetary museum, the Carollessa offered to replace the fleet with another, identical in design but wrought from up-to-date materials. Ever grateful to their generous neighbours, the Razalians declined, opting instead to keep the fleet going with a mixture of trust and improvisation. This decision, it has to be said, was not without calculation. Throughout the arc of the sixteen planets, Razalia was loved for its antique quaintness. The proud Sehundan, the gruff Baraskian, the barmpot of Galladeelee and many more – all came to the planet as believers might enter the room of a chosen child: frail, tiny but possessed, they were sure, of unfathomable wisdom. How could that image benefit from a pack of chara-jets, however primitive of aspect, zipping dependably about, dodging the vagaries of Razalian time and keeping their noses straight?

Hands loose at his sides, gaze just above the flow of the Billomingow, Tharle kept his thoughts light for a moment longer, considering the events of that morning. As usual, half-a-dozen chara-jets had flown nose-to-tail above Mopatakeh's western bridge, bearing artisans to their work in the capital, relatives to their families and alien travellers agog for their main destination. As befitted his position and power, Tharle's was the first face on the island to be fully aglow. Like all other Tharles in all other settlements, he used this advantage to act as a kind of dawn-watchman, doubling his height so that he could stroll at speed from the eastern bridge, through the capital proper and out to the west, checking that all was well. After standing for a while at the middle of the western bridge, gazing on the Billomingow, he began to hear those familiar noises – rattling wheels, cries of greeting – which announced the traffic of work on and off the island. Shortly after, the incoming chara-jets came ambling down the sky, their engines blessing the new day with their trademark noise, a cross between a cleared throat and the snapping strings of a cello.

Tharle stared at them in some amazement. The line was holding steady, not lashing like a speared snake as it normally did. For once, it looked as though there wouldn't be the usual ballet – the spirals, the bucking-bronco capers – as they tried to land in the airfield on the far side of the capital. Soon, the western bridge was thronged. Everyone else stopped too, pointing upwards, mouths taking shape in faces for cries of astonishment, ears flowering on heads to acknowledge them. As more mouths and ears appeared on more heads, speculation flew about. The jets were perfectly, almost freakishly aligned because the intimidating sun had disappeared. Everything – animate and inanimate – was relaxed, composed, like schoolkids after the king bully has been dealt with. Or Razalian time, itself relieved that the sun had gone, was making a special effort, suppressing its tics and glitches and creating a tunnel of smoothly ticking minutes for the landing. Or the extra-planetary visitors on board had bet the pilots that the Mopatakeh touchdown would be as endearingly shambolic as ever. Nothing supported these theories. The sun had abandoned Razalia a million times. The alien visitors were usually too engrossed in the view to talk, never mind lay bets. But this did not diminish the joy with which they were advanced.

In fact, the visitor theory was nearest the mark. As the jets went slowly over, Tharle reared up to twice his height again and began striding to the airfield. Flying low now, they were clear to his view. He tracked them as they began their final descent, their path still as straight as an arrow's. But then the second jet sprang out of line, the fourth thrashed like a beached fish and the sixth wavered and dropped below the rest like a great-aunt dying for a sit down. Something burst from the windows of all three – a convulsion of eels, it seemed. At the edge of the airfield, Tharle stopped and groaned, as did the stream of Mopatakehans jostling breathlessly behind him. They should have known – could have done, too, with a little telepathic oomph. But it hadn't been strictly necessary. After all, the three jets hadn't been in actual peril. They had, however, been commandeered by a singular species of tourist: a tribe of Galladeelee youngbloods who, it turned out, were visiting Razalia (or rather, extending their endless home-party) to witness the sun's disdainful transit. Sure enough, the eels turned into the familiar, apparently uncontrollable arms and legs of the goofy Galladeelean, which proceeded to wallop the roofs of the jets or kick out at thin air. From inside the jets came the sounds of whoops, shrieks and the traditional Galladeelee salutation, raucous yet somehow respectful, to the glowing Razalian faces: "Hey! Hey, you stars! You stars in the water!" Then, through the rear window of the last jet, one of them spotted and recognised Tharle and gave a long, three-mouthed, hiccuppy cry. It must have carried down the whole haphazard line: the thumps and whoops ceased instantly. And, next moment, the jets were neatly aligned again, and the countless arms were sculling the air in unison, ensuring a landing that was gentle, quiet and most un-Galladeelean.

Tharle smiled at this recollection. Boisterous they may have been (though they were ungainly charm itself when they emerged from the jets) – but at least the Galladeeleans had made a proper visit. More frequently, they used their huge catapults to *boing* clear across the eastern stretch of the system and yell their cheery, crazy greetings. Of course, a few Galladeelean wildmen always tagged along for the Baraskians' yearly festival – their brash yet somehow mystical celebration of the famed gaps of nothing in the Razalian landscape, their often trance-like worship of the whiteness that their planet didn't know. Tharle stopped himself and took a deep, mind-swirling breath. He'd sprung the moment on himself. He had to look now. Making a half-circle on the knoll, he gazed towards the eastern limits of Mopatakeh. Far off to the right a hillock rose up, round at the sides, level at the top, like a bottle sliced at the neck. Once upon a time, Razalians believed that the hillock was their creator's first stab at a landmark on the planet. Though that belief had long died on Razalia, it had been taken up among those Baraskians who believed that – in some special, inexplicable way – Razalia was the mother of the whole system. Some of them devoted a good half-day of their festival to circling the hillock, claws interlocked, creviced brows a-sweat, intoning gruffly, their words roughly translating as *O prime bloom of life, O firstborn of nature.* Far off to the left was the airfield, from which, before long, the last fleet of chara-jets would depart for the day. Artisans and relatives would return to their remote settlements; the Galladeeleans (who had promised Tharle that they would all depart on the same jet, even paying for its shell to be specially expanded and reinforced) would go whooping off westwards, pretending that they, in fact, had forced the sun to scarper. Between airfield and hillock was the usual run of Razalian landscape: gentle undulations, copses, a ridge or two. And, in the middle of all that, Mopatakeh's gap of white – site of the tragedy half-an-aeon ago, that dark hour in the annals of the Baraskian Festival. Like everyone else, leader and led, Tharle knew the whole grim story: the Baraskian chorus standing in attitudes of bravado against the gap; the squabble over some small word from their extraordinary anthem; the heated words; the tugging and swaying; the choral plunge into the white, whose raised surface remained as still as a summer pond; the gawping, fatally curious Galladeelean whose errant jaw was likewise claimed by the unfathomable nothing. By all accounts, uproar wasn't the word for what had followed – chiefly among the Razalians, who feared that the Baraskians would take their yearly trances elsewhere and that, far from being the mascot of the system, Razalia would become its pariah. But the Baraskians, with their characteristic, growly geniality, had immediately acknowledged the stupidity of their songsters, seeing their fate as an even stronger argument for worshipping Razalia's lethal patches of white. Indeed, next day, they had arranged the next Festival, down to the last lodging and flagon-cart. As for the jawless Gallideelean, it had long been thought that he would have been better off staying on Razalia, rather than submitting to the charge of freakery and its attendant punishment back home. Certainly, it would have been better for his kith and kin. Who could possibly count all of Galladeelee's rouge catacombs? It was said that he'd only managed three thousand at the time of his death, the sentence then passing to his wife, then son, then daughter, then son-in-law (who counted eight before being buried in a rock-fall) – then to a nephew who was apprehended on the day he was due to emigrate to Carolles. Around that time, however, a sea-change had occurred in the Galladeelean style of government, which shifted itself into line with the general goofiness of its population. The nephew was reprieved after his first hundred catacombs. He lived out the rest of his life on Carolles, a beneficiary of a Galladeelean pension which would have kept the dozen inhabitants of Lachbourigg, planet of the roving forests, in food and drink for an aeon.

"A good end to a bitter story," thought Tharle. "I need that now." And, reaching into the deeps of his mind, he drew up every last drop of visionary strength and stared across the east of the island to the Mopatakeh gap. His gaze, heightened a thousandfold, travelled all round its limits, drinking in every inch. They looked as they always did, perfectly still, as though the white had been penned in with invisible wire. But then they quivered and blurred, suggesting the reproductive jostle of cells beneath a microscope. The demands of focus nearly sent Tharle into a swoon, but he planted his feet yet further apart, he held on. A moment later, the limits sharpened again, and his fear hit him harder and colder than ever. Yes. They had moved. Outwards.

Like a mile-long telescope collapsing section by section, Tharle's vision shrank to its everyday strength. He turned away, staring out again over the Billomingow. Only recently had his suspicions been aroused. Two nights before, white had entered his dreams, flapping, spilling, upending like a sail maddened by gales. The following dawn, he had visited the controller of the airfield for their usual conference about the post-solar glitches in time and their possible impact on flight schedules. The controller was herself a naturally early riser. After Tharle's, her face was the first to reach optimum glow. Tharle had made his usual dawn patrol, then doubled back to the airfield. As always, the controller had devised contingencies galore for even the most volatile time-storm. The citizens of Mopatakeh were just stirring when the conference finished. With time on his hands (pretty stable, too, since the sun wasn't due for another day), he'd made a consitutional of his return to the capital, passing along beside the gap and rounding the hillock. He'd just emerged from the far side of the hillock when his mind was filled again with his dream. Though gazing on rolling fields and gentle crests, all he could see was an ecstasy of white. Then his gaze had cleared and he looked back at the gap. Its further limits seemed to be settling like the edge of a shaken blanket. He'd trebled his vision and looked again. The very lowest swell of a ridge seemed to have vanished.

As soon as he reached The Guiding, his official house near the main market-square, he'd thought his puzzlement off to Tharle of Kidresh, the second largest settlement on Razalia. On the other side of the planet, Kidresh lay at the foot of Maker's mountain, the very one that had figured in the planet's creation theories. It, too, had a gap, which partly skirted a wood to the north of the settlement and had claimed not a few foolhardy lumberjacks. Tharle of Kidresh had thought back immediately. He too had dreamt in white. And, after his morning patrol, he had been drawn to the wood. On its gapward side, two trees had been left branchless and hollow, as if in the wake of blight. A rivulet of white fingered its way between them.

Sensing that Tharle of Mopatakeh was about to sense the need to make an official request, Tharle of Kidresh promised to be on the island next day, once the sun had fully vanished. He could have come sooner, but there was prudence in his delay, an admixture of sense and superstition which Tharle of Mopatakeh endorsed. If the sun suspected that something was amiss – indeed, that Razalia was starting to eat itself up – who knew if or when it would return, or what spite it might visit on its cuckoo? After this exchange, Tharle of Mopatakeh had sat tight, his mind full again – not with daydreams of white but with messages from Tharles all over the planet. The gaps in their dispensation, too, were twitching into hungry life. But he also established that ordinary Razalians knew nothing about the alarming development – yet.

So, that very day, the sun had arrived to find Razalian business as usual. Its presence went unremarked by most – certainly on Mopatakeh, where talk was all of the chara-jets. It was only the young who delighted in the scant handfuls of heat and light the sun threw down, devoting their schoolbreaks to splashing about in the brightness as though it were a levitating puddle. Adult Razalians simply attended to their affairs. Like the generations before them, some briefly regretted the sun's scorn for their half-finished world. But, like Tharle of Mopatakeh, all rejected any culpability in the matter. Not that Tharle had time to spend pondering his planet's gentle defiance of the moody sun. After ensuring that the Galladeelean roisterers had every last foot planted on firm land, he had returned to the Guiding, spending much of the day thinking back and forth with fellow Tharles from all four corners. Again and again, the debate had veered towards the same questions. What was to be done? The gaps' rate of advance was between slow and standstill at present, but who knew when they might start acting like Razalian time, leaping forth, pouncing on hills, rivers – people? What had caused the encroachment? Could it be stopped? Reversed? Amid the warm colours and sturdy beams of the Notionary, his special conference room, Tharle had shuddered as his peers' anxious musings flowed through his head. He wondered if the bounds between creation and non-creation had always been so fragile – the former a crust of bread, the latter a cavernous mouth simply biding its time. He'd intended to keep the thought silent, since it wasn't strictly relevant to the present moment. But out it had slipped. From all over the planet – town and hamlet, headland and plain – the other Tharles had echoed and endorsed it. "Vital point" had been the characteristically clipped thinking of Tharle of Venacarr, Razalia's smallest, hilliest settlement. "Kind of thing we need to get on top of. Sentient being, is it? Been planning and hatching, has it?"

The conference and questions filled Tharle's mind again. Absently, he peered over the knoll, as if assuring himself that no white was lapping against its base. Then his face briefly flickered. A message was coming through from Tharle of Kidresh, who estimated that he would be on the knoll in twenty or fifty or five minutes: "I'd incline to twenty," he thought. "Sun's way off now. The hours look to be settling down."

As soon as his words had echoed away, they were replaced by a chorus of twangs and ticklish throats. The chara-jets were lifting clear of the airfield. Tharle watched their cabin and tail-lights as they lolloped into the sky. Though hardly as clean as it had been that morning, their formation was passable. The controller must have reached the same conclusion as Tharle of Kidresh: time was beginning to settle, providing a smooth enough tunnel in which to release the jets. Doubling the strength of his vision, he could see that the third jet was appreciably thicker than the rest, its casing unusually bright: "Ahh," he said involuntarily and, his vision now quadrupled, he looked inside its cabin. The Galladeeleans were unwontedly calm, their many arms and legs laced about them. "I wonder how much they paid to have the jet expanded." His eyes went into a momentary swoon. "Hmm," he said then, as the figure settled on a ledge of his mind. "Reasonable – we should get the whole fleet seen to." Their jet gained height with something approaching grace. "Well, they're being good as gold," he said to himself – then almost instantly panicked. Did their behaviour mean that they knew about the gaps?

"No, they don't," Tharle of Kidresh rang out in his mind. "And stop trying to keep your worries to yourself, Mopatakeh. Now, I shall join you in twel – fifteen minutes. Oh, and I'm bringing a companion."

Tharle was about to divine who it was, but a distracting peal of hiccuppy laughter streamed down from the skies. The third jet was now swinging about like washing on a windy line. Before he knew it, he was laughing aloud. Those Galladeeleans and their attempt at serenity – as unnatural to them as an unlit Razalian face at noon. Still, he saluted their effort.

Descending a little way down the knoll, Tharle let his gaze sweep from south to north of the capital. The young had left their street corners. Now, ploughman and blacksmith, apothecary and scribe were quitting their labours. In scores of homes, pots were being stirred, tables given a final rub prior to setting. He rubbed his chin and sighed, his laughter at the Galladeeleans now seeming misplaced, almost wicked. He'd just have to put up with Kidresh's good-natured chiding, for there was nothing he could do to stop his anxiety. What if, tomorrow morning, the whole island was just a pool of white? And what about that sound it was supposed to make if you went right up to it – that ghostly murmuring? Tharle had never heard it himself with either outward nor inward ear. He'd never met anyone who had, either, though the belief persisted: part of the fear, no doubt. Anyway, what if the morrow brought not a murmur but a shriek of hideous jubilation, rising from the white like the thickest steam? And would he be there to hear it? Would he have been wolfed down with everyone else?

Tharle blinked. On the thoroughfare nearest the knoll, three or four ovals of light had clustered and were beaming straight at him. Reflexively, he trebled his vision, discovering that they were engineers from the airfield who, having recognised his unmistakable form, were flourishing their hands as if indicating a priceless jewel: the Razalian gesture of good-night. Tharle's mind swept through theirs – ah, they were the ones who'd kitted out the Galladeeleans' jet. He flourished back. His thanks for their labour slipped into their minds and they moved away. As their ovals dwindled, Tharle felt a pang of fatherly keenness for their safety, for Mopatakeh's, for the planet's. Chiding himself for indulging thoughts of white islands and deafening shrieks, he applied himself to practicalities.

First among these was his decision not to hold what translates roughly as *a Candling of Eyes,* a counsel at the Guiding with all Tharles present. Not a few of his peers had clamoured for one during the day's discussion, but Tharle had declared – and declared again to himself now – that a *Candling* was the shortest way to panic. *Candling*s were infrequent and, anyway, tradition decreed that Razalians were always consulted on the reason for holding one, even before it was officially arranged. If their Tharles said nothing and simply turned up in Mopatakeh, they would be breaking a whole skein of confidences between them and the people. Worse, the people would forsake their usual, careful attitude to their own telepathic powers, which some dwellers on Earth might best understand through the words "Sunday best". The thoughtways of Razalia would instantly clog up with bafflement, then speculation, then discovery, and all would be chaos. In time, perhaps, a *Candling* might be all too necessary. For now, it was best to see what could be done by remote conference alone. Of course, it wasn't uncommon for Tharles to meet in twos and threes, be their dispensations adjacent or distant. So there'd be nothing untoward about Kidresh arriving with – again Tharle wondered who his companion was and, with no raucous Galladeelean to distract him now, flickered the question to Kidresh.

"Ten minutes," came the reply. "It was seven a second ago. Sorry, Mopatakeh, still a few twitches of time to beat. Taking up all our efforts. Who is my companion? Ah, you'll see when you – nine minutes – when you see." And Tharle heard a kind of crump, as of a huge book being closed with care: the unmistakable sound of Kidresh sealing his mind.

"Well, I hope the twitches let them through soon," thought Tharle, stroking his face, suddenly aware of his isolation. For a brief, un-Tharlian moment, he wondered if, in addition to creeping, the Mopatakeh gap could see. He imagined a spur of white spotting him alone and lunging like the tongue of a colossal lizard. To shake off this child's fancy, he sought the rough path that ringed the knoll, walked round to the west and faced Carolles. If asked, a delegation of Carollessa would be there as soon as they could – brimful of concern for their dearest sibling, laden with instruments to measure this, that and the other, even – he could hear them now – offering to take Razalia back with them – people, houses, schools, workshops and all. The Carollessa were indeed a good, kind, not to say handsome people, albeit that their world of whooshing gadgetry stupefied the average Razalian head. But what could they actually do about the wakening gaps of white? Tharle knew that, since nothing comparable distinguished Carolles, their Aeonodrome would contain neither account nor experiment of practical use. Besides, wondrous and unerring though their spacecraft were, it would still take them a while to arrive. Then there was the matter of Razalian time, which, in turbulent mood, had been known to catch visiting craft just at the point of landing and bounce them back by as much as three weeks. The thought of turbulence made Tharle groan inwardly. The first of the bi-monthly alignment times was approaching, when Razalia's three umber moons strung themselves out south-west to north-east. It would happen with a precision that was somehow in the moons' gift, for, in all senses, they were above the planet's temporal shenanigans. And then, of course, the dazzling shoreline that marked the place of the Nine Oceans would go berserk, heaving and furrowing as though eager to run the whole gamut of shape. If the whiteness were a sentient being, as Tharle of Venacarr had curtly suggested, might it use that time of convulsion to do its own heaving across meadow and ridge? He groaned again – audibly, loudly now. And the Baraskian Festival! It was due to start between the next two alignments! Miserably, Tharle pictured the sealess tides, surging and scrambling on the Nine Oceans shore; and, beyond them, the modest, mud-like plain separating shore from ocean. On the very night that the Festival was due to commence – give or take hours lost or gained – the cracks of the plains would hold their own celebration of frenzy, knotting and whipping for all they were worth. And there was nothing to stop Razalia's famed sliceblossom from joining in: it was as apt to feed by night as by day. Tharle imagined it curving out of the cracks, taking deep draughts of Razalia's air, puffing its leaves like inflatable fans, then jewelling the mud and the amethyst skies with its petals of breathtaking red. The whole carnival fascinated some Baraskians – almost as much as the white did. Often, if they arrived in time, they'd all troop down to the Nine Oceans shore, each with a sort of surfboard under a treelike arm. Riding the lone tides, they would watch the whole spectacle. Before them, on the plainward side of the tides, flanks of figures would kneel: Razalians who had slept during the day for a whole week, so that their glowing faces would light up the night scene for their guests. Tharle's groaning became a long, weary sigh. What if the white pounced on that night of interplanetary joy, spilling death over surfer and tide, washing along the flanks of light like a demon river? It would be the fate of the Baraskian anthem-singers again, magnified a thousandfold. The Baraskian temper was reflexively well-disposed to all – save their sometime adversaries the Sehundans, where some effort was required. But it would hardly tolerate the – well, the consumption of a festival's-worth of subjects. Razalia would become the new Sehunda. Barask would wage a ferocious war against – what? If the gaps pounced everywhere, what would be left to attack but a ball of white, far more lethal than the biggest, ugliest Baraskian war-machine? Or perhaps just a wisp of white smoke hanging frozen in space, sole reminder of the cuckoo of the arc? He'd simply have to make contact with Barask, soon, and – and what? Arouse the very suspicions he sought to avoid – on two planets? Again he thought of the Razalian people telepathising like mad – and, this time, of word spreading like a plague across the whole arc. Tharle beat his brow with a broad hand. He was no nearer a practical solution than he had been when –

"Five minutes," cut in Tharle of Kidresh. "We can see the western bridge." Kidresh's mind crumped closed again.

Tharle looked dully about – at the path, the capital, the airfield. For a moment he thought to meet Kidresh and his companion on the thoroughfare from which the engineers had greeted him. But the soothing flow of the Billomingow filled his ears; for a self-indulgent moment, he sprouted a third ear at the back of his head to absorb it fully. Far better to talk, he decided, overlooking the river, that symbol of reliability, of comforting ceaselessness. As he ascended the knoll again, he willed himself not to wonder if anything was reliable or ceaseless any more. But he couldn't stop Tharle of Venacarr's words slipping in again. Was the white itself a thinking being? Had it blocked all Tharlian thought-waves on some unknown level? Was that why not a single one of them had known what was coming?

"The sun!" Tharle of Kidresh's words flew in with such force that, about to gain the top of the knoll, Tharle nearly lost his balance. Vision quadrupling, he looked back towards the western bridge. Two figures were just leaving it, about to turn onto the thoroughfare that would lead towards the knoll. As Tharle had been that morning, they were double their height – understandably, since they'd had half a planet to travel and, drawing on their special powers (and abjuring the vagaries of a chara-jet), had done so on foot. Tharle recognised the features of Kidresh, kindly if a little severe. He smiled – in anticipation of their meeting, but also because Kidresh could never tower convincingly. Even now, he was appreciably smaller than his companion. This, however, was no disadvantage. If anything, Kidresh's stride was the more focused and assured. It was the companion who kept falling behind, having to double his steps to catch up. This, Tharle saw, was partly because of a shoulder bag, capacious and unwieldy, which kept swinging about as if with a life of its own, at one point nearly toppling him over; and partly because of who he was

– Tharle of Dreest. Boyish of face and temperament, unable to shed the puppy-fat of his youth, he had been Tharle for little over two months. Hesitant and bashful, he had distinguished himself in his one *Candling* so far by alternating between his own kind of silence, a sort of breathy blubbing, and a torrent of words which, at one point, had been so forceful that, clutching his Guiding Seat for support, Tharle had seen octuple. Tharle of Dreest seemed to breathe his own air, a compound of bewilderment and anxiety which thickened when he reflected, as he often did, that his election must be a mistake. His predecessor had led Dreest, by no means a small settlement, with due humility but also clear-eyed wisdom, making him admired through-out the whole planet. Like all Tharles, he'd been at liberty to eat the otherwise poisonous sliceblossom. And, as Razalians liked to believe, this power expanded the already formidable frontiers of their leaders' minds. Yet Dreest's predecessor had never touched a morsel, appar-ently. Thus, it was said by all – and with particular veneration by the citizens of Dreest – that his mind had happily expanded itself, and his wisdom was its own, natural, bonny child. By contrast, his successor harvested sliceblossom whenever he could, keeping a specially treated jar of it in a secret cupboard at his residence and reaching for it as some dwellers on Earth might reach for what, it seems, they are pleased to call a snifter.

The other Tharles knew that the years would bring no change in his style, that he would never grow into the job. During wakeful nights, when the glow came and went in confusion on his face, he recognised as much. "Sham-bling, stout, un-gain-ly boy!" was Tharle of Venacarr's sing-song estimation. Yet Tharlian regard for him echoed the system's regard for Razalia. Beneath his unpromising mien and behaviour lay something they could never hope to possess. Only he couldn't see it. "I know we are simply chosen, Mopatakeh, no bones about it. But when your last hour comes tiptoeing in, press for Dreest to fill your boots. The planet's soul is within him." That was Venacarr, too.

Mopatakeh considered these words as the two figures came strid-ing towards the knoll – or rather, as Kidresh came striding and Dreest hopped one way and the other like a man crossing a ravine on two widely-spaced planks: yet another effect of his impossible bag.

"The sun," repeated Kidresh, aloud this time. "I think, Mopatakeh, we were wiser than we knew to delay our meeting. It's not just a question –"

But Tharle silenced him with a raised hand. In the air, his finger traced the traditional greeting of Tharle to Tharle: in rough translation, *the doubled-oval*, a figure-of-eight pattern symbolising two Razalian faces with the glow of life flowing between them. Kidresh stopped, open-mouthed: "Oh, yes, yes," he said in mild irritation and returned the sign. By now Tharle of Dreest had hauled himself alongside Kidresh. "Dreest," said Tharle of Mopatakeh quietly, at which the novice Tharle cried, "Master! Trimmer of the Glow!" and prostrated himself at the foot of the knoll, his bag square across his back as though it had dropped from the skies and felled him. This form of address for the planet's leader had last seen regular adult use a good three aeons ago; now, it was only used by schoolchildren if Tharle of Mopatakeh made an especially formal visit to their settlement. But Dreest practised it, and a score of other moribund customs besides, in hopes of subduing the idea that he couldn't lead a toddler by the hand, let alone a settlement.

In reply, Tharle narrowed his eyes and held both hands out. Dreest levitated, hanging in the air a moment like an indecisive chara-jet. Then he landed gently on his feet to a welcoming smile from Tharle and, from Kidresh, a sigh which turned into, "The *doubled-oval*, Dreest. How many times did I remind you on the way here?" No answer forthcoming, verbal or mental, Kidresh furrowed his brow: "You managed it at your first *Candling* didn't you?" he said, half to himself; but then he conjured a memory of the occasion, with Dreest's well-covered form dropping to one knee and pitching sideways, a form of greeting known only to Galladeelean funsters with too much Baraskian serpent-river ale inside them. "Hmm," he added, his tone fainter still. "Of course – no *oval* there."

His smile now fatherly, Tharle gave the sign again. This time, Dreest copied him but so zealously that it he looked as though he were hanging on to an uncontrollable sword. At this, Tharle decided that the air was thick enough with formality, and he bade Dreest put down his bag. Rattles and thuds filled the air round the knoll. Tharle's inner eyes were about to rummage in the bag, but Kidresh raised a forestalling hand: "In good time, Mopatakeh." So instead, Tharle gestured that they should ascend and take their ease on the knoll's summit. Shrinking to his usual height, Kidresh started forward. Forgetting both his bag and the need to copy Kidresh, Dreest followed. For a petrifying moment, Tharle saw and felt what life, or rather its end, would be like if he were a teeny Carollessan elder, caught in the careless shadow of a Razalian boot. There was no time for formalities or even a bark of fear. Lunging at Dreest's mind, he shrank him as deftly as a Sehundan genie-bottler. For his part, Dreest didn't notice a thing. At last they settled down, facing the Billomingow: Kidresh compact and purposeful, Tharle momentarily faint-brained from his efforts, Dreest a picture of bottomless anguish between them.

"Now, two questions fall to my charge," said Kidresh, who could match Venacarr for briskness when he chose. "First, why are we wiser than we know, Mopatakeh, in delaying our meeting? The sun! It's my belief that the sun is behind this dreadful business. But I'd estimate that it's larking about above Carolles right now, so we can at least think and talk in safety."

Tharle said nothing for a moment. Still steadying himself from his vision of accidental death beneath the lolloping, puppyish Dreest, he let his eyes rest upon the river. Shards of light clustered and danced on its surface. Reflections of his face, they joined and broke apart like so many uneasy spirits. He, too, had pondered whether the sun had any part in the present peril. But there was protocol to observe, and he knew Kidresh of old. Even now he could sense Kidresh's chest expanding as he prepared to deliver himself of a full-blown theory on the sun's malice, complete with his familiar lobe-tickling and hand-rubbing.

"And the second question in your charge?" asked Tharle, smiling inwardly as he heard Kidresh deflate. He knew it already, of course, having turned aside a flap of Kidresh's mind as he was about to lambast the sun. But no Tharle, least of all the leader of the planet, ever openly anticipates the words of another in a meeting, however informal. The malpractice – which translates as *filching gold from the gullet* – is dismissed as offensiveness itself. Even Dreest, for whom protocol was almost as terrible as a ravening patch of white, had that rule by heart.

In reply, Kidresh patted the novice's arm: "Why does good Dreest keep me company? Because, Mopatakeh, a mere handful of time after I informed you of my visit" – here an exploratory finger got busy with the folds of his ear – "he troubled me for my attention. And very interesting trouble it is, too."

Tharle turned to regard Dreest, whose glow bulged and rippled with nerves: "You communicated with Kidresh?" Too late he realised that the question, meant neutrally, would flood the novice with guilt. Dreest's glow looked fit to explode.

"I should have," he blurted, "I would have, had it been… well, it was, but I thought, well, should have thought, should have known, really…" He looked fearfully at Tharle, who was now attending to his own ear, seeking to hush the wind that Dreest's outburst had set whistling.

Kidresh rubbed his hands, as though the business of speaking for Dreest would be physically akin to hauling wood.

"What he means to say," he began, "is that he felt he could not think to you directly. He desired the benefit of a second opinion."

Tharle was intrigued: "Opinion on?"

"His invention – which may, Mopatakeh, be the saving of us all."

"Ah… an invention, Dreest." This time Tharle ensured that his tone was encouraging. For, prior to his elevation, Dreest had been a full-time inventor. In a million different ways, his creations and refinements had improved the life, domestic and commercial, of his settlement. Their fame had spread wide – and how could they not? Who, after all, would impugn the usefulness of a device for luring mallowberries – a Razalian staple for garnish and pie – from inaccessible bushes? Or that polished and thickened the ice on ponds during *The Silver Quiet*, Razalia's winter, for the delight and physical advancement of the skating young? Dreest's inventions, or variations thereon, had popped up all over the planet. In fact, his name had crossed Tharle's mind but a short while ago, when he'd pondered the re-fitment of the chara-jets. Again, Tharle considered his newest colleague in a fatherly way. Poor lad: in his previous life, he knew, Dreest been steady of eye, calm of mind. Thus had his inventions, large and small, succeeded. Now, as leader of his settlement, he was all psychic fingers and thumbs. Would he ever accept that he was chosen fair and square? Would he ever believe that, in Venacarr's words, he had the soul of the planet within him? Tharle felt the answers staring at him like a pair of Baraskians at the foot of his bed, enthralled by the way his face-glow danced at the point of sleep. Like his counterparts all over the planet, he knew Dreest was probably unchangeable. But that didn't preclude any attempts to guide and embolden him, to… well, give him an occasional holiday from himself, however brief. Of course, such guidance was no more than Tharle's duty. It was just that, in the two months since Dreest had shambled into his new responsibilities, Tharle had been as nonplussed by him as everyone else. But he could hardly spin that out as an excuse. Telepathic tongues would start wagging. He could just imagine Venacarr's clipped tones bearding him as he squirmed in the Guiding Seat: "Have to try taking Dreest in hand somehow. Save him from his turmoil whenever you can. Rest of us will support you to the hilt, Mopatakeh – but-it's-up-to-you." (It should be noted that, were Venacarr a creature of Earth and a member of that sub-sect dubbed "English", he would possibly top his sentences with "Thing is, old man" and tail them with "chum".) But now Tharle was smiling again, and not only at the imaginary counsel of the bluff, well-meaning Venacarr. Here was the perfect chance to still Dreest's many agitations, if only for a while. Here was his new invention, which had obviously lit up Kidresh's seasoned, deliberation-worn eyes. He laid a hand on Dreest's arm, which almost stopped jigging about.

"Show me what you've brought with you, Dreest," he said gently.

Free of any deliberation for now, Kidresh's eyes simply rolled and one of his lobes got a furious tickle. He could see Dreest mouthing "What I've brought with me," sense his mind slipping its slender leash. Careless of Tharle's kindly pressure on his arm, Dreest began gingerly patting the folds of his cloak. Tharle guessed what was happening and, despite himself, felt a twinge of vexation where his fatherliness had been.

Hearing the change of mood from deep within Tharle's mind, Kidresh muttered, "Here we go again, Mopatakeh."

Tharle, eager to make sure of his suspicions, leaned into Dreest's thoughts like a watcher over a parapet. Sure enough, Dreest had misinterpreted his request. All thoughts of his invention gone, he was fumbling about for a clipping of shrub from Maker's mountain. Protocol once dictated that any Tharle visiting Mopatakeh should bring the shrub as an offering of respect for Razalia's leader. But the protocol had lapsed even before the use of "Trimmer of the Glow". Yet again, Dreest had enlisted a scrap of arcana in a bid to make his new destiny intelligible to himself. Besides that, he had never actually clipped any shrub from the mountain. His settlement lying at its foot, Kidresh would have known if he had. In fact, both he and Tharle knew that Dreest had brought no offering of any kind. More, they knew that Dreest knew it, that naked anxiety had tucked the truth under a cloak-thick fold of his mind. Vexation did not come naturally to Tharle – nor, fundamentally, to Kidresh, though he could make more colourful use of it when it did. So it was that, with a preparatory flick of a lobe, Kidresh reached into Tharle's mind, extricating his spasm as though it were a ripe mallowberry and he, with a family pie to bake, were using Dreest's famed contraption to hook it free. Then he placed an apparently kindly hand on Dreest's other arm and squeezed. At this, Dreest let out a yelp, shook himself free of both Tharles, dug deep in his cloak, produced a jar of grated sliceblossom and stuck the neck, teat-wise, into his mouth.

"No shrub," he wheezed between gulps. "Oh, I forgot, forgot, forgot. So what have I brought, what did I – ?" Dropping the jar in his lap, he pressed his fingers to his brow like a vaudeville mesmerist. "Bear with me, Trimmer of the Glow," he pleaded, rocking to right and left.

The motion becoming more dramatic, Tharle leaned out of his way, and was about to drop the simple nudge, "Your new invention, Dreest," into his mind when Dreest rocked low in the other direction, found no resistance from Kidresh, cried, "Oh, Trimmer! What have I done with him?" and froze bolt upright. Very gingerly, he pawed the ground to his left. It was deserted. In the midst of his panic about being shrubless – and giftless altogether – Dreest thought that he'd pulled a wrong lever in his mind and spirited Kidresh away to – where? The Mopatakeh gap? The waves of the Billomingow? The forsaken midnight?

Not daring to look round, Dreest cried, "My Master Trimmer, un-Tharle me this moment! I have *enchaffed* Kidresh (another Razalian archaism, meaning to scatter something or reduce it to nothing; Tharle remembered that, when he was a child, the planet's oldest farmers and brewers used it, but only *when the lone tides wove into a fountain,* which roughly translates as "once in a blue moon").

Now Dreest was almost sobbing: "And he was so kind, my Master Trimmer. He it was who –" He stopped, slack-mouthed, as though a tale from long ago were drifting back to him. "He it was who had such faith… in what I" – his eyes widened – "have brought to you… my –" At that moment, the hand that had squeezed his arm clamped itself on his shoulder. All a-tremble, Dreest turned to his left. There stood Kidresh.

Emphatically unenchaffed, so to speak, he had decided that the easiest thing all round would be to leave Tharle to the novice's mad pantomime, descend the knoll and drag up the invention-bag himself. Now he laid it across Dreest's lap. Tugging its mouth open, the novice gazed on the response to Tharle's command from, it seemed, aeons ago. "My invention," he mouthed.

A briskly purposeful hand-rub challenged the sound of the river. "Tomorrow, Mopatakeh," said Kidresh, "we hasten to your Guiding, install ourselves in your Notionary and spend a demanding but, I hope against hope, not fruitless hour in ridding our young friend's mind of every pick and speck of antique *folderol*." He sighed to himself. "*Maker's shrub... Enchaffed...* Oceans lave us!" ("God help us" comes nearest to his last phrase. Given the planet's provisional state – and now, the threat from the gaps of white – it would be foolishness itself for a Razalian to invoke any kind of god in a pleading oath. Ever pragmatic, the Razalians direct what passes for their prayers to something they can see and depend on in their planet's singular nature.) The next moment, however, Kidresh surprised himself with a yelp and stepped back, nearly pitching down the knoll. For Dreest had gently cast the bag aside, pocketed the jar of sliceblossom, stood up and taken a pace or two towards him. Tharle plumbed the novice's mind on Kidresh's behalf. There was no wrongful assumption that Kidresh had played some trick on him, no intent to offer violence – nor did Tharle think there would be. Instead, there was the imminent threat of a deliriously grateful bear-hug, one that would do for Kidresh as surely as, a little while before, the double-sized Dreest would have done for Tharle himself. Summoning twice the power he'd used to shrink the novice, and nearly as much as when, alone and troubled, he'd scrutinised Mopatakeh's creeping gap, he brought Dreest to a dead halt. Hastily collecting himself, Kidresh laid hand again on the novice's arm. This time he didn't squeeze, but drew the novice into a biddable consciousness.

"Set it up, Dreest," he whispered. "Here on the knoll." Then he pressed his hands together, at which Tharle intervened deep in his thinking: "Rest your palms and earlobes, Kidresh, until good Dreest is done."

A great and merciful change came over Dreest as, with Tharle and Kidresh standing either side and a little away from him, he emptied the bag and set to. In this moment, he was no longer a baffled leader but an inventor only, his mind on nothing but why he and Kidresh were on Mopatakeh and what he had devised. With relief, Tharle realised that this had nothing to do with any telepathic prod from Kidresh or himself. Dreest's clear-sighted focus was all his own work. Briefly, Tharle pondered his duty of care to the novice. Might it not be a good idea to ensure that he always had some invention bubbling in his head? That way, he could always have at least one sizeable foot planted back in his old life. Wouldn't that keep him… well, on the steadyish side of confusion? Sealing his mind against any remote rummaging, he thought again about Razalia's chara-jets. Facts had to be faced: it was no good just reinforcing them here, expanding them there. Refitment on the hoof wasn't enough – ordinary Razalian know-how had its limits. Look at the way that extra-fat Galladeeleean charter had flapped about just a short time before. Dreest, though – he could see to them, all right: keep the same quaint design, but re-build them from the nose backwards with completely new material, stuff that he could work his magic on so that they would fly without their old, familiar lurch and swing, withstand Galladeelean high jinks and the concertina solo that was Razalian time. As for what that stuff might be – well, Razalia had nothing suitable, and everyone knew that Carolles, the jets' planet of origin, was now clean out of the material from which they'd been made. Of course, the Carollessa had offered to build new ones for their sister planet, to the same curious specifications. Most folk knew that, too – Dreest among them, no doubt. He'd probably give Tharle some rambling, bashfully-worded reason why Razalia should still take up the Carollessan offer, asserting – as far as he could assert anything – that he was unequal to such a task. But Tharle could command – no, firmly suggest that he forget Carolles and go scouring other planets in the arc. Bound to be something somewhere. Lachbourigg was rumoured to have rich deposits of anything you cared to name. Getting at them might be a problem, of course. Tharle thought of the planet's strange forests, how they were apt to rove about at each Lachbourriggian sunset. But its inhabitants were notable wizards – surely they'd conjure up a way. They'd be happy to, Tharle hazarded, since almost no-one visited them. Not surprising, really: there were only a dozen of them, and they spent their time either quelling restless trees or lost in wild incantations. But Venacarr had spent some time there (accidentally, after a trip to Galladeelee, when one of the goofy planet's catapults had lost its *boing* halfway to Razalia) and had found them uncommonly hospitable. They would make a proper fuss of Dreest. Then there were the arc's infamously martial races. Tharle could imagine the Sehundans and Baraskians falling over themselves to mine, melt and press some indestructible substance – leagues and leagues of it – and ship it out to their little sibling without hearing of any recompense. Yes… Dreest could go roving through the arc – at and for a specified time. As for his settlement, Kidresh could keep an eye it. Capable to a happy fault, able to brook no nonsense while somehow endearing himself to Tharle and commoner alike, Kidresh could run at least three settlements on his own – Mopatakeh included, thought Tharle, without a hint of false humility. And who was it that Dreest had turned to about his invention? A bond was obviously there, for all Kidresh's displays of annoyance – in which, Tharle had anyway observed, there was irrepressible affection.

Tharle was dimly aware of some rattling and clanking, a voice saying, "Now for the deep angle… hope this knoll's sturdy enough." But his mind, at that moment, was tight around Dreest's future like wadding round an heirloom. Yes – say two Razalian years for the chara-jet project, from Dreest's voyage to the last tap of… well, whatever he last tapped with. Razalia could put up with its present fleet for that much longer. Anyway, two Razalian years sometimes had a way of folding into a tiny pile of months like a half-baked mallowberry fancy. Long or short, it would surely be time enough for the resourceful Dreest. Of course, this wasn't a question of barring him from his Tharlian duties. The good people of Dreest would be up in arms if they suspected that. Dropping the commoner's usual coyness about telepathy, they'd fire off chunks of their mind at Tharle like so much Sehundan *quashbuckshot* (bullets which, in Earth terms, would compare in shape and effect to an unripe Cox's Pippin). Tharle could just see himself, so vividly that it almost hurt, gripping the arms of his Guiding Seat as their indignation battered his brain. Then, of course, there'd be the delegation, the whole of the settlement clumping along to his Guiding, with dire consequences for its joists and foundations. No: the whole point, impossible though it may seem, would be to settle Dreest into his new calling with a reaffirmed sense of his old one. Couldn't his confidence in the latter drip onto – or preferably flood – his dread of the former? The odds might be… yes, longer than the whole planetary arc. But Dreest couldn't simply be left to welter in his anxiety. Who knows, it just might –

"Mopatakeh, where have you got to? Flame up! Flame up!"

Bundling his thoughts away, Tharle saw Kidresh just as his mouth was settling from his command. He saw Dreest's invention, which looked just like – but then an avalanche started in his head, a thousand knife-edged pebbles dashed themselves about from his crown to his neck. Oceans lave us! He'd clean forgotten his own glow, his watching light. Razalian day was nearly at its end now. All over the planet, people's faces were darkening in readiness for sleep. But he and the others had to stave sleep off, which meant *flaming up*, a special Tharlian power which allowed the boost of watching light. This had to happen in good time – otherwise it was like waiting with a new candle until the old one had guttered, and the attendant torrent of mental pebbles was enough to split wide the most sagacious head. Usually, whenever the need arose to shine into the Razalian night, Tharles flamed up without thinking. Tharle of Mopatakeh had done so himself, a thousand times, often when he was distracted by far weightier matters than Dreest and the chara-jets. But, he realised as the knife-pebbles rained down, the Dreest business hadn't been the real distraction. He'd taken his eye off the lower caverns of his mind. And now, wafting up from these, seeming to cloud the pebbles in a noxious mist, there returned the image that had somehow hoodwinked his automatic flaming-point: Razalia's gaps, their white now as baleful as the form of malign spirits, their edges terrifyingly on the move. Screwing his eyes shut, he flamed up at double-speed, experiencing the usual sensation (equivalent, in Earth terms, to flipping backwards over a high-jump bar, then bouncing up and flipping backwards again, at least half-a-dozen times). The pebbles disappeared like marbles rattling down a chute. The plans for Dreest rolled quietly onto a secure shelf in Tharle's mind, to be lifted out again at a proper time. Opening his eyes, he saw that Dreest was a little to his left, having stepped back to the edge of the knoll, his assemblage complete. On the novice's far side, Kidresh was standing as before. Both had flamed up when necessary. Now, three Tharlian faces converged on what looked like a colander stuck on the burnished pole of a hatrack. Jutting out from the middle of the pole was a pair of something between straps and stirrups.

Kidresh flicked his eyes in Tharle's direction: "None of your

Carollessan flash here, Mopatakeh," he thought to him. This was no derision at the expense of their bright and shiny neighbour. Tharle saw that, yet again, Kidresh's admiration for their unlikely colleague had fought through all the usual perils, the grumps and agitations, emerging as a plaudit which, for him, was almost Galladeelean in its playfulness. Then Kidresh leaned back, flipping up his hands in a sorry-to-interrupt manner. For Dreest was stepping gravely forward, as if to accept a great prize. Gripping the strap-stirrups with either hand, he pressed his bulk against the pole and stuck his head in the colander. After a moment, the knoll vibrated to a string of determined inbreaths. Anyone passing the landward side of the knoll might have concluded that some creature – perhaps the beast at the core of Razalia, famed as the maker's nemesis in one of the planet's dusty old theories – was breaking the surface of the Billomingow after a leisurely thrashabout. Anyone watching from Earth might have concluded that Dreest was lamenting a fifth pint of beer, that the colander was a bowl paying dearly for a night's excess. Dreest's own behaviour would have encouraged the notion. Raising his head for a second, he seemed to deflate round a dying groan. Then he sank forward again.

Tharle and Kidresh's watching lights played around the colander's curves and the shoulders of their novice-colleague. For a moment or two, Tharle toyed with a matter of protocol, then decided that he couldn't wait for Dreest to finish his singular performance and explain all. His thoughts tiptoed up to the crest of Dreest's mind, as though he were physically closing in on the man himself. But all at once two interdictions seemed to fly up in his face like the crossed sabres of a Paladin guard: "Wait, good Mopatakeh," said one. "Can you not trudge one final mile of bafflement?" the other demanded. Respectful but insistent, the silent voice belonged to Kidresh. Tharle swung his glow up at him, at which Kidresh shook his head: "Dreest won't let us in till he's ready," he added in Tharle's mind. Suddenly, Kidresh's glow wavered a little, and in that brief weakness Tharle saw the whole tale of his colleague's wearying day. There was his surprise role as the novice's confidant – what a storm he must have withstood there. Then there was the journey across half the planet, with Kidresh doubtless having to wait again and again while his ungainly companion slung down the bag and hitched it to his other shoulder, or stopped dead and checked his cloak for the sliceblossom jar. Tharle could just see the pair of them miles from the western bridge – Kidresh rolling his eyes like peas in a shaken cup while Dreest intoned his unearthed relics of popular speech and Tharlian civility; or reminding the novice about how to execute the *doubled-oval*, the modest but proper greeting for the present times, and then rolling his eyes anew as his advice whistled through Dreest's ears like the swooper-bird of the Venacarr region, returned from some far corner of the planet to familiar eaves again. For all that, Kidresh clearly didn't begrudge an elastic minute of his journey.

Realising this, Tharle thought profuse apologies to Kidresh for his uncustomary impatience.

"I understand, Mopatakeh," Kidresh thought back. "And he is almost done, I think. You and I are but half-a-dozen paces from the moment." Tharle's apology seemed to steady Kidresh's glow. For a second his eyes twinkled, as though Tharle were another and more excitable Dreest, fit to bust from all this waiting, about to shoulder the novice aside and push his own head deep into strangeness.

Dreest raised his head again. Something else seemed to be weaving through his patterns of breath. Kidresh inclined his head as though this change were precisely what he'd been expecting. But Tharle watched the novice anxiously. What had Dreest caught in the net of his breathing? Was it the murmurs that reputedly played on the surface of the creeping gaps? The cries of lost souls within them? Was it the crackle of some doomed traveller's last words, uttered a hundred aeons ago out in the forsaken midnight and only now coming to rest in their hearing? Was it Razalia's Maker itself, filling Dreest's body with a plan for their salvation or a declaration of their end? Now the sound divided, seeming to become a duet between a child and a dying man, but still unintelligible. Lifting his hands, Dreest traced the colander's rim, then stepped back and fell silent. But the duet continued from the mouth of the colander. Gradually, Tharle and Kidresh began to make some sense of it, although the eerie sound that had first coloured Dreest's breathing still broke in.

"I got it to translate itself," whispered Dreest, "except for" – he made an apologetic face – "well, some things wouldn't give up their meaning. And" – apology turned to agony in his eyes – "I couldn't steady the voices out. They both go high and low."

So it was that Tharle and Kidresh heard a Razalian minute of talk between, it seemed, two voices that could not decide between the morning and the dusk of their years:

"Are you?" asked the reedy pipe of one voice, before sinking into hoarse old age with, *"because it won't take a moment."*

"No, I said not." The second voice took over the hoarseness, then soared into childhood, then crashed again. *"When do I ever go out on a –"* Here, and at certain points following, the eerie sound broke in like a neatly folding tide. *"Anyway, I'll have to wait in for ... won't I? Did she tell you what time she'd be back from ...?"*

"I thought," said the first voice, rising as uncertainly as a chara-jet, *"she was staying over at ... That's what she told me."*

"Well, she never ... a word about that. Still" – the second voice, fluttering between youth and age, suddenly managed a tone which even struck the three leaders as false – *"don't you go worrying about it. And she deserves ... with friends after all her work. I can ... her at ... and get some approximate time."*

"Someone else pestered by approximate time!" cried Kidresh. "That's heartening."

Tharle silenced him. The first voice was swinging from angelic to catarrhal, insisting that whatever it had said before wouldn't take a moment.

"Well," tooted the second voice, *"all right, go on – then it's done for when... get here tomorrow."* And now it growled: *"especially since ... nearly broke his... off last time they came."*

"So he's definitely coming as well?"

"Oh, honestly... I did say." There was that troubling false tone again. *"He was supposed to be ... up to ... but now they want him ... And ... said he was well and truly ... about it. Well, he can make a killing when they have to pay him for ..."*

A shared frown shone down the three watching lights. Shared questions baffled their owners. How were killings made? Since when was death an act of creation? What manner of creature possessed such dark skill?

"I'll tuck the ... right against the ... They won't have any bother ... either side then." Despite its haphazard twitch from bass to soprano, the first voice clearly sounded agitated.

"Actually – no, look, I'll move it," said the second voice. *"You get going. Don't want ... and ... wondering where you are."*

"I'll see to it."

"... you'll be late!"

"Won't take a second... it's a ... of a clamber up into the ... you know that. And the key needs a good ... in the ... All right, I was thinking of your –"

The eerie tide folded in on the last word, but Tharle was sure he'd grabbed it.

"Back," he said.

"What, us?" His eye still on the colander, Kidresh began an awkward, reverse shuffle to the edge of the knoll. "Is there danger, Mopatakeh? What, is your gap splashing round this very –?"

"Back!" Tharle accompanied the repetition with a single thump to his own spine. "That's what it said. The agitated one." Dreest involuntarily shushed them, then plunged into more agony at his presumption, then was ignored as the second voice said,

"Told you, it's fine ... not one twinge ... a half-hour's soak and stroke with the ... then five minutes ... on my ... while I played the ... of the ... skybells ... and a quick, light... to finish. Had my doubts, but it worked a treat. Better than those bathsalt pyramids I got from ... but they're best as preparation anyway, when you need to give your ... a proper ... so there was no harm using them last night."

Above river and knoll, three watching lights clashed in delirious confusion.

Then Dreest raised a hand. The voices were fading. *"Leave me your key, then,"* said the second voice, hollowly affectionate as before. The first voice said that it would be back by – then the tide folded in for good.

Kidresh started to think something to the other two, then changed his mind. Suddenly, silent chat seemed a bit cloak-and-dagger. This was a matter for clear words on the night air. In that very moment, the other two decided the same.

"Actually, Dreest," he said, "I couldn't help thinking – all those trills and grizzles back and forth – are you sure there weren't more than two?"

The novice shook his head: "I just couldn't undistort them enough – they've come a long way."

"Very long," said Kidresh. "Making killings, indeed. You wouldn't even hear that from a Sehundan." He nearly gave a lobe a concerted twang but collected himself in time. A brief silence fell. Then, slowly and reverently, Kidresh and Dreest swung their watching lights towards Tharle, who, distracted, was playing his own light across the Billomingow, watching it break up gently on the sleepy ripples.

"So," said Tharle, "we have learnt of beings visiting other beings, an object that must be moved, an irksome key and a bathing ritual unlike any on which Razalian time has been wasted. Who have you fished from your bowl of voices, Dreest?"

Dreest gave the colander a last peek, as though another rogue word or two might come wisping up. Then, stepping back again, he said, "The... well, affectionate one –"

"Pah! If that's affection," broke in Kidresh, at which Tharle raised a hand, stilling his peevishness. "The troubling one," Dreest corrected himself. "That's the consort, I'd say."

"The consort of?" his companions demanded. Tharle's light threatened to set the novice's face aflame. The brightness seemed to wear Dreest's features away, until there was nothing but a pair of anxious eyes flickering between Tharle and Kidresh. "Of?" they repeated, voices raised.

"Of the one responsible," said Dreest.

"Responsible for?" Dreest couldn't bear their chorusing. While he had assembled his invention, bent to the colander and set the voices in motion, he had seemed to assume – give or take the odd quake and apology – exactly that confidence which Tharle sought to draw out through the chara-jet project. But now – if ever eyes could squirm, Dreest's did.

"For Razalia," Dreest managed, his eyes now swooning away as though he were twisting his body in anticipation of a blow. "He of the agitated voice – the one who was worrying about a –" He trailed off and Tharle's light lost its fierceness – just in time to reveal the novice mimicking his master's thump to the spine.

Dreest's words reduced Tharle and Kidresh to a pair of fish, mouths opening and closing on words that would not come. At last, Kidresh managed "Our Maker," in the voice of a penitent who craves blessing at his moment of death. Tharle, his mind on the Mopatakeh gap, on all the gaps across Razalia, made a sort of singing noise which seemed to slide from hope to anger and then to despair, before dropping into his boots. After that, neither made a sound. Astonishment emptied all thought from their minds like mallowberries from a baking-gourd. Even when the power to think came back, it dragged them where it pleased. Tharle tried to hear again those edgy, bitten-off phrases. It made no sense that they'd been uttered by Razalia's Maker. No, that wasn't right: look at the state of the planet, all that white where proper creation should be. In fact, it made perfect sense that their Maker's words should be unfinished – never mind Dreest saying he couldn't translate the lot. But if someone, something, were so inept, how did they become a Maker in the first place? There must have been something there… enough for some… well, say some master-teacher to draw out, to nurture. Or did Makers just happen? Did creation itself say *yes,* as Razalians did when new Tharles were chosen, and there it was? If so, perhaps Razalia's Maker was another Dreest, formidably capable but plagued by cruel doubts. Or had something external intervened? Had Razalia's Maker been distracted by something that challenged its Makerhood? All the ancient theories about the planet ended with its creator's demise. But what if the Maker had been called away to deal with some threat to its project… some danger from…. Tharle's inward sigh was weary indeed: "Oceans lave us," he thought, "danger from what?" Speculation defeated him. He felt that he was prodding about with a newborn's helpless hand. He gave up.

Meanwhile, Kidresh had fastened on the voice of the consort. Consorts, as far as he knew, were wives or husbands with gilded bells on. In this case, however, the phrase *licensed leech* had stuck fast in his mind and would not be shaken out. Kidresh recalled the consort's tone of voice. No, untrue: it needed no recollection but broke hard over his thoughts, dousing them like a noxious downpour. Glittery and hollow, it was a wheedler's voice – and as easily a moaner's. No wonder Razalia's Maker was all agitation. Presumably she, or it, had been there as the planet bloomed in forsaken midnight. Kidresh imagined her, or it, dogging him, or it – but there he stopped and breathed deep. It was no good riddling this fancy with qualifications. Slippery already, it would vanish altogether, abandoning his mind to scraps of words and images that made no sense at all. So: he imagined *her* dogging *him* as he fashioned a hill and went up it, carved a valley and scrambled down. He heard her voice in full moan: "Call this a planet? Look at all that you've missed. Where's the green for this bit? You'll be doing something with all the white, I presume? No? Planning to cart it off? Well, I tell you this, boy, you needn't expect me to roll up my sleeves –" Kidresh clapped his hands to his head. This was worse than thrashing about in senselessness. Never mind imagination: it was as though she were right there – as though he were the Maker and she was lambasting his every effort, made or to come, deriding him before he so much as drew the first shoot from the first cake of soil. And since when had that word *boy* sounded so vicious and ugly? No-one on Razalia would use it thus. His head felt like Tharle's when he'd neglected his *flaming up*. Pebble-storms lashed and pounded it, till he was convinced that his skull was done for. At the last second, something freed him from that terrible inquisition, and he reverted, like Tharle, to utter blankness.

Dreest stared at the two statues his revelations had created. He'd planned – no, hoped – well, prayed, really – that his words would emerge, and be received, in perfect calm. Instead, they'd brought up the rear in a skirmish of questions. Just his luck: just his destiny. He felt his old, capacious glumness taking hold. But then, reflexively doubling his height, he pulled clear of it, even stamping his feet as if to close it off. This was no time for shambling and whimpering, for calling on the skies to *enchaff* him for good and all. His elders were dead before him. He had to bring them back to life. Resuming his normal height, he played his glow from one face to the other: "I found him yesterday," he began. "Our Maker." So pleased was he with this show of assurance that he didn't notice uncertainty looming behind his relief: "Well, their yesterday," he babbled now, "about two days ago for us, though sometimes it was two-and-a-half... no, two-and-a-bit... no, it was less than... more like" – he paused to count on his fingers, seemed to make a hash of it, then started again with his ear-lobes.

Still, his performance had the desired effect. At least, it gave Tharle and Kidresh time to come to. Blinking, working his shoulders as though he'd been sleeping upright, Tharle told himself that rolling his mind into a ball was hardly suitable behaviour for a leader faced with staggering news. Despite Tharle's earlier request, Kidresh went through a full work-out of handrubs and lobe-twangs, the end of which was a silent but impassioned declaration that he hadn't found the *oomph* to trek across Razalia only to swoon away like a Galladeelean over an empty keg. But this shared mortification did elasticate their minds. They were able to reach behind them, so to speak, and catch Dreest's half-confident, half-shambolic words just as they finished quivering the air.

"Our apologies, Dreest," said Tharle. "Mine especially. We should have waited on your words, not bearded you like Sehundan helots. Your news astounds, but that hardly excuses our –"

"No excuse at all," Kidresh chipped in, giving his hands a single, dramatic rub as though such un-Tharlian behaviour were dirt to be wiped clean away. "And look how we paid for it" – he pretended to goggle like a circus clown.

But still Dreest hopped and twitched. Watching him, Tharle regretted turning his light so ferociously on the novice's face. That, really, had precipitated the whole episode, along with the way he and Kidresh had pelted him with questions like a pair of bullies. He hadn't intended to stoke his light – hadn't known it was happening, in fact, until Dreest was nothing but a pair of wide eyes. He wasn't, he realised grimly, having much luck with his glow that evening. And for someone of his position, falling back on luck was hardly the way to maintain –

"Compose yourself, good Dreest." Kidresh was all kindliness. "We assure you that henceforth we are all sober attention. Now, the swooping and scouring – tell Mopatakeh that."

"Yes, Trimmer of – Mast – Mopata–" Giving up his mish-mash address with a gesture that could have been half a *doubled-oval,* Dreest cleared his throat and fought for the confidence which, in his summoning of the voices, had come so naturally to him. "I swooped and scoured these many days past, called up spiral and planet-shower. The voices of all creation poured themselves into my head."

"And then you heard his voice." Kidresh shook his head in amazement. "And now, so have we."

Tharle turned to him: "So you didn't know until now, Kidresh? What Dreest had actually found?"

"Wasn't I parroting those fool questions along with you? No, as I said when we arrived, Mopatakeh, I could tell that his invention might be the saving of us all. And I knew of the swooping and scouring." Kidresh sighed in mock weariness. "Yes, I knew mightily about that." Gentle laughter rolled along the beam of Tharle's light; he could imagine – no, why simply do that? He folded back Kidresh's memories of his journey and, sure enough, heard Dreest's endless incantation at his ear: "Swooped, scoured, they emptied themselves… swooped, scoured…"

"But," said Kidresh, "when I asked him what the end of all this" – he waved a hand, supplying Dreest's incantatory words – "actually was, he wouldn't say. Which was only right," he hurried on, in case Dreest should hear a charge of rudeness in his words and drown him in apologies. "He wanted my opinion on the general worth of the thing, and I was happy to give it. As for what we've just heard... oh, he hinted alright – after a fashion – but then he sealed off again. Still, his knowing coughs were our companions." Kidresh's hand rose to his ear – not for a good flick this time, but because, through mere rec-ollection, Dreest's explosive hints were trouncing his head anew. "But as for his triumph, he could not tell me before he told you." Having delivered himself of all this, and once Dreest's coughing had sunk again into the pit of memory, Kidresh couldn't help setting up a slow hand-rub, topped off with a graceful tickle of a lobe. Pride in the novice shone through his unlikely pantomime. Like a magician with power over water, Dreest had carried his discovery in cupped hands until he stood before Tharle. Despite himself, he had honoured the most signal point of protocol. "I didn't even know, Mopatakeh, if he'd set out to find our Maker."

"Did you know yourself, Dreest?" asked Tharle. In reply, the novice begged their pardon and sank to the ground. Inventing, jour-neying, babbling, demonstrating – all now exacted their toll. Again the jar of sliceblossom appeared from his cloak; again the draught was deep and, it seemed, restorative. Tharle motioned to Kidresh that they should copy the novice, and they sank in unison either side of him. For his part, Tharle was happy to take Dreest's lead. Only now was he taking in the full significance of what they'd heard. With the Billomingow lapping gently below them, with Dreest's invention ris-ing before them like a baptismal font, he tried his question again.

"I knew I'd find something," said Dreest, sounding only slightly less exhausted than he looked. "Of course, I had to look beyond our arc first. Past all that yukking on Galladeelee, the Baraskian growls, the whooshing on Lachbourigg."

"You don't think of Lachbouriggians as whooshers, do you?" Kidresh was reflective and amused at the same time. "Venacarr never mentioned whooshing when he told me about them. But then he was down among them and their jumpy forests. A different matter, I sup-pose, getting an earful of their spells from" – he gestured at Dreest's invention – "the miraculous basin." He stopped, his face burning in the heat of two incredulous beams. "Tree-proof, that house they live in," he finished lamely. "Venacarr told me. Enchanted grouting."

"Sober attention, Kidresh," said Tharle. "You promised." He urged the novice gently on, relieved to see that Kidresh's singular discourse hadn't jangled his nerves. Probably he was too fatigued to be anxious about anything. Tharle could have tested his theory with a quick gawp into that wondrous mind, but chose not to.

"Once I was hunting beyond our system, though – how to describe it? The things that came up over that rim. When you're hearing your way over our sixteen planets, yes, it's a gabble, shrieks and barks and whispers. But there's… there's a level floor to it, it's your system, you know you won't smack into a mountain of sudden noise or fall down a hole of silence. You move like a stately land-ship, translating as you go. But after that – you're in quicksand. Sometimes it hardens. You could be hearing along, I don't know, something like the cracked plains of our outwater. Then, without warning, you're thrown as high as a Baraskian surfing our sealess tides."

The comparison unsettled Tharle, who thought again of the Baraskians' imminent Festival on Razalia. Would there be tides for them to surf? Would there be any cracks twisting and flexing, mimicking all the known shapes of the galaxy? Would any of Dreest's beloved sliceblossom rise up, flapping and puffing? Or would there just be a white sea, petrified, unwitnessed?

"Patience, Mopatakeh," thought Kidresh at him, sensing some change in his mood. "Hear the boy out." Not bothering to explain his unease, Tharle attended again to the quiet words.

"Or the quicksand opens like a well," Dreest was saying, "and you're tumbling down hundreds of leagues. And the noises – on the crest of those sand-tides, in the caverns deep down. Some are just untranslatable, though not unpleasant – like birdsong, or a mother's wordless lullaby. But some – I heard along a whole system, easily forty planets, that was just one long scream; and another one, three planets wide, which was the same noise repeated over and over, a kind of sob that… well, it didn't translate, exactly, but it sounded like *oh, no... oh, no,* as if all the bad luck in creation had landed on one sorry soul."

Hands planted behind him, Tharle was leaning back. "All these sounds," he said dreamily, as though quite alone. "Seeing with the ears."

"And eyes, Master," said Dreest, at which Tharle sat bolt upright. "Eyes, Dreest? You really saw as well?"

"Whenever I sensed that I might be near something to help us. Then there were deserts in the bowl, Master, swirled with reds and blacks and yellows; and floating valleys that swung like cradles in summer skies; and cities that were toppled pyramids, and other cities that were tiny humpbacked houses in lines like the underside of footprints. Then… whether it was some extra power I can't explain, or" – Dreest smiled – "well, just a most un-Razalian wishfulness… then I could translate, then understanding came. But there was nothing for our case after all. In the whole of the desert galaxy, I found only four beings on one planet, and they'd just placed the roof on a hut. One hut in quintillions of leagues. And they were saying that it was something, what they'd done, it was a start after all that had happened, whatever that was. And in the valley galaxies they were whistling and cooing because flowers had bloomed for the first time ever, and this one was asking that one what they should call them, what you did with them."

"And in the cities, Dreest?" Kidresh sounded like a child, amazed and scared by fresh tales of Razalia's beginnings.

"Questions," said Dreest. "Questions without answers, even though they were all about things the beings had created themselves. *So what do we do with this now? How can we start it again? Do we have any left? Doesn't anyone know?"*

Tharle looked at Kidresh: "He told you nothing of this?"

His fellow-leader looked nightwards: "He gave me a picture of swirls and running colours, Mopatakeh. A notion, an outline." He placed a hand on the novice's shoulder. "The best you could do at the time, eh, Dreest? Even you, good Mopatakeh, would have a deal of waiting until such visions, such wonders made any sense to you."

Tharle remembered his problem with *flaming up* and how his fatherly glow had nearly crisped the novice. If he'd been Dreest, he feared, these visions and wonders would have had him slumped and gibbering under the Guiding Seat.

"Yes, Kidresh," he murmured, keeping his thoughts close in a pocket of his mind, "I rather think I would."

"Mmm, me too." Suddenly, Kidresh's voice seemed different. Had the business of *flaming up* been too much for him as well? But then Tharle saw that, having prevailed upon Dreest, he was chewing a fistful of sliceblossom. "Haven't had this for years," he said. "Tastes like early mallowberries."

"I crushed some in," said the novice.

"Is that because you're partial to them, Dreest, or did you have a mountain of 'em stashed away after you'd perfected your magic berry-catcher? You know" – he stuffed another mouthful home – "I met our district berry-man just last week. Having a mighty rummage, he was, stripping all the bushes for miles. Big celebration on – Dame Pennater turning twice-ninety in three days, or a week, or tomorrow. Or perhaps she's been twice-ninety for a year. Really, you'd think our time would stabilise out of respect for the elderly." He leaned forward and winked. "She's all agog for your birthday visit, Mopatakeh. *If you're thinking to him,* says she to me, *remind him about his duty. Twice-ninety, sir, gilded milestone. If he forgets I'll dunk him in the Billomingow.* Her husband was there, picture of exasperation. Well, she's been thinking the news all over the planet, like she was the first to be gilded. Old Gent Pennater rolls his eyes. A year younger than she is, you know... doesn't reckon he'll make his gilding, the way she's carrying on."

"My visit to Dame Pennater is at the crest of my mind, Kidresh," said Tharle, watching as his colleague put paid to another mouthful, wondering where his sober attention had got to now. Never before had Kidresh simply dropped his interest in any matter of grave consequence. But now... Tharle's mind roved at tenfold speed through Razalia's lore of medicine, returning none the wiser. No, no-one had written or proclaimed that sliceblossom was a quick intoxicant, or the juice of the mallowberry. But the two mixed together? Another quick sprint, this time through the annals of sliceblossom (Tharles, for the use of), showed him that Dreest was the first to try the concoction. It had had no effect on him. He was young, though, and his invention and discoveries had kept him sharp as a thorn from a Sehundan snow-tree. Trying not to notice the hand that was again busy at the slice-blossom jar, Tharle quietly asked Dreest to continue, hoping that hearing more about sounds and galaxies would remind Kidresh of his wonted gravity.

"How far had your hearing taken you, then, Dreest? When you looked down on the cities filled with questions?"

"Far, far," said the novice, his bright eyes suggesting that he was there again. "Imagine our arc stretched fifty, a hundred times over – then as far again. There were vast expanses, oceans of dark with nothing to hear or see. Then it grew cold, colder than the deepest days of our *Silver Quiet.* All I knew –"

"Anyway, our berry-man." Despite a full mouth, Kidresh's bellow was fine indeed. "Gathering 'em up for Dame Pennater's Twice-Ninety Pie. Three portions for every mouth in the settlement." His arms seemed to fly apart of their own accord. "Big, big, big, big, big. *Morning, Gent Satherfall,* says I. *Scaring the bushes for the good Dame, I see.* Satherfall" – he snorted and brayed together – "Satherfool, more like. He swings round from the bush, Dreest's marvellous catcher *pyoinnging* here and *tottertipping* there in his hand – nearly has my nose off with the thing. And I'd only grown it out a second before. Kept it furled away, you see, till I was good and ready to enjoy the scents of the morn. *Oh, the scents of the morn,*" he extemporised tunelessly, "*and the per-dee-perp of the dawn.*" Then, seeming to think that he was Dreest's cloak, he lunged at the novice and wrapped his arms over his shoulders. "Not-that-I'm-blaming-you-Dreest-not-in-the-slightest-wouldn't-dream-of-it." Like a cloak itself, his voice fell in a draggled chant about the knoll. "No, Satherfool – my good Satherfooooool – he should have brought the thing to heel." Now Kidresh flailed about as though gaps of white had him in a murderous circle.

Aghast, Dreest tried to hunch clear of him, only to catch a pummelling as Kidresh fought his way upright. Meantime, the sliceblossom jar had made its escape and, contents frothing, was rolling easefully towards the Billomingow. With a scream to match a Galladeelean's at the words *you must toil for your keep,* Kidresh dived after it, gathered it in one becloaked arm, scooped a pile of rogue sliceblossom from the knoll and resumed.

"Not that I'm really blaming Satherfool either, for" – clasping his hands, he juddered about, miming a possessed berry-catcher with an old party on the end of it. "He probably couldn't tell where I was. Got a rotten case of half-glow at the moment. Left side in darkness every day. Common among berry-men, did you know that?" Kidresh pulled his cloak about him with righteous fussiness. "I blame the umber moons. Well" – his hand delved deep in the jar – "what use are they? Eh? All our twinges and sores, they could sort them out. Wrap the planet in healing rhythms, calm it, regulate it. But do they care, jigging and alley-ooping about? Every Razalian should reach double-ninety, you know, but do they? Do they?" He rounded on Dreest, who was wondering what strange, zig-zag arc had led the talk from his own discoveries to these wayward imprecations. "Look at them!" cried Kidresh, pointing up at nothing. "They see how the sun treats us, but do they lift a finger to help? Call yourself moons! You're rubbish! All your alignment business – what's that about? Just gets the cracks and shingle in a tizz." He staggered to his feet. "Oi! Fairybeads! I'm talking to you! Right, then –" He stood up, just about, and approached Dreest's colander. "You're for stuffing into this, my lads! See how you like life in the only hut in a desert." Swaying, trying to grab hold of the strap-stirrups, he cried, "Be it known, I am de-mooning Razalia!"

"Master!" The cry had been a long time swimming into Tharle's awareness. Dreest had uttered it the moment the jar had got away from Kidresh – the moment after Tharle had gone into another trance of astonishment. But now Dreest's cry rang clear in his head. He stared hard at Kidresh, who was alternately grabbing for the straps and swaying like a mallowberry bush in a gust of elastic time. He hoped he could do this. He'd only had to do it once before, when he'd come upon a group of foolish young playing a game of chicken at the Mopatakeh gap, racing up to the white, making to plunge in, then skidding to a heartstopping halt. He'd unskidded them, unplunged them, had them all running backwards to their several homes, the urge to play at dying purged from their minds. Now, his watching glow trebled its power. It worked. In less than a Razalian minute, Kidresh had stumbled backwards from the colander, unstood, unsat, unscrambled for the fugitive jar and unlunged at Dreest. Like a pumping-mule at an oil-well, his hand had risen and fallen over the jar, which had rapidly filled with uneaten sliceblossom. A minute later, Tharle's glow had subsided and the jar was back in Dreest's lap. Leaning in with grave solicitude, Kidresh was again saying that, even if Tharle himself had devised the contraption on the knoll, he would still have had a deal of waiting to do until its wonders made sense. "Now, Dreest," he added, "you were describing cities full of questions." And he pushed one lobe upwards to show he was all concentration. With a brief look of amazed gratitude at Tharle, the novice continued:

"Yes… yes, I said that my ears and eyes were far from here when I came upon the cities."

"You said that?" Kidresh chuckled. "Oceans lave us, my memory's playing the fool." Then, frowning, he glued fingers to lobe again. "Actually, I do feel a bit –" His words trailed into a helpless shake of his other hand.

"No, I can't remember that part, either," said Tharle, eyes widening at Dreest.

"Oh… oh, well, perhaps I… yes… yes, I was far and far. Farther than – than –"

"*Our arc stretched fifty, a hundred times over,*" Tharle thought at him. "*Expanses… oceans… nothing to see or hear… then cold… colder than deepest days of Silver Quiet.*" With a thankful look at his Master, Dreest repeated his own words. This time he sounded uncharacteristically dramatic, more like the decisive Venacarr, so that Kidresh forgot the oddness buzzing about his head and breathed "Goodness" as though he were an ordinary Razalian who, just that minute, had finished a dip in the Billomingow and stumbled on the leaders' parley.

"And then," said Dreest, "I found us."

"Us?" Surprise flashed from Tharle to Kidresh and back, as though Dreest's simple words had set their own glow weaving about the knoll. Independently, it seemed, Kidresh's fingers made a speculative voyage of either ear.

"Us," repeated Tharle in a whisper. As the word sank in, his glow made an aimless sweep of the knoll, Dreest's contraption and the quiet run of the Billomingow, returning at last to the novice. His lips shaped themselves for his next word. For a moment they stayed that way, as though he wasn't sure what the word was or what would follow it. At last, reminding himself that he was not a Sehundan helot, he gently managed:

"And where were we?"

"In our Maker's book."

Whatever Dreest answered, Kidresh had determined to be as encouraging as Tharle. The novice's response, however, was even more bewildering than *I found us,* and Kidresh's sense of sounds and meanings folded itself away. "Book," he repeated almost nervously, as though he had come upon the word floating in a gap of white. Razalia was filled with books of all sorts: compendia, puzzles for the young, lives of Razalians notable and ordinary. His own Settlement House bulged with them, to the point where Dame Pennater – who saw her imminent gilding as justification for pitching up daily at his door – declared that he was at the point of self-eviction. Still, repeating the word again – stretching it, reducing it to two consonants knocking together – he seemed flummoxed by it. As for Tharle, it looked as though he, not Kidresh, had gorged on the sliceblossom. His watching light played on the air like a distended firefly, finally coming to rest on his own lap. Then he sat motionless, as though he were no longer the leader of Razalia but some elaborate, forgotten storm-lamp.

Between them, Dreest twitched and shuffled. His old anxiety was reclaiming him. A moment longer and he might have been on his feet again, addressing Tharle as *Trimmer of the Glow*, praising Kidresh for dodging his unintentional *enchaffment*. Luckily, Tharle began to think aloud and, realising his duty to lead his Master from the deeps of confusion, the novice calmed himself again.

"So," Tharle said, laying his words out like cards, "our Maker still exists and has us fast in a book."

"Book," intoned Kidresh again, this time letting its vowel flutter and fall to rest against the *k*.

"It grew so cold," Dreest continued quickly, "that I thought I must have reached the end of everything. There was nothing but the rustle of freezing currents, the moan of gathering ice. I wondered if I was hearing pure forsaken midnight, stripped of any clusters or galaxies, rolling out like a one-way tide through the ever and ever."

At these last words, the sound of the Billomingow spread disconcertingly through Tharle's mind. By then, however, Kidresh had somehow made his peace with *book* and caught up, steeling himself for whatever new perplexity Dreest might throw at them. So it was that he stoically shared the image which now possessed Tharle. They saw themselves with Dreest on his astonishing journey – or rather, they saw the novice as he negotiated the pits and ranges of space, dragging them in his wake as if on leading-strings, their ears filled with the tumult or static of other Makers' works. Reflexively, Kidresh rubbed hands and then ears, momentarily convinced that the fire of life was deserting him.

"But then other noises awoke," said Dreest, "and started to move about. I think I must have reached the last galaxy, or at least a forgotten one, decillions of leagues from the question-cities, the valleys with their first flowers. I heard my way over planets again – tiny planets that spoke in mists and gases, and a larger planet girdled with a sound like a… like a carousel of rocks… and another that had tantrums of red heat and fierce winds."

At this, his hearers relaxed a little. Now, Dreest seemed to speak of living sound, of sights such as Razalia itself might offer. They imagined the tiny planets he described, their babble of mists and gases, and heard the swoosh of their own shores as they bunched and hollowed at the umber moons' command. They pictured the carousel of rocks as a million such moons, leapfrogging and figure-of-eighting as they swung round their circle.

"Fancy," murmured Kidresh, feeling no rancour at all at this far grander display of pointless energy. Gradually, their image faded of themselves as intergalactic toddlers, stumbling behind the pioneering Dreest. They even managed a sigh of relief, albeit barely audible. On the knoll, the air began to warm and comfort. Again the Billomingow was merely lazy, not a torrent of strangeness.

By now, Dreest had shuffled back a little, so that his glow could move with more ease between the two faces gravely agog:

"Suddenly, I sensed help for our case again – stronger than ever. Up to then, I was hearing much, seeing little. Now I had to see properly, deep down." But here he broke off with a long, whinnying laugh.

Tharle and Kidresh jumped as one. What comfort and relief was this noise meant to offer? How could it possibly aid his tale? Convinced anyway that Dreest couldn't run to an amiable chuckle, they found his explosion as frightening as the prospect of a night among the gliding trees of Lachbourigg. They tried to get into his mind, but the way was blocked. Kidresh thought to Tharle that the sheer weight of some hideous recollection must have pushed Dreest's reason off its perch. Tharle wondered if Dreest's special compound was finally doing its worst but, mindful of Kidresh's performance a short while before, he chose not to share this for fear of triggering in him a fresh need to assault the jar.

"Let us see," he thought back instead. "The peal of bells can green the brownest grasses" (an old Razalian saying which roughly translates as "Laughter is the best medicine"). "Perhaps he is merely recalling some fancy too foolish to share." But then he saw Dreest's eyes and berated himself for a fool. Why was he dragging up whiskery old proverbs? Why was he lugging such stuff around in his head at all? The novice looked terrified. Had Kidresh thought true? If he had – oh, oceans lave us, there was no precedent for this, a leader lost in madness. They'd have to get another Dreest – but how long would that take? And how would anyone find out, now, how to use the… well, the bowl on a stick before them? And would they want to, even if Razalia's Maker was floating about at the bottom of it?

"Mopatakeh!" Reprimand rather than name, the word rang hugely in Tharle's head. It hadn't come from Kidresh. He was chiding himself. Again he'd dropped his duty of care, letting it skitter off like that infernal jar of sliceblossom. If Kidresh was right, the novice had sacrificed his reason for Razalia. This was nobility in action, not a fleeting inconvenience. The first thing to do was try, however great the odds, to coax that poor brain back to sanity. The bowl and stick could wait – and the gaps of white. Why, if need be, he'd bring the things to heel with one long stare, fiercer than any pyre-rocket Sehunda had ever launched at Barask. The main thing –

Something was bothering his vision. It was Dreest's glow, which was wobbling about as though the sun's pulses were having their way with it. His hands were clapped to the side of his face. He was still laughing, but now it was just that kind of chuckle of which Tharle had thought him incapable. "Fool, fool, fool," Tharle heard, and for a moment he thought it was his own mind, still on at him for clogging it up with old, cosy-sounding saws, for his cold pragmatism in the face of his novice's distress. But it was Dreest, ticking himself off.

"Forgive me, Master, good Kidresh," he said, steadying his glow. "A proper horror just rushed through me, and I clean forgot I'd survived it. Had I not, how could I be here?" His tone was self-mocking, but quietly so. There was no hint of imminent mortification, not the slightest shuffle or helpless jig of the hands. Tharle wondered if he was growing up after all – if he was realising that his shambling, puppyish self could play no part in these present revelations. He tried his best smile of encouragement to the novice, an effort only partly undermined by his noticing, at the edge of his glow, that Kidresh was eyeing the sliceblossom jar with something like – like what? Dipping into his seasoned colleague's mind, he found only a bewildered question – *what does a wonder like Dreest need with all that shrubbery?* – and withdrew in relief.

"The thing is," Dreest went on, "as soon as I gazed deep down, I found something strong all right – but not what a Razalian would call help. White came at me."

"White!" exclaimed Tharle.

"Leagues of it. At first I thought one of our gaps had streamed along in the wake of my hearing, ready to snuff me out. Never mind just creeping. It was energy itself. It became its own planet, ridges and lakes and all, rolling away to the very edge of my sight. Then it was a crazed thing, mad to wrap itself about me, to get into my mouth, down to my heart. I hung on to the straps for dear life – the bowl spun like a wheel about my face. My sight was dropping, dropping like a sun-scorched bird, the white still hard round me."

"What did it feel like?" Kidresh asked.

"Like the brush of a million tiny hairs. Hairs wet and cold from a proper dousing. Hairs that would any moment turn to briars, even nails, and press deep."

At this, Tharle sprang up and, boosting his glow and vision to their extremes, trained a long look upon the Mopatakeh gap. Taking his cue, Kidresh stood and flickered his eyes shut. His glow broke apart like plumes of breath from a horse pulling fuel or provisions in the depths of *The Silver Quiet*. Doggedly, his inner eye roved all the other gaps of Razalia. They had sat down again before Dreest quite knew what was happening – sat down in guarded thankfulness.

"No movement from our neighbour-gap," Tharle said to Dreest.

"Nor elsewhere," added Kidresh. "Sorry, Dreest, it was all that about briars and nails. Didn't want to turn and find our white was brushing its way over the whole planet."

Dreest understood: "I can't say that my ambush of white was the same as lurks in our gaps. If it was, my escape was merciful – it tore apart at last, loosed its hold on me. Now I was seeing down faster, through a kind of blue – nearly what we get when the sun bestirs itself to call, but brighter, more evenly spread across that vastness in my bowl."

"The kind it bestows on everything else in our arc," grumbled Kidresh. "Yes, the sun has a furnace-hand in our predicament. Mark me."

Dreest chuckled again: "Not that it lasted long – not even as long as the fortnightly crumb it throws us. Grey was rising towards me, great bulks and spurs of it."

At once, Kidresh looked up and flung his arms apart. Tharle wondered if, sliceblossom or no, he was about to flay the umber moons again, damning them as the sun's henchmen. But he was warming further to his theme of the moment: "Grey! Doleful grey! Exactly how our beloved sun would love to see us wrapped for good and all! Oceans lave us, you can always feel – you can even hear – its reluctance to cross our threshold. I can, anyway. Wheezing down from the forsaken midnight, all its fancy fireworks popping and pffutting –"

"Kidresh." Tharle's hand was light but determined on his arm. "The sun is as it is. We Razalians may lament that... but we accept. You know that." He glowed purposefully at Kidresh's brow. "Now, seal the sun away. Our present business is otherwise. If the sun indeed has some part to play in our gaps' encroachment –"

"Dreest will discover!" Kidresh sailed in, jabbing a hand at the colander-and-stick. "With his miracle!"

"Ah... I'm not altogether sure – ah." Dreest's mouth worked between agreement and denial. "Thing is, I haven't yet –"

"Yet isn't never, Dreest. No bashfulness, at this of all moments. Proceed."

"Bulks and spurs of grey, Dreest," prompted Tharle; then, into the mind of their splenetic companion, *Leave be, Kidresh. See how confident the boy's tale makes him. We mustn't jitter him up again. Come to that, we mustn't crumple like dolls again at any new marvel. We shall consider the sun when we consider the sun.* Kidresh laid his hands upon his chest in mainly gracious, slightly irked accession to his leader's wishes. "Apologies, Dreest. Let's have the bulks and spurs."

"For a moment I thought the white had shot down past me into hostile altitudes and was starting to die. All was dollops of grey. Then came other spurs and twists – dark blue, darker than our amethyst skies. But as I looked, the grey performed wondrously – changed itself to settlements, tiny and huge. And the blue became inland seas, fingers of rivers, and the settlements clung to the blue or raced away from it, climbing hills, tumbling into valleys."

"Are you sure you hadn't heard and seen your way back home, Dreest? And didn't know it?" Tharle felt his puzzlement expand as he spoke. It was as if he was asking more than he properly knew.

"So it sounds, Master. I might say, yes – apart from the birds' eggs."

"Birds' eggs?" Tharle leaned a little away from the novice. Uncharacteristically, Kidresh stretched out and propped his head on one hand (but not before he'd given both lobes the ghost of a tickle).

Dreest craved Tharle's pardon: "That's how they looked to me, nestled among all that grey. At first I thought them speckled with – well, no colours we have on Razalia. But then they declared themselves. Red like the egg of a Carolles sheenaloft. Yellow like the Sehundan snow-duster. Lemon like our own hop-ridge. And they weren't inert. They were moving on pepper-covered stoneways, lurching and bouncing like the roisterers will doubtless be at Dame Pennater's Twice-Ninety gilding."

"How true," sighed Kidresh.

"So these eggs," said Tharle, "were rolling themselves in drunken lines."

"When they weren't spinning round circles of green – sorrier than the stoneways, those. Grim little attempts at shrubs and flowers on them. They reminded me of that galaxy of valleys I'd heard along, leagues back, where the first flowers had come and no-one knew whether to eat them or marry them or what."

"Hmph," said Kidresh. "They remind me of the average Baraskian's efforts at raising a garden." He shook his head. "Oceans lave us. And eggs spinning about them. I must say, Dreest, you got yourself into a queer nook of creation."

"Not so queer, in the end." Dreest smiled. "It took me some while to shake off the 'egg' notion – to see things as they really were." He gave another chuckle, which Tharle copied encouragingly, thinking that mirth suited their young colleague after all. "No," Dreest continued, "when I magnified my gaze, I saw they weren't eggs – but even then I didn't get it right. Primeval Galladeeleans was my next guess."

"Good Dreest, in the grand long ago, Galladeelee flowered exactly as it is now," Kidresh sounded as though he were orating to Razalia's massed schoolchildren. Like many others, he found it difficult to credit that something had actually troubled itself to create Galladeelee. More appealing was the idea that it had popped out of nothing, like a self-made firework which, instead of dissipating, hung in the air, refining its gaudiness. "The planet of the rouge catacombs never had a primeval phase. Though I suppose, if you want to look at it the other way round, primeval is the only phase it will ever know."

"But what could he do, Kidresh, save use his knowledge of us, of our planets?" As he spoke, even Tharle's finger now closed discreetly on an earlobe. "Assume, connect, eliminate. I should have done likewise. So should you. He didn't have the name for these drunken oddities. It's doubtful they would have shouted it out as they rolled along.

So" – he beamed at Dreest – "what were these non-eggs? And why did you think of riotous Galladeelee?"

"Busy little boxes," said Dreest, "with crazy wheels. Not that they were all little. There were some real bruisers among them, as long as a chara-jet. They had wheels all over, even up off the stoneways, just for show – like a child's drawing of a market-cart. And it was all the jostling – the drunkenness, as I called it – that made me think of our wild-limbed neighbours. Every last box was rocking and shoving away. I actually expected them to sprout a tangle of arms and legs – to start a mighty old flap."

Tharle thought of the chara-jets that morning and evening, their freight of roisterers. He could see why Dreest had assumed and connected thus.

"So these were actual creatures?" Astonishment had narrowed Kidresh's light to a glowing sheet. "Not closed carts with mad... things inside them?"

"So it seemed." Dreest flapped his arms helplessly. "Imagine yourself in a blizzard, good Kidresh. Or on Lachbourigg at midnight with all those trees roving about you. Imagine so much coming at you – not just through eyes and ears but over your whole being. That's how it was for me. I felt that I wasn't just bent over that bowl, seeing and hearing. I was there. The great slabs of distance were crushed. I was hovering right above them. That's why I hung onto the Galladeelee notion, I suppose. It was either that or lose myself completely. And I couldn't do that – I just knew there was something for our case down there."

"Among boxy creatures," mused Kidresh, "dancing about for the sheer foolery of it."

"Well, as for that" – Dreest shuffled about; his glow betrayed a well-reddened face – "I wondered if it was foolery. I wondered," he mumbled shyly, "if they weren't... preparing."

Tharle and Kidresh frowned together: "And what," said Tharle, "might such frenzy be preparation for?"

Dreest drew a deep breath. Hesitantly, he brought his hands to within an inch of each other, twisting them this way and that as if demonstrating a stringless cat's-cradle. He didn't seem wholly aware of what he was doing. Certainly, the three kisses he blew at the Billomingow were a shock all round.

"For mating," he said.

The two other lights turned awkwardly aside. A cough funnelled along Kidresh's.

"It was the noise they made," persisted Dreest. "Little parps and weeps, then a long bellow, then a bit of squawking. I wondered if they were trying to... you know, select... pair up... off... so that..." He sought about for a conclusion to his theory. It was like looking for a pinhead of light at the end of an impassable tunnel.

"Hundreds mating in the open," said Kidresh. "Yes, Dreest, you found something primeval. I doubt if Galladeelee itself could boast such sport. Most troublesome," he concluded wearily. His mind ran on courting couples who, thanks to the zealous patrolling of such as Dame Pennater, would from time to time be drawn shamefaced from wood or copse around his settlement. Personally, despite his present words, it didn't bother him that much. He was rather of the opinion that love should have its way. But he had to be seen to be properly Tharlian about it, delivering homilies, inserting fleas in ears. It was irksome. And Dreest's theory made him picture, most unwillingly, what would happen if mass passion took hold back home. He could hear Dame Pennater and her cronies holding him personally responsible for the evaporation of all morals. "Decency?" came the Dame's imperious tone. "Decency? Gone from this settlement, Kidresh. See now? There's the last shred of it going *pffft* on the top of Maker's Mountain."

"Mind you," said Dreest, "the moons would stop them, ever and again."

"Moons?" repeated Tharle. Like Kidresh, he had been reflecting on courting couples, but they hadn't made him doleful. His strategy for dealing with them spared blushes and forestalled the gripes of his own Dame Pennaters. He exploited his throat, clearing it mightily whenever his patrol of Mopatakeh took him deep into nature, then sealing off his eyes and ears so that anyone who had to could retreat undetected. A little hum topped off his efforts, meaning *don't let me fail to see you again.* Thus far, no ardent youth or maiden had ignored his bidding.

"Trios of moons," Dreest was saying now. "Everywhere. As nimble as ours, too, though hardly as adventurous. They cling to poles like fat old grapes on a vine. Like this –" He trained his glow on the ground before him. The others followed suit. By the tripled light, Tharle and Kidresh saw Dreest's finger score a line in the grass, then prod three points at the top. "And they leapfrog, like ours, so fast you don't see them jump out and back. But they never slide down the pole, or shoot off it. Just the same motions in the same space – no urge to dart about – not like ours – you know, when the sun vanishes and they blow raspberries at its tail."

"And these, too, are natural beings, like the boxes?" asked Tharle. "Not some artificial contrivance?"

Dreest nodded vigorously: "They leap as blithely as fish in a stream," he declared in bardic tones. "A sad little stream, but there it is. And they do their bit for public order. When a particular moon hops to the very top of the pole, whole lines of boxes stop their wheezing and parping. And when another moon does, they start their jostling again, and another lot shut down."

"Moons like proper acrobats," mused Kidresh, "and with restraining effect. They sound positively mannerly – just the thing for our skies." Picking a point where he supposed the umber moons to be, he glowered up, his light sweeping the forsaken midnight like an emulsion-brush. Tharle quaked a moment, fearing an inexplicable return of his sliceblossom turmoil. But Kidresh was content to hiss, "Your days could well be numbered," before returning his attention to Dreest's line in the grass.

"And you still thought," said Tharle, "that you'd found some ancient Galladeelee?"

"Not after watching the moons for a while. I saw – method there – a pride in cause and effect – however unseemly the general spectacle might have been. That's just not the Galladeelee way."

"No," Tharle added, "I should have discarded that notion myself." Despite a look of prompting enquiry from Kidresh, he fell silent. Cause and effect, he was thinking. Nature organising nature. And moons again. Kidresh would hardly agree with him, but wasn't there some correspondence with their own gadfly moons? They align: the burning shingle makes new landscapes, veritable worlds of itself. Exactly between their alignments, the cracks beyond the tides flex their way through every last shape in the galaxy. And always there is precision: always the moons elude the scrunch and drag of Razalian time – which is far worse, anyway, than their clowning. Yes, the umber moons perplex and exasperate. Yes, you would think they were Galladeeleans themselves, the way they cheek the sun at its departure. But mightn't that be play well earned – for duties whose method and aim Razalia doesn't yet understand? He'd had his doubts. Part of him had thought that, despite his conviction, Dreest had dropped down any-old-where. But that assumption was fading; a connection was firming up. Yes, this was indeed sounding like their Maker's home. New home. His – what? – second go at creation? A new Razalia? True, the notion that their Maker might be a lascivious box on wheels didn't bear overmuch thinking. Still, best to be patient until Dreest – suddenly Tharle felt something stir at the edge of his mind. *I couldn't help it, Mopatakeh*, thought Kidresh at him. *I know what we agreed: outer talk for each new revelation this night. But I really had to know what you felt* – there was a long silence then: Kidresh was considering Tharle's thoughts, as if standing on the bank of his own Billomingow while they streamed past his inward eye. Finally, *Our moons?* thought Kidresh sharply. *With a purpose? Oceans lave us, Mopatakeh, as tall orders go...* But then a softening in his tone: *I was doubtful myself. But no-one will ever hear and see as much as Dreest – no, not even the admirable Carollessa. And if he's right, we have indeed heard our Maker. And I think that, if we simply –*

Simply what, Tharle never knew. Nor in fact did Kidresh, who'd decided to raise Tharle's roof with some grand final pronouncement but had neither words nor sentiment to hand. Dreest's voice came showering down on them: "So strong I thought I'd explode!" They stared at the novice, who seemed to be shining on all Razalia, his glow waving about like a huge, errant flame. "I was close. Help for our case – the best and only help – was as near as that" – he pointed down the Billomingow to where an islet split the waters. "Once I felt it as strong as that, I couldn't loiter. So – one minute I was looking down at one of those green circles, with its derelict shrubs and those passionate boxes skeltering round. The next, I was off down a stoneway as if something gigantic was drawing breath and I was aimed straight for its mouth. There were dwellings – as alive as the boxes, it seemed, though that might have been the speed of my eyes. Some came bellying right up to the road; others scuttled back, petrified of something, and hid behind crook-necked flowers and tatty little greens – not a mallowberry in sight, by the way. I just missed a huge creature, a chara-jet and a half – parping away, heaving its rump to the road. And the road! Mad as anything I'd seen, twisting this way and that –"

"Like the crack-plains!" cried Kidresh.

"Exactly so!" Tharle rejoined.

"– dragging me along as if it had me by the nose. And I saw a grey cliff with scores of mirror-windows and lines of the creatures all quiet outside. And the cliff was splashing and squealing –"

Fearfully, Kidresh raised a hand: "Good Dreest, I may not be as crammed with time as Razalia, but I've eaten years enough and my face is lined from the chore. I implore you, humour a fading Tharle and spare us your theory on squealing cliffs."

"I have none," said Dreest. "I had scarcely a moment to see it before the wall."

This he had seen in some detail. He described its restless coping, the way it buckled out and swayed back. He dwelt on its curious cuts of stone, some sticking out like a fist, others seeming to hang unsupported from its side.

"That's the wall round the Guiding," said Tharle. "If it's not, I'm a stranger to my own sight. I stared hard enough at it yesterday, Kidresh, while I was thinking to you of the gaps."

Kidresh didn't seem to hear: "That's the wall Gent Pennater and Satherfall built," he declared, "to keep the settlement hogs from snouting the Maker's mountain geese to death."

"It was playing a game," said Dreest. "There was thwacking and cries and different parps and beeps."

"Oh, well, you get that with walls." Kidresh sounded as solemnly knowing as when he'd meditated on Lachbourigg and its solitary, tree-proof house. Ideally, after the excitement of recognition, he and Tharle would have enjoyed the chance to sigh in unison, lapse into brief repose and catch their breath for the end of the novice's journey. But Dreest was already leaving the wall behind:

" – like something had my ears by the lobes – hauling me into this curious dwelling. Stairs flapped down past my eyes, then I was plonked on flatness, then more stairs, more flatness – then my eyes shinned a berry-man's ladder, up into a brown triangle of dust and planking – and there it was, there he was – our Maker, with us in his book."

His hearers swayed like the exposed roots of the Nine Oceans. Their hands sought the firm earth beneath the grass. No repose now: they felt as though they'd burst up through the dwelling on Dreest's back. Tharle shook his head vigorously:

"And was he… is he… a wheeled box? Did he parp?"

Kidresh recalled the novice's mating theory: "Did he pant?"

Dreest, now worn out himself, fanned his face with a fold of cloak: "Just like us," he said quietly. "Except he seemed smaller."

"Ah," said Tharle, "so he made two prime species for his new planet." On behalf of Razalia, he sounded a little hard done by.

Kidresh glowed steadily at Dreest: "What does he call this planet, Dreest?"

The novice pressed his fingers lightly to his brow. The name fluttered out over the knoll.

"What an odd sound," said Tharle. "Like someone trying to work a Sehundan sournut from the back of their throat."

Save for the odd lapse by Kidresh, that was the end of all extraneous comment. No more did watching lights bob and flash in astonishment or irritation. There were no further imprecations against the umber moons. To Tharle and Dreest's relief, there was no further chaotic business with the sliceblossom jar (which, in any case, Dreest tucked into his cloak and, a while later, transferred to his invention-bag).

"His book," said Kidresh. "Was it a map of Razalia?"

Dreest scratched his head: "No, not really. It was a queer-looking thing. Sort of an almanac, or – just on the line where an almanac becomes a scrap-book."

His hearers hmm'd recognition. In their official houses, there was a goodly shelf of such books, whose name is best translated as *Knowscapes*. They were half-printed with general principles and philosophies of use to the practising Tharle; but the other half was blank, so that each settlement's incumbent could add, verbally or diagrammatically, any experience whose worth might benefit a successor. By the time a volume was filled, the next was ready for the shelf. The printed half varied little, unless a particular *Candling of Eyes*, the counsel of Tharles, led to the adoption of a new general principle or modification of Tharlian philosophy. As for the blank part, its sometimes close-written, sometimes sketched, sometimes three-dimensional contents were shared on an *ad hoc* basis across the planet. One leader might, for example, think most anxiously to his peers about a poor mallowberry season. Another might discover a predecessor's record of a similar famine in his own settlement, together with opinions on ending the misfortune. At such times, however dire the problem, the telepathically-charged air was almost merry. This, after all, was an exchange-and-mart between some of the most singular thinkers in creation; and a solution to the problem, or at least a brake on any further deterioration, was usually not long in coming. For a moment, Tharle and Kidresh wondered if future *knowscapes* would boast the heading *White, gaps, curtailment of. Eradication*, of course, would be the ideal.

The two of them shared their thoughts with Dreest.

"I don't know if I'd call his book a *Knowscape*," said the novice. "*Hopescape,* perhaps. It seemed to be mainly plans for planets he'd like to create. I didn't get a feeling that they were records of real places. I didn't get any feeling at all, until he found a page and lost it. Then there was the sharpest pain in my head, like strings pulling themselves out of my temples and entwining before my eyes – or a finger jabbing out of my skull. Somehow, I'd just seen us! I might have rediscovered the page for him – I can't remember. In any event, he turned back to it – and there were our valleys, our outwaters" – he nodded to Kidresh – "and Maker's mountain to its very tip."

Tharle's voice came softly: "And the white?"

"That, too." At this, Dreest's hearers sighed.

"I didn't see it immediately," said Dreest, "nor any of it – not in detail. I had to expand the whole picture to make sure. I think it shocked him."

"I wonder if he planned it?" said Tharle. "The white. For some purpose. As our umber moons might be." He blinked before Kidresh's gaze: "Might incredibly be," he corrected himself.

"There was… something else." For a second, Dreest looked about to succumb to a fresh burst of twisting and apologies and pleas to be *enchaffed.* Tharle laid a firm hand on his arm.

"Good Dreest, it is hardly as though we know this tale you tell us – every scrap from dawn to eve – and are testing your knowledge of it. In all of this, you are our leader. Who contrived this voyage of ear and eye to make these discoveries? Not Kidresh, not me. We are resolved not to" – he turned to Kidresh – "what did I say we shouldn't do, however astonishing his news?"

"Crumple like dolls," muttered Kidresh. "Though I should much have preferred 'Like the Razalian rose at glowfall.' I've been called some things in my time, most of them by Dame Pennater, but a doll is –"

"The something else, Dreest." Tharle raised a hand square into Kidresh's glow, which dimmed grudgingly.

"There was so much in the picture. Hard against its left was a cluster of dots and blobs. I'm sure they were the planets I'd heard and seen along, just before I reached – again he pronounced the name of the Maker's new planet; his hearers winced.

"He'll have to call it something better than that," said Kidresh. "Come to think of it, I heard the very same noise at one of our Baraskian Festivals once. A Galladeelean waiter – waiter, mark you! When did Galladeeleans ever wait, except till the danger of honest work disappeared? – anyway, a so-called waiter was just draining the dregs of a flagon when he let fly –"

"His new planet must have been amongst them," the novice drove on. "But then the picture glided into something different. Our arc. From such a strange angle. Such as the sun might see if it circled our eastward side alone. I could make out Sehunda. I think I saw Carolles. But they fell away in a line of curves and satellites. Razalia was at the head, right against my eyes."

His words warmed Tharle and Kidresh, reminding them of how the other planets in the arc saw theirs: as keeper of time before their times, image of their long-buried, fledgling selves – a beguiling conundrum of wisdom and frailty. Razalia at the head: right that it should be. They smiled benignly on Dreest, who now spoke of writing.

"It was above the picture, strung from left to right. Exactly what it meant, I couldn't tell. I was weakening quickly. It was… the end of some record. A *knowscape* memorandum? An account of Razalia's creation, perhaps? An epic of storm and battle? Something, it said, was speeding past the Arc of the Sixteen planets, right over us." In his weakened state, Dreest had got only the barest gist of the writing on the Maker's page. The embroidery – describing Razalia as *unfinished, overlooked, the very runt of that system* – had happily defeated him. "I could see it, too," he added emphatically. "The creature in the sky."

"What was it?" Kidresh was agog. "What was speeding?"

By his own confession, Dreest had seen nothing of the epic over which their Maker had pored. He knew nothing of "The Magenta Line", or what it might signify. He knew nothing of the creatures Broom and Anstey, or Goody Trower or Squire Evershed. Still, he'd gleaned enough to provide an answer for Kidresh – though he feared that it would take a prodigious effort to find the intelligible Razalian for "Farhanva, Planet of the Rising Age" or "twenty-foot pregnant seahorse".

Again he pressed his brow like a medium, as he had when conjuring the name that seemed so crude for their Maker's new home.

"A *curiotwist*," he said finally.

Tharle and Kidresh started. A *curiotwist* was a Razalian question-mark, far more elaborately inscribed than its abused counterpart on Earth.

"A flying *curiotwist*?" Kidresh's lobes came in for some mighty prodding.

"Shaped like that... no, it was... a limbless, baby-bubbled horse with fans for shoulders, three Razalians high. It was from –" But "Planet of the Rising Age" emerged as "old clod waking up". As for "Farhanva", the name seemed to make his voice melt, so that Tharle and Kidresh were treated to a gargle, a whistle and a belch. Understanding that, whatever it was, the word had stuck fast between Dreest's brain and his gullet, they didn't press him. Besides, the baby-bubbled horse was enough for now. Not that Tharle or Kidresh were especially dismayed by the sound of it. In their own system, several planets were home to creatures as bizarre – even more so. Sehundans, for example, were so improbable of structure and aspect that, on Razalia, a kind of proverb had developed about them, best translated as *once seen, never remembered*, implying that they were so hard to credit, except as the stuff of night-fever, that the average mind voided their image. Most of the other planets had similar sayings about them – with the inevitable exception of Barask, whose inhabitants, never noted for abstraction, had spent much of their remoter history trying to ensure that there was no Sehunda to forget. But it was the very existence of this horse, this limbless *curiotwist*, that filled Dreest's hearers with awe. Here was a creature which had played some part, crucial or literally fleeting, in Razalia's conception. Why else would he be in the Maker's book?

Now Dreest had a fresh surprise for them; "I can... I think I can conjure its likeness," he said. "Weak I might have been, but its image went deep." He thumped his chest. Tharle nodded assent, at which Dreest stood up and began lightly drumming his brow with the fingers of both hands. From centre to temples and back they moved, as if stuck in one figure of an eternal dance. Slowly, the limbless *curi-*

otwist rose over the Billomingow, its tail just clearing the water. Once at rest, it resembled a moon which, having found its place in the heavens, starts to melt and flow back to its lair below the horizon. Dreest had managed a fair approximation of the creature in the Maker's book, save for its bodily texture. The book presented its skin like crazy paving. But Dreest had so much on his mind when he looked upon the book – enough, indeed, for two more minds besides – that he'd been momentarily distracted when his Maker lost the page, thereby absorbing a blink of an image from elsewhere. So it was that, from curled head to questioning tale, the *curiotwist* was now clad in the discreet check sometimes favoured by Eddie Beplate, "Clarinettist Against Crime".

The image compelled attention. Tharle and Kidresh didn't hear Dreest when, fatigued by the conjuration, he groaned and sank back down between them. Under its spell, Tharle began throwing out theories as though compiling a list of highly speculative advice for the Mopatakeh *knowscape:* "Perhaps it was the Maker's apprentice, and it went rummaging through the system for ideas to complete us... as far as Sehunda, where they took one look at it and" – here his finger described the creature's ignominious trajectory. "Or was it a rival Maker, an adversary who went boasting of how it had thwarted the Maker's plans to finish Razalia – even stolen them from his head – so that there was only white where there should have been natural beauty? And did our sister planets tire of its boast – even fear that it might have terrible plans to reshape them? Did they catch it off-guard and hurl it from our midst?"

At this, Kidresh's concentration broke. He pulled his cloak tight round him, tut-tutting away. "Yes, yes, Mopatakeh," he said, "but its business wasn't with the Sixteen Planets alone. Dreest said it had travelled over the galaxy where the wonder-boy is hiding his face."

Tharle arched an eyebrow: "Wonder-boy?"

"Our Maker, so-called." Kidresh was decidedly peevish. "My apologies, Mopatakeh, but at present I'm none too impressed by him. Ah" – he held up his hands in a forestalling gesture – "I'm not courting agreement. I don't even wish to sound your minds in the matter. But Dreest only found him at the uttermost end of the line. What being skedaddles that far from its offspring? Even Sehundans acknowledge their young until they can stand upright. As for your theories, Mopatakeh, I don't discount them, but I'm much oppressed by the thought that they might be true." Now he spread his hands wide, as if determined to grab the knoll by its sides and uproot it. "Self-respecting Makers don't have rivals, do they, in or out of their systems? Or if they do, surely they see them off before getting down to the business of making. And you vet apprentices, don't you? Every last Razalian farrier will tell you that."

Tharle said nothing. He didn't resent Kidresh's words – which were, after all, food for much meditation. But his mind was presently in thrall to the *curiotwist*. There its likeness was, hanging resplendent before them. At that moment, it was more real than their Maker. It looked as if it would turn its head and charm fresh speculation from him. Besides, for all his prodigious powers, Dreest couldn't keep it there much longer. Luckily, Kidresh gave his special string of coughs, which always struck any stranger as one cough and a stutter of echoes. Simultaneously, he lowered his hands, rubbed them with exquisite lightness, then gave three claps. Tharle knew what his antics meant: *profound grump suspended.* So did Dreest, who'd seen them more than once on the way to the capital, and who now broke in with, "I think it's at my lips... the name of the *curiotwist's* home." The others looked at him as he wrestled again with "Farhanva, Planet of the Rising Age". This time, after a near-swoon, he got the words out.

"The Rising Age," repeated Tharle, gazing on the *enceinte* shape before them. His voice grew gentle, almost fatherly. "Perhaps I do it a disservice. Perhaps its flight across the Maker's page was intended – nothing to do with banishment." He pointed with a child's finger. "Brimming with young – you see? A benefactress of the universe, birthing planets on its way, hanging comets by their tails in the sky. A master-Maker, aiding our own – bringing forth umber moons, so that the Razalian sky might not be barren." As Tharle uttered the last words, Dreest gave a long sigh of relief, and the image gracefully vanished. Disregarding the sigh, Tharle couldn't resist the idea that the image had lingered until he was right.

"Perhaps, Mopatakeh, perhaps." Kidresh sounded sleepy. "Perhaps all of it at different times – perhaps none. But why bequeath all that infernal white, without telling our Maker what it was or should become?" Again he flicked up a hand. Though seeming to invite it, he didn't have the stomach for further reflection. "All I know now is that my glow is near done for this night. As yours must be. And especially –" He gestured at Dreest, who was now rocking slowly, all but spent from his exertions. "And, Mopatakeh, I can no longer fight you about our umber moons. See? That's how tired I am."

For several moments, the only sounds came from the knoll's rustling grass and the ripples of the Billomingow. At last, Tharle stroked his face, then studied his own glow. Yes, he too had boosted his last for that night. The light was thinning away, beyond even Tharlian command. He gazed at Dreest, who stretched, yawned, then turned his attention to husbanding his own light till the meeting was done.

"What you have shown us, Dreest," said Tharle, shaking his head, "is beyond miraculous." He wasn't sure where the next utterance came from. Perhaps it was tiredness. Perhaps, all that evening, his no-nonsense colleague from Razalia's smallest settlement had been mad to get into his thoughts. At any rate, his next words were Venacarr's. "You have the soul of the planet within you, Dreest," he blurted.

Sadly, the blessing seemed to transport Dreest back through the hours to the foot of the knoll. Again, the novice squirmed and fumbled – if anything, worse than when he came staggering up with his magic bag – until Tharle feared that he might double his height and go stomping into the Billomingow, simply to shake his mind loose from this redoubled attack of agony: "Master," he said, "I hardly feel that, as if I, as if such praise, as if I should acknowledge it – I mean I *do* acknowledge it, accept it, but when I say 'acknowledge' –" His voice folded into his waning light. "When I say 'accept'," he tacked on in a miserable whisper.

During all this, Tharle could only shake his head. Venacarr having spoken through him, he had no words of his own, brusque or soothing, to add. He was therefore relief itself when, despite his own confession of weariness, Kidresh fixed the novice in a final bright glare: "Dreest!" he said. "You have taken us on a journey of journeys. You have gathered all that is into your sight. We have listened like children at Gent Satherfall's knee, while he tells old tales of the first berry-men on Razalia. You are no petrified puppy."

As though hypnotised, Dreest began intoning heavily, "I am no –"

"No, no, good Dreest," Kidresh pressed on. "No need of that. What I tell you is, Mopatakeh blesses you truly, with all good cause. And one day, we hope, you will know it."

Awoken and emboldened by these words, Tharle laid a gentle hand on the novice's shoulder. His gaze unwavering, he looked like a maker of galaxies lodging the final moon in place.

"Indeed, Dreest," he murmured. "Now – our beds hail us. But Kidresh and I must know the journey's end. Can you do it?"

Kidresh looked bewildered, then annoyed: "Oh, speak it out, Mopatakeh. I *am* about to crumple like a doll." But Tharle said nothing and so, with an *oh-very-well* sigh, he stood alongside Dreest in their leader's mind. He stared at the words, smiled and echoed them aloud.

After a final spasm, the petrified puppy disappeared. Dreest gave a three confident nods, as if to bounce his reply out into the night: "Yes. Yes, I'm sure so. I'll need four days – provided our time holds steady. Five or three if not."

"How many of his days is that?" asked Kidresh.

"Two, I think. So that should be –" Pausing, he raised leaden hands to his brow and ran through the days of his Maker's week. "Yes, that should be the day he calls… Soo… Sana… Sunday."

The others gasped. The word was a pointless noise – even worse, really, than the name for the Maker's new hidey-hole. Kidresh spoke, but this time with great reluctance:

"I suppose… I suppose she'll be coming with him." Deliberately, he avoided saying "the consort". He was mindful of the run of his thoughts after Dreest had conjured the voices – the way her imagined moan had roamed about his head. But it was too late. *Call this a planet?* she shrilled anew. *Look at all that you've missed. Where's the green for this bit? You'll be doing something with all the white, I presume?* Somehow, Dreest's response broke through, fighting her off: "No, good Kidresh, I doubt I could manage the two – not the first time, at least."

"Oh." Suddenly Kidresh sounded as breezy as if he'd just got up. "Ah, well, right that you shouldn't. We need… time alone with wonder-boy. Time to see what fist he makes of our questions. About Mopatakeh's beloved *curiotwist*. About" – he snapped his fingers, recalling the first question he'd fired at Tharle when they settled down on the knoll – "about our singular sun." Sitting bolt upright, he thrust out a dramatic arm. "Maker," he said sonorously, before breaking up his words like Tharle of Venacarr at his most insistent. "A-bout our sun. Our twi-sting, lur-ching, snee-ring sun. Friend-or-foe?" He tapped his brow. "Now," he muttered, "there was that saying the consort used in their extraordinary chatter. Ah, exactly" – and he reverted to his drama – "life source or ma-ker of ki-llings?"

Dreest chuckled. Tharle, however, simply stared at his over-weary colleague.

"And our other question, Kidresh?" he inquired quietly. Then, like a mother coaching her child through a speech, he mouthed, *Peril.*

"Oceans lave us!" cried Kidresh, dropping his arm. "Has it moved again? Leave it to me, Mopatakeh. I can do it – I can survey all! I'll gee up some light from somewhere. Just let me –"

"Kidresh, give up your agitation." Tharle spread his hands. "I just gee'd some up myself. And I roved the whole planet, though where I got the strength from, I hardly know. No movement. The white is as it was when we ascended this knoll."

"Ah… ah… ah." Kidresh sounded worse than Dreest at his most bashful. "Now I understand you, Mopatakeh. What does he pro-pose… does he know… can he vanquish – ?" He broke off and, copy-ing Tharle, mouthed *gaps.* Then, in a single breath, "Well, of course, that would be my final, my steeliest question, that was where I'd lead him, I'd fully intend – lulling, you see, a good inquisitor lulls, feints, works his way about, you see – think of a boat, Mopatakeh, on the Billomingow, tacking, you see, bringing its prow –"

"Our Maker has work to do," Tharle cut in. "If it involves explain-ing suns and *curiotwists* – as well it might – then that will be more work besides. But our planet stands to be eaten alive. Before all else, our Maker must roll up his sleeves against that."

Chastened, Kidresh ruckled and unruckled a handful of cloak. "Well, yes," he said quietly. "Of course, Mopatakeh. I assure you, the white was at the peak of my mind." Despite his awkwardness, how-ever, he was all admiration for Tharle. He'd spoken like the leader he was.

"Good Dreest," said Tharle now. "Whatever you need – I mean, in addition to" – he gestured at the colander and stirrups – "I shall pro-vide for you. Tomorrow, we shall plan."

"What about Venacarr and the others?" Kidresh asked, cocking his head. "Surely you can't delay a *Candling*, Mopatakeh. But how do we manage it without telling Razalia? How do we avoid suspicion, rumour, all-out telepathy?"

"Tomorrow, Kidresh, tomorrow we unlock our minds to Venacarr and all our colleagues. Tomorrow we decide everything. At this moment, we are three lights that need their dark rest."

"Vales and ridges." Dreamily, Dreest's voice lapped round the others' practicalities. With a start, they turned to find him staring far down the Billomingow. On tiptoe, they crept into his thoughts. Whether through fatigue or thankfulness that this present, covert *Candling* was done, they were fastened on one thing. At last, the novice was pondering the dimensions of what he'd achieved – and the demands of what he would shortly do. "Our Maker leaves Razalia – the vales and ridges he himself has fashioned – the heathland and tides. He goes far, far… horizon after horizon… brow of a hill, brow of another, out and out. Peaks and ocean floors. A desert planet with one hut to its name – whatever that name is. Valleys where flowers are a mystery. Planets that rage, planets that weep. Out and out, far and far. And I follow… a leaf in a storm. Somehow I follow."

"Hardly as erratic as that, Dreest," said Kidresh kindly. "Though you may never know it. As for your quarry, well, he can just come back and back. Gallumph his way over all his pretty horizons. What choice does he have? Good Dreest, he is fixed like a star in your eye –" He broke off. A boyish grin, such as he hadn't managed for countless years, now tricked out his face. "No, I shouldn't. Mustn't."

"Kidresh." Tharle spoke his name in some alarm. Kidresh gave him a faintly pleading look, then continued in yet another rush:

"Dreest – yes, I know, our glows must be off to their beds, and if you can't, you can't, and if you won't, you won't, but" – his voice sank to a bare whisper – "can we see him? Could you drop him in the bowl? For a second, Dreest – no more. So we can" – he shrugged – "fix him in our own eyes?"

Dreest looked at Tharle, who couldn't deny the same boyish urge. "It is for you to pronounce, Dreest," he said, secretly hating to sound so proper. "We shall be fixing on him enough before long. We've waited aeons – we can wait on the morrow. You more than anyone need deep, earnest rest."

"It's not so much that," said Dreest. "It's – well, I conjured the voices a goodly while ago. They'll be deep in their own sleep. You see, it's early their next morning now."

"Of which of their days?" asked Tharle. "I'm sorry, Dreest, there was something of the Sehundan about the noises you made. They're gone from me."

Again, Dreest made use of their Maker's tongue.

"Sa-tur-day." Repeated Kidresh, sounding now like Venacarr uncharacteristically stumped. "It's not a language, really, is it? More a riot of the throat. I can just hear some of the roisterers at Dame Pennater's Gilding – especially if a brace of Galladeeleans drop in. They'll all be hacking it fluently."

Instantly, all three were knocked flat on their backs. The knoll swung from side to side like a warning finger. The rich spray of the Billomingow soused their cloaks. Dreest's contraption shuddered like a lightning-rod. "Sorry, Maker!" cried a petrified Kidresh. "Sorry, umber moons! Forgive, oh, forgive an old Tharle's unbelief!"

As quickly as it had stirred, the tumult faded. The knoll stilled itself; the contraption stood motionless, almost upright. The trio scrambled to their feet. Tharle and Dreest had known instantly what had befallen them – and the whole planet. As for Kidresh, mortification at his foolishness, at the childish fear that had found shape on his lips, left him in a rare old froth. "Our infernal, useless, drunkard time!" he cried. "I thought it had been too quiet while we were up here. Saving us up for a right old shake. And those moons egging it on, no doubt – falling about up there, chortling like those Galladeelee topers who'll drink Dame Pennater dry." He goggled at the others. "Mark me, both of you, mark me, when our Maker sets his foot on our sorely-used planet, I shall fling him into a mallowberry –"

"Wait!" Dreest looked wildly about. Then, once more, he began that semi-chant of inbreaths he'd emitted with his head deep in the colander. At last he broke off: "Our time! It has shaken us back through his. Now it's just after I found their voices – hours before their sleep." He turned to Kidresh. "You can see him."

And so the three Tharles clean forgot fatigue, *curiotwists,* umber moons and consorts – and even, briefly, the capricious gaps of Razalia. The Billomingow flowed smoothly. The grass on the knoll stirred as gently as could be. Slowly, they advanced on Dreest's contraption. Setting it properly upright again, the novice motioned to them to take a strap-stirrup each, while he cupped his right hand against the colander's rim. Then, at his signal, all three inclined their heads.

At the far side of Razalia's nine oceans, a Carolla who is not keeps guard on a free-floating pier. In shape and beauty, she is as the

Carollessa, but they have no record of her being. Nor did any Carollessan or Razalian hand construct her vantage-point. Nor has any living Razalian spoken with her. Nor has she in any way revealed the secret of her mysteriously comforting presence. Still, while Razalia toils or feasts, while light creeps into its faces or whirls on their drooping lids, she glides back and forth between splendid white columns, under a canopy of teal green, scanning land, ocean and beyond, a graceful hand shading her vision.

That, at least, is her usual, inscrutable round. But while three astonished Tharles bent over a colander on a pole, a further cause of astonishment came gliding toward them. A boat moved under its own motion, leaving silken traces on the Billomingow.

TO BE CONTINUED

Lightning Source UK Ltd.
Milton Keynes UK
01 September 2009

143248UK00001B/212/P